To Lori

[signature]

JAKE'S RUN

By Jerome R. Mahoney

This book is a work of fiction. Any resemblance to actual events or persons, living or dead, is entirely coincidental.

"Jake's Run," by Jerome R. Mahoney. ISBN 1-58939-749-5.

Published 2006 by Virtualbookworm.com Publishing Inc., P.O. Box 9949, College Station, TX 77842, US. ©2006, Jerome R. Mahoney. All rights reserved. No part of this publication may be reproduced, stored in a retrieval system, or transmitted in any form or by any means, electronic, mechanical, recording or otherwise, without the prior written permission of Jerome R. Mahoney.

Manufactured in the United States of America.

ACKNOWLEDGMENTS

Many thanks to my friend Connie Underhill for bringing her editing skills to bear on *Jake's Run*. Thanks as well to Oliver Wittasek, another friend and former colleague who was for many years the Sommelier at the Woodstock Inn & Resort in Vermont, for selecting the wines to accompany the Rehearsal Dinner. Most of all, thanks to my family for putting up with Jake and the author from beginning to end.

For Darts lore, I relied on *All About Darts*, by Ivan Brackin and William Fitzgerald, 1975, Contemporary Books, Inc., Chicago, Illinois.

EARLY MONDAY MORNING

J acob Mulligan's Meticulous Rumpus the Third, com-
monly known as Jake, roused from a peaceful and stupid slumber to scratch. He moved his great body, three
years old and near full grown, back and forth along the
two-by-eight planks that formed the side of his pen, slowly
moving along the length of the pen, drooping his broad
snoot to meet the door boards at the end, following his
usual routine, as regular as some old retired Brigadier
General in a London club.

But something different! Bert Grantham, 16 years old
and undone by an encounter that afternoon with the most
beautiful creature in all of central Vermont—one Beatrice
English, age 15, heiress to nothing at all, shapeless still, but
endowed with a hypnotizing effect on poor Bert—had insuf-
ficiently latched the door to Jake's pen, mooning as he was
over the lost opportunity of the afternoon when he had
said "hi" in a squeaky sort of way when he knew that it
should have been *basso profundo* to impress his priceless
gem.

Jake, anticipating his usual early morning nose scratch
on the door boards, was initially disappointed when the
door swung slowly open to his powerful nudge. He stood, a

great menacing bull over five feet tall at the shoulder, wondering what it was all about, staring dully into the dark. He heard the brook across the road and it occurred to him to get a drink of water. He walked slowly out of the yard into the night, stopping to finally get his nose scratch on the front of the pickup truck, the thick ring in his nose making a slight scraping noise on the grill, then ambling on out of sight.

MONDAY

At 6 a.m. on the last day of May Bingo Reilly stepped out on his porch, savored the early morning sharpness of the air and scratched his belly, thinking he could practically hear the buds popping in the trees.

Checking the bird feeder hanging from the eaves, he scuffed into his chore boots and went about the morning's unchanging business: trudging to the barn through the damp, grain for the horses, grain and hay for the beef critters and lambs, whole corn in the goose yard, water for everybody and a good word where it was needed.

If you were standing outside the barn it made quite a racket. The lambs set up a blatting as soon as they heard him at the door, but they weren't the first to be tended. The horses came first because they had a habit of knocking the daylights out of the sides of the stalls if they weren't first on the list. "Kick the goddam barn down, why don'tcha," was something Bingo said every morning of the year.

The tops of feed storage cans clanged, bales of hay thumped onto the loft floor from the top of the pile, grain rattled in coffee cans, and a general conversation went on to the satisfaction and understanding of all concerned.

Saved until last, in the shed attached to the side of the barn, was Jake, purebred, pedigreed, pride of the Reilly herd, a prize-winner for sure. A bale of hay in one hand and a three pound coffee can full of grain in the other, Bingo approached the door of the shed.

He went inside and stopped short, startled by the emptiness. "Damn," he said. He climbed into the pen itself, stepped across it and pushed the outside door. It swung open slowly, creaking a bit, and he again said, "Damn." Louder this time.

———

Laura Brookings stirred awake at 8:30 a.m., slowly realized the phone was ringing, and fumbled the receiver on the pillow. The covers were flung back on Thad's side; he was probably out in the barn seeing to the horses.

"LO! BINGO HERE!" It was Mr. Reilly from down the hill, who really didn't like phones and so yelled into them at the top of his lungs.

"Yes, Mr. Reilly," she sighed.

"THREE YEAR OLD HEFFID RUNNING LOOSE! SEEN'IM?"

"What does it look like Mr. Reilly," she asked.

"KEY-RIST," said Bingo in disgust, and hung up.

Laura thought that she never seemed to measure up to Bingo Reilly's standards. Awake now, she went over in her mind the arrangements for Kimberly's wedding on Saturday, wondering if she had overlooked anything.

The invitations had precipitated the first major disagreement, and what a fuss it was. Ancient history now, the invitation fuss had seen the battle lines drawn with Kim insisting on an informal affair and Laura holding out for formality.

Now, several major arguments later, the moment was almost at hand and Laura was suffering the last minute jitters. Caterer, music, ceremony on the front lawn, flowers, the Universalist minister so as not to offend anyone, Kim's dress and veil, dresses for the other girls, tuxes that fit the ushers properly, the rented tents for the possibility of rain, places for the wedding party to stay, vehicles, parking in the upper pasture, china, silver, waiters, bartenders, portapotties for God's sake, her own dress and shoes, the right amount of jewelry, things to do and little time to do them.

And Thad offering little help through all this. A very sweet man, her husband, but he absolutely refused to be drawn into the center of the hullabaloo, regarding all the fuss as unnecessary, nothing but female foolishness.

She put her hand on his side of the bed, testing the temperature, and concluded he'd been up long enough to be out of the bathroom.

Laura heard a truck of some kind grinding into the barnyard across the road and swung her feet onto the floor. Must be the men come to clean the barn. If the weather allowed, wedding guests were to be encouraged to wander about the farm, admiring the view and the horses, each with spic and span stall, fresh bedding, freshly painted sign with name and pedigree, combed, curried, gleaming beauties snorting and high spirited. Show these people.

Ten minutes later, teeth brushed and hair combed quickly, still nicely shaped in her Calvin Klein jeans at the age of 47, she strode to the barn to supervise the cleaning operation.

It had been, thought Bingo later driving into the village, altogether too nice a year. Should have expected something like this to happen. Mild winter, but plenty of snow. Good runoff and plenty of rain in April. No late snow storms. What a few weeks ago was a yellow haze over the woods had become a light green mantle of small leaves, the early green of May now turning a deeper green. Hayfield, on a south-facing slope, looking good and a bit ahead for the date. Could be a good second cutting in August. If the apple trees just made it through blossom without a late frost, they'd be all right and a fresh barrel of cider would go down cellar in late October.

Things had been going good. But starting yesterday Milly was all mad about something, he couldn't figure out what. And now the damn bull flew the coop.

First thing he'd looked around. In the orchard. Behind the equipment shed. In the lower pasture.

Then, back at the barn, he went to serious tracking. Jake had stood around some, then gone down the road 50 yards to the brook for a drink. Then he crossed the road into Peterson's front yard and made manure, then went around the house and up the hill toward the ridge, where Bingo lost the trail. Could be anyplace on the ridge between Woodbine and South Woodbine.

The Reilly property–41 acres with a house, a rambling barn bigger than the house, an equipment shed, and a half-finished garage–lay along the South Road about halfway between Woodbine and South Woodbine. The Oglesby Farm Road, usually referred to as the Farm Road, is a dirt road that goes east, climbing the western side of Mt. Harriet, coming off the South Road just a few yards from

Bingo's house; in fact access to the Reilly barn and garage is from this dirt road.

Past Bingo's place at the foot of the Farm Road was a 265-acre farm known as the Chester place, now owned by the Brookings family and the bustling scene this week of wedding preparations. Beyond the Chester place was a 194-acre piece on the north side of the road where Frank Hickham and his lovely second wife had built their dream house two years ago. On the south, or right hand, side of the road was a 60-acre piece that was extremely difficult of access due to a combination of deep gullies gouged by spring runoff, a line of ledges, and the thrust up and tumbled boulders that are the wreckage of the last ice age. This last piece of property was the old Oglesby Farm, and Bingo Reilly had had his eye on it for a long time.

The Oglesby family had been on that land since shortly after the civil war, Scotch-English-Irish folk who moved north from the Carolinas to get away from the fighting. Recent immigrants, clannish, isolated back-country people, their attitude was "We ain't got no dog in this fight." After some wandering and some false starts elsewhere, they filtered into Woodbine and settled on this isolated and difficult piece of land.

At one time the Oglesbys owned 353 acres along the tumbled and rocky flank of Mt. Harriet, raising sheep like everybody else. Then in the 1880s and 1890s the impact of the transcontinental railroads began to be felt, in conjunction with the growth of the stockyards and slaughtering operations in the mid-west. Western beef became readily available in the east and the sheep business went to hell in New England, never to recover, and the Oglesbys suffered along with everyone else.

Pretty soon they had to sell bits and pieces of land, and their holdings began to shrink. By the time Black Jack Pershing sailed off to Europe to put the Kaiser in his place, the Oglesbys were feeling crowded on the 60 or so acres that Bingo Reilly now so dearly wanted.

The first World War played hell with the Oglesbys. The best of the lot, three boys, ended up buried in France. The ones that came back, or didn't go, never had been much for schooling or having anything to do with outsiders, and they pretty much stayed on their hill, settling into shiftlessness and dubious pursuits, such as jacking deer, stealing anything loose, and making illegal strong beverages.

When the great depression came along the Oglesbys didn't even notice; things didn't get any worse for them than they had been already. Woodbine folks considered them more as oddities than as neighbors, when they thought of them at all, which wasn't often. In fact, about the only time the Oglesbys came to mind was if a bicycle was stolen or a calf turned up missing or something like that.

Then in 1934 they had the fire.

It was January and cold as hell and a three-day snowstorm brought things pretty much to a halt. In those days they didn't have a bunch of big old plows to push the snow around. Many people still got around on horseback, and when a big storm like that came along everybody just sort of went to ground, made sure there was plenty of firewood handy to the back door, and waited it out.

The fire started some time during the storm, probably the first day, and nobody knew about it. Well Roscoe Logan, who lived a couple of miles further down the valley towards South Woodbine, later claimed he'd smelled smoke throughout the storm but folks discounted that because he was a known blowhard and liar.

It might have been another month before anybody knew about it except that Plutarch Oglesby, age 15, had ridden a big workhorse into town with a shopping list of coffee and tobacco and such for the next six or eight weeks, and then got accused of shoplifting by Nathanial Waterford at the general store and detained by the Constable. Before they got it straightened out, young Plutarch had been remanded to the custody of the Universalist minister and his wife, he being too young to put in the slammer on Central Street. By morning it was snowing hard and Plutarch settled down to wait out the storm.

By the time he got home four days later, leading the horse up the Oglesby Farm Road through the deep drifts, the fire was out and snow was heavy across the ruins. Years later he would say that the thing he remembered most about the whole affair was coming into the clearing, stopping and being aware of silence, an additional vivid silence on top of the normal winter silence, what he remembered as "the terrible silence."

Late in the afternoon, as the winter darkness gloomed the ridge, Plutarch presented himself at the Reilly's house and, while two-year-old Calvin Reilly lustily banged a spoon on his highchair, brought the news that the Oglesby place was burned to the ground, outbuildings included, and no trace of anybody anywhere on the ridge.

Next day the Constable and some others went up there and looked around and they couldn't find anything either. The only tracks were those that Plutarch had made; the only life a few wild-eyed cattle up in the cedars. While they were poking around the place it began snowing; a second storm following right behind the other. So they gave up on it after making sure that nobody was around.

In the first part of May that year a bunch of them went up again, this time finding four skeletons in the cellar under the charred remains of the house timbers, two women and two men according to old Doc Skallet, who looked them over before they were buried. But the funny thing was that Plutarch said there were seven people on the property when he left early that Monday morning. Nobody could confirm that, though, because the Oglesbys had a way keeping to themselves and of running people off who came around the place, always a deer rifle somewhere close, even the truant officer was afraid to go up that hill. And the younger Oglesbys were known to come and go, slipping down off the hill, sometimes months going by without anybody seeing this one or that one. So nobody really knew what happened.

It was one of those mysteries. Oldtimers still wonder about it around Woodbine. Other than Plutarch, nobody ever saw any other Oglesby around Woodbine again. As for Plutarch, the Reillys took him in and he stayed with them until he was 19, helping around the place to earn his keep. By then it was 1940 and Plutarch went off to the army, "$21 a month and all you can eat."

Nobody had lived up on the Oglesby place since the fire. The road to the house washed out some time in the 40s, heavy winter runoff gouging a deep rocky gully that raged in the spring of the year, and a shivery kind of menace attached to the place. It was a hard place to get to and people didn't like to go there anyway. Anybody who did go there felt uneasy, stopping often and listening, sometimes taking a quick look backwards, feeling as if some unblinking eyes were off in the gloom sizing things up, maybe squinting a little, gauging the range.

When Plutarch came back from the war he lived around Woodbine, but never on that property. He worked in the woods, logging, or helped on farms, when there were still farms, cut firewood, raked leaves, shoveled sidewalks, always a good worker. He always paid the taxes on the property, which didn't amount to much until recent years, but he never lived on it. Matter of fact, he seldom even talked about it.

Mulling things around over the last few months, Bingo had figured out a way to get fairly easy access to the property at a fairly reasonable cost and he was waiting for the right time to make an offer to Plutarch, 75 years old by now and getting his miseries.

Anyway, if Jake was on the Oglesby property, there was nobody to call to ask about it. If he was there he was probably listening to the hum of insects around the brush and berry bushes choking the pasture, and maybe wondering at the cellarhole and the blackened stones of the foundation.

Bingo got along pretty well with the Brookings, his nearest neighbors up the hill, and liked the family, despite his brusque manner on the phone this morning. They paid their bills and were reasonable and fair in any questions that arose and, as far as Bingo Reilly was concerned, you couldn't ask for anything more than that.

As for the Hickhams further up the hill, Bingo had better things to do than waste his time talking to that mealy-mouthed flatlander. And that's all there was to that.

How that came to be the case was really an object lesson in how not to deal with Bingo Reilly, or any other independent-minded cuss.

Frank Hickham was a 52-year-old Long Island boy who took the train into Manhattan five days a week for 25 years and made a ton of money as a stock broker. He retired at the top of his game, like Joe DiMaggio. The stocks he picked went up, his clients made money, and he acquired a name as a shrewd investor, an assessment he was inclined to agree with. Looking back now, of course, it seems obvious that everything went up in the 80s and that a blind man with a handful of darts could have done as well.

Caroline Palmerston Hickham, 33, went to work at Frank's firm in the mid-80s fresh out of Harvard and a mistake of a marriage. She soon set her sights on Frank, who was rolling in dough, both kids grown, and bored with Marilyn, his wife of 25 years. Soon the two were an item at fashionable restaurants and art show openings, and it wasn't long before Marilyn and the suburbs were history.

He retired and married Caroline at the same time. They took an apartment in the village of Woodbine, joined all the obvious organizations, and set about looking for a piece of land upon which to build a gentleman's farm, although they wouldn't have called it that. The property on the Oglesby Farm Road was perfect, nice view, open to the southwest, and plenty of privacy.

The Hickhams spent January, February and March in their Fort Lauderdale condo, returning just before tax time to the lovely post and beam quasi-barn on Oglesby Farm Road. Their automobile license plates were clever: Frank's said HICK and Caroline's said SAVETREE, reflecting her concern over the imminent deforestation of the world and the problems that would bring. Caroline even approached Milly on the sidewalk in front of the Woodbine Drug Store one time, explaining that she had noticed the Reilly woodpile by the house and wanted to object in the strongest terms to the wholesale destruction of trees that was the consequence of heating with wood stoves. Milly explained to her, holding her temper admirably, that a well-managed woodlot could provide two to three cords of wood per acre per year ad infinitum and that the Reillys were not such horses' asses as to mismanage such a resource. Caroline dismissed this answer as self-serving misinformation and every day felt the anger rise as she drove by the Reilly place at the foot of the hill.

The Hickhams were on the hill every day the summer their house was built, supervising every inch of the way. They ended up with an elegant post and beam beauty with cathedral ceilings and a nice view off to the mountains, with plenty of lawn and flower beds that would look better if relations with Bingo were better, a big swimming pool and a telephone system. As Frank often remarked with a rueful shake of the head: "You wouldn't believe how many people just stick a phone in the house and that's it." Another shake of the head. "First thing I told the contractor was make provisions for a proper phone system." Still another rueful shake. "Want something done right, you've got to keep an eye on these locals every minute."

Their lives had settled into a busy uselessness, weekend trips here and there, planned around golf tournaments and visits from his grown children. There were shopping and concert-going trips to Boston, charity initiatives, and carefully selected environmental undertakings by Caroline. Frank earned an occasional finder's fee from an old client of his who had retired and was developing an expensive retirement complex on the shores of Lake Champlain. The Golden Sunset Independent Assisted Living Village had everything from tennis courts to a 10-bed nursing home. The condos were priced from expensive to outrageous but they sold briskly and Frank had steered a few prospects from Woodbine in its general direction, just to keep his hand in at pitching a proposition.

They ate out frequently. The tourist business, summer and winter, ensured that there were a number of good restaurants within 30 or 40 minutes of Woodbine and the Hickhams became familiar faces at the most expensive of these. Caroline made it a point to send her meal back to the kitchen at least every third visit to a restaurant, keeping track in a little notebook she carried in her purse. Too hot, too cold, too spicy, too bland, too thick, too thin, too tough, too mushy, she could always come up with something. "Keeps them on their toes in the kitchen," she explained to Frank, and he agreed wholeheartedly.

At the outset Frank thought he might be helpful in straightening out the local town and village government, but after a few tries he gave up on them. He had expected his sound advice and sage counsel to bring a respectful silence followed by humble gratitude and questions from the local folk hoping to learn from his vast experience. Instead, there were steady appraising looks and questions such as: "Ain't you the fella built up there above Bingo Reilly?"

Frank Hickham never felt the rebuffs. In fact he didn't recognize them as rebuffs, putting it all down as the stupidity of the "locals."

His first meeting with Bingo was typical. Driving down the hill after a morning spent supervising the pouring of the foundation for the combined horse barn and garage, Frank stopped at the Reilly house and knocked. When Bingo appeared in the doorway eating an apple, Frank thrust a paper and pen at him. "Need your signature on this to get the road paved," he declared.

"What road's that?" Bingo inquired. "And who might you be?" Actually he knew damn well who it was but had never met his new neighbor-to-be. You'd think, wouldn't you, in all that time of traipsing up and down the hill, first with the real estate lady, then with the architect and the builder and the wife, you'd think, by God, that he could have stopped once and said hello I'm so-and-so and nice to meet you. Well, Bingo knew how to play that standoffish game himself.

"The road up the hill," Frank said, trying to be patient. "That one right there." His arm swept around, pointing.

"What the hell for?" Bingo was honestly puzzled. Lived there over 60 years and it had never occurred to him or anybody else to want the road paved. Perfectly good road, maybe a little sloppy come April, but a perfectly good road all the same.

Well, Frank could see that some of the talk he'd heard about the locals was probably not exaggerated. This one didn't seem too smart at all. He tried again, speaking very slowly, enunciating each syllable carefully. "So . . that . . cars . . can . . go . . a-long . . chug-a-chug . . nice-ly . . and . . not . . get . . all . . mud-dy."

The door slammed shut just four inches from the end of Frank's nose, since he had leaned forward the better to make his explanation clear to this rustic. He started back in surprise, which quickly became fury. Stomping back to the BMW, he looked around the yard, wondering how much it would take to buy the place, fix it up and sell it to some intelligent people.

Since that day Bingo and Frank had exchanged little more than grunts of acknowledgment. Add on the wood-burning scolding delivered to Milly by Frank's wife, and it made sense that relations between the top of the hill and the bottom were not cordial.

So now, even with Jake running loose, there would be no call to the Hickham residence seeking information. Not in a pig's eye would there be such a phone call.

Bingo drove around some, looking for some sign of Jake. But there was nothing. Home again, he made a few more calls but nobody had seen Jake. Finally, conceding it wouldn't be a quick recovery, he notified the Town Constables that a bull named Jake was running loose, somewhere in South Woodbine. It started right away. "Ain't surprising a man your age has trouble keeping track of his critters," said First Constable Euclid Armstrong. "You fed him now and then maybe he wouldn't leave home," said Second Constable Artie Hortinger.

Jake's escape was a delicious news item, in certain circles, as is the case when the mighty are fallen. Bingo Reilly, who acted as if he knew more about farming than just about anybody, or at least had a whole bunch of loud opinions on the subject, who at the age of 62 still carried himself with a brash and challenging self confidence, who just last year had dropped Henry Lafferton with one swift right hand punch to conclude a discussion of a disputed boundary line, this Bingo Reilly had a bull running loose and didn't have any idea where the critter was.

Bingo at a disadvantage was not only delicious, it was downright unusual. Here was a man who could fix your plumbing or rewire your barn (although not legally any more since they put in all those damned regulations and licensing and so on), who was a fine carpenter (as long as you left him alone), who could tinker and get the baler working or replace the transmission in your truck.

Here was a man who got his nickname as a child. After attending a few bingo evenings with his mother and noting the excitement and elation that seemed to accompany the shout "BINGO," he took to congratulating himself with the phrase whenever he did something admirable, which in his opinion was often.

Every base hit, every passing grade, every punch that landed, every chore completed, every pigtail yanked, was celebrated with a roar of "BINGO!" This was partly due to the natural boisterousness of a strong young lad excelling at almost everything he did. But it was also due in part to the fact that he had been christened Calvin, his parents being strong admirers of President Coolidge, who was born and grew up not far from Woodbine.

Bingo didn't like the name Calvin and it took years of scraped knuckles and shiners and shirts hopelessly torn to get the point across to his classmates and various older boys who mistook their greater size for unbeatable advantage. When he reached voting age he looked into the possibility of changing his given name, finally deciding it would cost too much. But there were strict orders in the strong box on the top shelf over the kitchen sink that his tombstone was to say Bingo Reilly and the pertinent dates and nothing else.

And he planned to be buried right here on his own property, same place he'd been born. His two older sisters were married and lived elsewhere in the state, so the property had come to Bingo when the old folks died.

As a young man he cut quite a swath through the Woodbine area, winning most of his fist fights and dancing till the band went home. Between being a good dancer and exuding a brash confidence, he attracted the prettiest girls and was generally considered a good catch. He worked

21

as hard and as deftly as he played, and soon had a name as a reliable and careful worker, who didn't take orders too well, especially stupid orders. "Meet 'im on the street and ya' don't know whether he'll tip his hat or spit in yer eye," as someone once said.

Mellowed over the years, Bingo had gradually attained a certain stature in the Woodbine community which varied depending on which part of the community was doing the judging. In the circles in which he lived his life, Jake's escape was an event to be relished, and Bingo knew he was in for some raucous needling before Jake was back in the barn.

———————

It was Bingo's way to meet things head on, for good or ill.

So it was that he ventured that same afternoon to the Milk House, the venue, from about 4:30 to 7 p.m. each working day, of fearsome cribbage encounters, cutthroat darts contests, industrial strength beer drinking, and banter that was as close to a fist fight as words can get.

News of Jake's escape preceded him, so the carpenters, plumbers, painters, truck drivers, farmers, pot-wallopers, waitresses, electricians, grocery clerks, and other working men and women who congregated there daily were united in their glee that one of the town's most respected pair of callused hands was helpless and reduced to dialing the Constables for the latest news on his prized bull.

The Milk House was in a rambling low, cinder block building on the edge of the village of Woodbine. Part of it, the part where the bar was, had actually been a milk house at one time, when it was part of the old Rushton Farm.

But, with the village growing and attracting wealthy flat-landers, Rushton cut the property up and sold it, making more in a year than he had in 35 years of dairy farming.

A man named John Bellamy from over to South Royalton had bought the milk house piece and fixed up the building some and opened it as a bar in 1968. Business was just picking up a couple of years later when his liver gave out on him. The property passed to his three daughters, who ran the place while the probate court struggled to make sense of Bellamy's mysterious and ambiguous financial records.

When all was finally said and done the girls sold out to Desmond Kiley, a great bearded behemoth who carried 320 pounds on his 6'5" frame with surprising agility. There were never any disturbances inside the Milk House. "Transposition this debate to the otherwise, boys," Desmond would say quietly, and they would. He ran a good place, poured a good drink, made a hefty sandwich and kept things from getting too loud. He added to the place from time to time so that now, when you got inside, it was bigger than it looked from outdoors. He liked old maps, and the walls were covered with them, mostly of different towns in Vermont, some dating back a hundred years.

About the only holdover from when Bellamy opened the place was the name, which had stayed the Milk House right from the beginning, although it was informally known as the Six Teats while the girls ran the place.

When Bingo walked in he was greeted with a roar of shouted wisecracks and jibes. Nearly everyone in the bar was wearing a hat of some sort, ranging from a red felt hunting fedora to billed caps with "John Deere" or "Caterpillar" on the front. Painters wore painter pants, some with bibs. Plumbers, truck drivers, farmers, and men who spent their days on bulldozers or back hoes wore dark olive-green workpants and workshirts bought off the back of the uniform company's truck.

Most, particularly those over a certain age like Bingo, wore their cuffs and collars buttoned, so face and hands and the back of the neck were permanently mahogany colored while the pale white skin visible at wrist and neck showed the color of the rest of them.

Carpenters were apt to be dressed any which way. A varied lot that included every sort from former New Jersey school teachers to farm boys who had never been further from home than the World's Fair up to Tunbridge, most of them were small builders working for themselves. Every one of them thought he was a better architect than any architect and a better engineer than any engineer. Work boots or running shoes, could be either one. You never knew with carpenters. Bingo dressed farmer himself. Although he had made his living over the years principally as a carpenter, he thought of himself as a farmer, doing carpentry on the side.

He lived in the house where he was born and always had lived there. He had worked off the farm throughout his adult life, carpentering and whathaveyou. At home there had always been animals to tend to; it wasn't a vegetable growing operation. Pasture and a hayfield, a patch of corn for winter feed, a well-managed woodlot, a section of just useless scrub wooded land, 41 fairly lumpy acres in all, that was it. There was a sizable vegetable garden that put a lot of their food on the table, but Milly took care of that.

The barn was pretty well filled at the moment. Two ram lambs, just weaned, bought from Mrs. Pamela Hathaway, that would go off to the slaughterhouse after Thanksgiving and provide the Reillys with some wonderful meals next winter. A matched pair of mighty Belgian work horses that won prizes at the Fairs, while earning their keep hauling tourists on hay rides and sleigh rides. A handful of geese, so there were six or eight young ones to dress at Christmas time. And the beef cattle, currently 13 nice cows and Jake. Carefully over the years, he had improved the small herd, getting better blood in there, breeding for size and strength and conformation, selling here, buying there, trading and dickering. Jake was a find, from up along the Canadian border, one of two really good young bulls in that barn, but the fellow couldn't use both of them. One or the other, but not both. He knew Bingo was looking for a good bull so he got in touch and they got visiting and dickering and the next thing you know Jake was on his way to Woodbine.

And right at the moment Jake's name was on everyone's lips. Ordinarily Bingo was eager to talk about Jake, such a marvelous specimen, bragging him up to anybody who would listen. Today was a little bit different.

"By God you 'spect ta lose the keys to the truck, things like that, but not a damn bull weighs about a ton!"

"Sure you looked everyplace there Bingo, like under the bed, down cellar, up'n the loft?"

"Git 'im back, better gitcha spare bull, case he gits lost again!"

"Better git Peter Larkin he'p ya find 'im!" Peter Larkin was a Woodbine boy, born without any sense of direction whatsoever; out of sight of a road he was lost and somebody had to go find him. Hunting season, they'd long since learned to just sit Peter on a stump someplace, and tell him not to move under any set of circumstances, and then they'd go fetch him when it was time to go home.

There wasn't much that Bingo could say, and that was not a common occurrence. He just accepted the inevitable, standing at the door with a big grin on his face, letting the rude and affectionate jeering wash over him like a bucket of water. During the first great hoot, he bowed and tipped his hat and bowed again. Still his nature was to counter-punch.

"FIGURED, BY GOD, IT'S TIME YOU BOYS GOT SOME EXPERIENCE CATCHIN' A BULL THAT'S RUNNIN' LOOSE." Pretty weak, but the best he could come up with at the moment.

After the initial chorus of whoops and smart remarks, Bingo settled down along the bar with his bottle of Donovan's Downtown Stout and considered the day. The damned day, as he thought of it.

Jake was not going to be easy to catch. Young and powerful, in perfect physical condition, wild enough to be dangerous and easily spooked, he was going to have to be lured into a pen someplace or subdued with a medicated dart.

The ridge he was most likely roaming was pretty much wooded and steep, tough going on foot and only a few logging roads and driveways for vehicles, mostly too wet to negotiate this first week of June. Getting close to him was going to be tough, and whoever shot the dart gun would do well to shoot from 10 feet up a tree.

At least the leaves weren't out at full summer peak. But they were filling in fast, especially on days like today, sunny and warm.

Bingo sighed, a bit down about the whole affair. He had plenty to do this next couple of weeks without all this business of chasing Jake around the puckerbrush. There was some trimming and planting up to Brookings that had to be done before the wedding on Saturday. Then as soon as it dried up enough he wanted to fertilize the east hay-field, bags of 20-10-10 setting in the barn ready to go, then there was fencing to fix in the pastures, a regular spring-time chore. And he had promised to build a storage shed for Perseus Burlington before the first of July.

And here he was probably going to lose a day or two getting Jake back in the barn, right at the start of the most productive time of the year. Damn nuisance, having to pay attention to the animals, which are a break-even proposi-tion at best, when there are better and more profitable things to do.

You can't make any money raising animals in Ver-mont, of course, what with land costing so much and taxes going up and government regulations getting tighter and tighter. And it's especially difficult in Woodbine, with all its wealthy retired people and younger wealthy people too. Not to mention the not so wealthy city people who thought of the village as a tourist town, while Bingo and his friends thought of Woodbine as the commercial center of a farming area. Drawn by the resort and the golf course and the sports center and the ski area and the beauty and the relaxed pace, and backed by the quarterly check from the trust fund at the Bank of Boston or Chase Manhattan, an inherited portfolio or both, the newcomers set up shop as lawyers or artists or merchants in Woodbine and for many of them it didn't make any difference if they showed a profit or not.

As the area changed from a fairly stable rural popula-tion to a growing exurban population, the demand for land and housing changed property values and just about made any kind of farming a waste of your land assets. There was so much more money in cutting it up and selling it off that working 14 to 16 hours a day, seven days a week, seemed like a pretty dumb thing to do. Bingo noticed that the ones who made the most noise about saving the family farm were folks who had never slaved on one year in, year out, with little reward but an aching back and a growing debt load.

This change in the texture of the community had been in progress for many years but picked up speed when the Interstates from Boston and Hartford opened up Vermont in the 1960s. Tumble-down old farmhouses were fetching outlandish prices and land you couldn't give away in 1950 was going up too. Like almost everybody else, Bingo figured it wrong. "It's goin' up, but you'll never see $1000 an acre land in Woodbine," he said.

Ha! Now he sat on $4,000 per acre land, and if it was further up the hill it'd be $6,000 an acre land. And taxes to go with it, by God. Flatlanders no more than moved in and they raised a big hullabaloo to get the perfectly good old school torn down and a new one built with a flat roof, for crying out loud, here in snow country. And taxes go to the moon to pay for it.

And they want this fixed and they want that fixed. Man pays a fortune for a tumble-down house and 30 scrubby acres at the end of a gravel road, and the first thing he does is complain that the road's muddy in the spring and narrow in the winter and dusty in the summer. What'd they expect, a white line down the middle?

It irritated Bingo. People buy a piece of land that a cow can't even stand up on, and after they build a fancy house on it they start yelling for the town to "do something about the road."

Every now and again, when he got bellyaching about no money in raising stock and taxes too high and such,

someone would ask him why he kept on with it. Why not
sell the place to some dummy for three or four times what
it was worth and retire, set for life. It was one of the few
questions that could shut him up; he didn't have a real
good answer for it. The folks had lived there and he'd always lived there and there had always been animals
around.

"Wal, you look out and see them critters over there on
the side hill and it gives you kind of a good feeling, you
know," he'd say.

Not a bad answer, at that.

Stumpy Parker dropped onto the stool next to him.

"Bingo," he said, "I was in the barn up to the old
Chester place today."

Where the Brookings lived, up the hill from Bingo,
was known as the old Chester place despite the fact that
Chester had sold out and retired to a mobile home in Flor-
ida some 23 years before and it had had two owners since.
The Chesters were the last ones to take the place serious, as
a farm, so it was the Chester place.

"That Philadelphia lady called up and wanted the barn
cleaned up," Stumpy went on, "and me and the boy went
over." He paused. "I been in and out of barns all my life
and I never been in a barn as clean as that one. And she's
got us up there to clean up. I said 'Clean what,' she says
'We're serving food in here next Saturday if it rains.' I says
'You're what?'"

Bingo sympathized. "She's running me ragged over the
flower beds, too. Daughter's getting married this Saturday
and she's all het up about it." He finished his stout and
signaled for another one. He poured the brew just so, not a
lot of foam and only a couple inches in the glass, and
thought about the coming week. Jake running loose, Laura

29

Brookings in a great hullabaloo over the wedding, Milly grumpy as hell over something or other. He sighed and shook his head. "It's a rocky road to Dublin, Stumpy, a rocky road to Dublin."

Bingo and Stumpy went way back. Back to growing up around Woodbine before it turned into a "god damned candy-assed flatlander do-gooder golfie-town," as Bingo was wont to put it. They went back to when you tied the deer over the front fender and went downtown to get it weighed and tagged and everyone–men, women, children–came over to look and say "OOH" and "AHH." Now, by God, you get a nice buck and the do-gooders are hissing at you about killing Bambi.

"You sign up for the tournament, yet?" Stumpy inquired.

"Damn no. Glad you said that; forgot all about it."

So he anteed up a ten-spot to enter the final darts tournament of the spring, a major event scheduled to commence right in this bar on Sunday. Summer was too busy a time for such tournaments, whether you were a farmer or a house painter or whatever. There wouldn't be another such until about the beginning of deer season in November.

And this last one carried the biggest purses for the top players. Starting right with that first one in November, and continuing through the winter and spring, there was a tournament every month or so. And at every one a little bit of the purse was held back, all to be added to the purse for this season finale. "By God, I guess I'll be here," Bingo growled.

Then Stumpy put another worry on his shoulders.

"Ya'know, Bingo, I run inta old Plutarch Oglesby yesterday afternoon down to the Reading firehouse 'n' he says

he's lookin' to move in closer ta town." In recent years
Plutarch had been living practically a recluse in an old
shack way the dickens up a road that's nothing but a dotted line on the town map, and when the Reading town
map goes to a dotted line it means that maybe somebody
got a skidder through there once in August of a dry year.

"Well he told me that last month, too, and I been
meaning to work up an offer on that land of his, thinking
maybe he could use the money to get a decent place,"
Bingo said. "Kinda' slipped my mind with all the spring
chores."

"Well he gave me a message for ya,'" Stumpy declared.
"He said to tell ya' that flatlander up the hill from you had
made 'im a big offer fer the property, but he ain't done
nothin' about it and won't till he hears from you."

"DAMN!" said Bingo Reilly. "One damned thing right
after another!"

This was a complication. He couldn't match the
money Hickham could spend and he couldn't ask old Plutarch to make a financial sacrifice for old times sake. At
one time Plutarch had been quite a drinker and he and
Bingo would run into one another in saloons and roadhouses. They had always liked each other's style, both independent, spit-in-your-eye type personalities, although
Plutarch was quiet and Bingo was loud. Plutarch was a big
strong man in his prime, worked in the woods a lot, built
like an ox, didn't take any guff from anybody. He had in-
tervened on Bingo's side at a crucial point in a brawl in
Bridgewater Corners one time that had surely saved Milly a
great deal of iodine and gauze bandages. It might have
been his remembrance of the kindness of Bingo's parents
in taking him in back in his youth. Whatever it was, Bingo
knew–other things being equal–that Plutarch would rather

31

sell to him than to that flatlander up the hill. The problem was how to make other things equal.

Jake and now this. Bingo ordered another Donovan's Downtown Stout and went to thinking.

Along towards 6 p.m. Darwin Blakely zipped right on up the scale on his harmonica and Bingo, starting to feel better, hummed a bit under his breath. And soon his fine baritone was leading the way:

"When I joined the Canadian Navy,
Sailed along the northern shore,
That's when I met sweet Bridget O'Shaughnessy,
Otherwise known as the Winnipeg Whore."

By 7 p.m., with six bottles of Donovan's Downtown Stout and 11 rowdy verses of *The Winnipeg Whore* under his belt, Bingo was on his way home to face the grumps of Milly.

———

Probably got something to do with some woman or other, Bingo figured, although how she could've found out about last week he couldn't imagine. Way the hell and gone down below Springfield looking at some cattle for Wellington Burbank, he'd met this girl he'd gone to school with, well not exactly a girl anymore, hadn't seen her since, hardly, and she's widowed, living alone, and why not have a cup of coffee, and one thing and another, and the next thing you know, Bingo!

Well, news travels, he thought, but he wasn't giving anything away until he was sure what Milly was so mad about.

Milly had set her cap for him when she was just 19 and he fell hard, to the dismay of a number of young hopefuls in the area. Milly played it cool in public, remarking often over the years that she "could've done better if she'd waited," but back then she managed to let him lure her into the loft at the Greenwood Farm, where they were both helping get the hay in, and he was a goner.

The relationship had its stormy moments over the years, especially in the early years when they were out drinking and dancing every weekend, down to Ludlow or over in Rochester. Those were some times back in the 50s and into the 60s; cheap liquor and fist fights was the way Bingo remembered it. And Milly was hell on wheels with a snoot-full, too.

Bingo had a tendency to stray, him having an easy way with the ladies, and now and then Milly found out things she'd probably been better off not knowing. And what she would do was: she would simmer. And once in a while she and Bingo would be out at a dance or some roadhouse or other and she would come face to face with the particular lady that she happened to be simmering about at the time and, as the Sheriff Department's report invariably noted, "violence ensued."

Milly was still a handsome woman, but she wasn't sylph-like by any measure. She stood 5'10," with black hair long and thick, and a serene face. And she could flip a bale of hay up on the truck with the best of the menfolks. The general consensus was that "she's a damned good-lookin' woman." Not beautiful, mind you, but damned good looking, although a minority judged her perhaps a bit too thick through the hips. "Built the strongest where the strain's the greatest," was Bingo's answer to that.

He pondered the possibilities on the way home, his old truck moving down the South Road at 35 miles per hour, his eyes missing very little along this road he'd traveled for over 60 years. A little spring runoff damage here, trunk of an old maple split there, new folks moving into this house, folks in that house got their tomato frames all ready to go.

Time he got to his house he usually had two or three cars piled up behind, tailgating, impatient, flatlanders in a hell of a hurry to get somewhere or other. He never budged or changed speed. To hell with them, he thought, as he swung onto the Farm Road, just past the house, hearing the four vehicles piled up behind him accelerate with the abruptness of intense irritation.

The house, built before the First World War, sat only 30 feet back from the highway because when it was built the road was dirt, tourism hadn't been invented, no traffic to speak of.

Bingo climbed the worn steps to the back porch, thinking the house should be painted but he'd be damned if he'd paint it this summer with a reappraisal coming up in the fall. Damned taxes too high already.

He filled the kitchen door, stopping for a moment to let his eyes get used to the different light, broad-shouldered, with a full head of black hair only slightly streaked with gray, just a hair over six feet tall, a dance or two in the old boy yet.

He stepped into a small kitchen with an old porcelain sink and drain board set on legs of two-inch lead pipe. The cold tap was connected to a spring across the road and up the hill, gravity feed, water even when the power went out. The hot water tap wasn't connected to anything; you want hot water, you heat it on the stove, an old gas model in the corner. The refrigerator was next to the doorway into the front room. The freezer, the single greatest boon to home gardening since the discovery that slugs willingly drown themselves in beer, was out on the back porch.

Milly stood at the stove, stirring a pot of the last of the winter's pea soup. Starting in October, she made big batches of pea soup, froze it in generous portions, and warmed their ribs with it on a regular basis. She gave him a look he couldn't interpret, then went back to stirring.

In the other corner were some cabinets he'd built, for dishes and such. Just visible under the cabinet was a mark on the floor where the rain barrel had sat when he was a boy. Before the spring was connected to the house the rain barrel was their source of water, and he remembered that his mother always kept a trout or two in it to keep it clean.

From the kitchen he stepped into the front room. Here was his worn leather chair, belonged to his father before him, with the table alongside piled with farm catalogs, Fair entry forms, notes on carpentry jobs, last week's newspapers and the like. There was a couch and a worn rug over the hardwood floor that needed sanding and finishing. The walls were decorated with pictures of cows and horses, ribbons won and framed, a photo of Bingo with the winning team at Fryeburg Fair in 1962, Bingo and a blue ribbon ram back in 1958, when it was still possible to keep from losing money on sheep.

The newest thing in the room was the wood stove, one of those air-tight European models that were so efficient and heated so evenly, provided, of course, you didn't burn down the house with a chimney fire from all the creosote they generated.

There was no fireplace, the house having been built when they were considered dust-producing heat-wasters.

Three boys had come along to grow up in this old farmhouse, and in due time went their own ways. All brought up the same way, they all turned out different. The oldest boy joined the Air Force and eventually decided to make a career out of it. The middle one was in and out of trouble and currently serving six months for possession of stolen property ("I got to own him," Bingo once remarked, "he turned up in my trap.") The youngest boy went to Colorado one summer to fight forest fires and stayed there. Last Christmas he came home with a new wife, at least they said they were married, and he was now living in Denver and working in an office.

There was a table in the corner of the room, by the front windows, where they ate lunch and dinner. Breakfast was in the kitchen. The front door was off to the right of the room and was opened just twice a year, for spring and fall housecleaning. He shooed Dobbin, a big old 13-year-old rascal of a neutered tomcat, off his chair and sat down in it.

After Dobbin jumped up in his lap and got himself settled just right, Bingo arranged the evening paper around the cat and tried to get interested in the news, but he was thinking about Jake and where he might be found. Dumb animal like that could get in trouble and hurt himself. Jake was too valuable for that! Damn right!

Dinner was pretty quiet, with some plate thumping and skirt swishing and wrinkly face. Not much talk, but what little there was seemed civil. But you never knew with Milly. She had a temper like a summer thunderstorm and when it let go, the best thing to do was take cover. He remembered times, back in their younger days, when she'd get in a certain mood and take on a certain amount of liquor and just look around searching for somebody to have trouble with.

And Milly never lost a public brawl, which was more than Bingo could say. And she ignited the most spectacular go-around Woodbine had seen in a generation when she ran into Clarissa Hodgsen at the annual Woodbine Volunteer Firemen's Ball at the Columbia Hotel in White River Junction. Milly knew for a fact that Bingo was with Clarissa in a motel in Island Pond for a three-day weekend the previous March when he was supposed to be at a hunting camp in the backwoods of Reading hunting rabbits with Stumpy Parker and his brother. The thought had been festering for months and when she turned around from getting a refill at the bar and found herself face to face with Clarissa, it just seemed like the natural thing to pitch that rum and coke in her face and follow with a solid left-right-left combination.

The hotel ballroom was real crowded, you could hardly move in there, and it was July and hot and humid and a full moon and everybody half crocked. Part of Milly's drink hit some other people, and Clarissa lurched into some others, and somebody threw an elbow, another person swung a backhand and all of a sudden the brawl was general. Even people with no interest in fighting were fighting, trying to get to the doors. Men and women were swinging chairs, people ducking under tables, the bar was one of those things with wheels you roll out of a storeroom and it went right over on the bartender, he's yelling and soaked with liquor, and they said afterward you could hear the din across the river in New Hampshire.

For once Bingo had nothing to do with it. He was up on the stage with a microphone in his hand bellowing out a song with *The Wayward Woodchucks*, a country band that was on hand for your listening and dancing pleasure. The guitar player usually did the singing but he was a shrimpy little fellow and Bingo, feeling like singing, just climbed up there and took the mike away from him and unleashed his vocal cords. He was into his second number when the riot started. He and the band carried on to the end of the song, watching incredulously as happy throng dissolved into brawling mob, feeling like the orchestra on the Titanic.

By the time things quieted down there was damage not only to the ballroom and its furniture but also to the lobby and its furniture. The plate glass window on the street was shattered, the barbershop door got busted in and the fights spread out onto the street. Also the kitchen, because celebrants too far from the regular doors tried to get out that way. But the chef was Polish and spoke only rudimentary English, and he thought it was the German army after him again, his worst nightmare come true, so he and his staff put up some stiff resistance, fighting a rearguard action while retreating into the walk-in cooler. There were seven arrests.

The damage was enormous throughout the hotel, and it had to be paid for by the Woodbine Firemen's Benevolent Association, which was the official sponsor of the event. The hotel was two weeks getting completely back to normal, had to move the Rotary luncheon to the Congregational Church Hall that Wednesday, and it was several years before the Woodbine Volunteer Fire Department ventured to hold another Firemen's Ball.

Later there were different stories on how the rumpus got started, but Milly knew from the word go that she was the culprit. Sure, conditions were just right for the blaze, but she was the spark and she knew it. Some of the injuries were verging on the serious and, all in all, the event took the fun out of the raucous weekends for both Bingo and Milly. They quit going out to dancehalls and roadhouses not long after, bored with it and taken aback by the potential for serious harm. Maturity, you might call it.

But tonight there was mostly silence, not even any sympathy about Jake getting away. Bingo went to bed in the dark, in more ways than one.

———

Darkness took Jake by surprise in the woods near the elegant home of Mr. & Mrs. Phillip Fosterworth Pennington, painstakingly constructed of Vermont fieldstone with part of the deodorant fortune that was so closely associated with the Pennington family name.

Perhaps appreciating that their circumstances rested completely on the proposition that everybody stinks, Mr. & Mrs. Pennington, militant do-gooders in their 40s, devoted considerable time to the planning, placement, planting, plucking and promotion of their extensive and fragrant flower gardens.

Indeed, when the property appeared in House Beautiful magazine the previous year as much attention went to the grounds as to the structure itself. It was, by some four pages, the longest such photo tour ever published by the magazine, although among the urbane lawn chairs and chaise lounges clustered about the pools and tennis courts of Woodbine, its principal impact was a wave of incredulity that the Penningtons would allow Banjo, a 93-pound Gordon Setter, to sprawl himself the full length of a $15,600 Italian couch in the living room, as pictured on page 78. The discussion raged sporadically for months, but few of the hard-liners of either side–couch, no-couch–knew Banjo personally. He was actually a well-trained and well-behaved animal, although something of a cad with the neighborhood bitches.

At any rate, when Jake ambled out of the woods and walked through the fence into the huge garden the first member of the household to become aware of his presence was the controversial Banjo, relaxing on the porch, who set up a great ululating howl and, forgetting his careful training, lunged into action.

Jake, startled, bolted away from this noisy threat, through the heart of Mrs. Pennington's freshly planted cutting garden, kicking seedlings and expensive, guaranteed-weed-free topsoil in all directions, hurtling the length of the garden before bursting through the fence at the end and into the woods. Beds and rows of cosmos, zinnias, marigolds, nasturtiums, gladiolas, impatiens, snapdragons, alyssum, asters, dianthus, gazania, daisies, ripped from the soil and tossed every which way, scattered, delicate stems crushed and broken, identifying signs yanked out and flipped aside. Along the way he took out three rose trellises and an elaborate grape arbor in addition to the damage his plunging hooves wreaked. Perhaps worse, because it ensured a daily reminder of this monstrous event, Mrs. Pennington's favorite trowel, in a bucket near the rose garden, was kicked about and buried in the melee, not to be recovered until it was turned up by the rototiller the following year. Not a day went by the rest of the summer that Mrs. Pennington didn't reach for that trowel, not find it, and begin thinking extremely murky thoughts about Jake.

TUESDAY

J ake lumbered down off the ridge just after dawn, crossed the road about a mile north of the Reilly farm, and ambled through the early summer mist onto the 15th hole of the Woodbine Country Club, heading for the brook for his morning slurp. The golf course and the road lay in a valley extending south from the village. Jake had come down off the western ridge, known as Kirkridge, and, attracted by some good-looking bushes, was now ambling toward the eastern ridge, called Mount Harriet, much to the embarrassment of the town's tourist industry. The Woodbine Chamber of Commerce had tried to promote changing the name of Mount Harriet to some fake Indian name but it didn't take.

He paused at the 15th tee long enough to scratch himself on the ball washer, then started off again toward Mount Harriet. At that moment Barton Bradley started up the fairway mower in the shed just off the 14th fairway and, imagining himself at the controls of an F-16 on the flight deck of the U.S.S. Kitty Hawk, careened out into the morning with a roar, squinting about for Iraqi MIGs and taking a chip out of the jamb with the left mower bank in the process.

Jake was caught unawares, enjoying, as he was, the taste and crunch of the succulent "globosa" arborvitae bushes that had been brought in special from New Jersey because they were the personal favorites of the very rich man who currently chaired the Governing Board of the Country Club, and was startled by the abrupt and rancorous noise of the F-16. Eighteen hundred pounds of perfectly conditioned bull went from standing still to full speed almost instantly, accelerating across the 14th green for the trees, leaving great heaved up gouges in the perfectly groomed surface, gouges which would brutally demonstrate the catastrophic effects of an escaped bull to the golfing community of Woodbine, who would talk of nothing but this atrocity for several days.

There were no witnesses to the crime, however, since the F-16 pilot's attention was on the danger from the sky and Ernestine Cartwright, who mowed the greens every day, didn't start until 5:30 a.m., some 15 minutes after the awful event. She found it first thing though, because the 14th was the furthest south on the course and the noisy mowing began there and worked back toward the clubhouse end of the course where the village lay sleeping.

After a bit the sound faded for Jake and soon after that he forgot why he was running and stopped. He spent the rest of the day moving in and out of the meadows that he found along the flank of Mount Harriet, unaware that the movers and shakers of Woodbine were turning their attention, their indignant attention one might add, to the problem of his freedom.

It was, Bingo thought, a different barn without Jake. The pen looked bigger without his bulk. The whole place seemed tame, washed out, without the power and the menace of him. Keeping a bull was a test of strength. Most dangerous animal on any farm, without question, and a creature that does not tame. No sir! Better not be too sleepy or distracted dealing with a bull; they do something ugly when you least expect it. Every year or two some farmer or some farm hand gets himself killed by a bull.

That danger is a big part of the challenge of keeping a bull. And a big part of the pleasure of it, too. Jake was Bingo's daily roller-coaster ride, ski run, barrel roll, his qualifying lap at Indianapolis, his ride in a hang glider. Feeding the other animals, Bingo realized how important it was to get Jake back in one piece, unharmed, before he hurt some retired flatlander moved up from Boston who couldn't tell a bull from a milk cow.

He went back to the house and called the miscreant Bert.

"I know you done it and it wa'nt too smart but what's done is done," he began, and could sense Bert's relief over the phone. "You smart enough to climb a tree if Jake catches sight of ya?" Bingo wanted to know. "O.K., I want you to get up on the ridge this afternoon after school and work down from the village line. Just move along, and stop and listen, and look for some sign of Jake and if you find him get to a phone and call."

Mrs. Pennington called at 8 a.m., the morning light having disclosed just exactly what the dog had made such a hullabaloo about the night before. She was not happy.

A gardener and nurturer of flowers himself, Bingo sympathized. He liked the Penningtons, had built a garage for them once and they treated him all right, paid on time, no quibbling or bellyaching. And he'd had a big hand in putting in that garden that Jake tore up.

"I'll come over next week and see what I can do," he promised. Damn Jake. Probably out looking for a china shop right now.

Bingo no sooner hung up than the phone rang again. Jake was seen just outside South Woodbine. Out on the Northbridge Road a lady nearly put her Volvo into "...an enormous animal, a moose or a buffalo . . .," and there was a report of Jake drinking from the brook right in the center of the village.

"Mebbe he's growed wings," growled Bingo.

"Town's getting Jake Fever," said the First Constable, beginning to enjoy himself.

Milly didn't help. "You shudda known better than give Bert the job of button up," she said, "that boy don't think of nuthin' but naked women."

By the time the Country Club manager called to describe the damage to the 14th green, Bingo was getting sick of it all.

"Walked right through the fence, did he?" he asked innocently.

"What fence?" said the manager. "We don't have any fence."

"WAL, HOW IN HELL D'YA 'SPECT TO KEEP 'IM OUT THEN?"

"Why should I have to worry about keeping him out?" The manager didn't enjoy arguing with some farmer.

"GUESS YOU AIN'T WORRIED TOO MUCH, SEEIN' AS YOU AIN'T GOT NO FENCE," said Bingo and hung up the phone with a clatter. "Damn flatlanders," he muttered.

By 9 a.m. an informal network of friends and neighbors were checking in with reports of sightings, non-sightings, advice and offers to help. This was a varied group, ranging from millionaire horse breeders–Woodbine and South Woodbine were noted centers of equine activity–to a mobile home resident who ate fresh venison year round and was thus much in the woods, to fellow small farmers.

The sense of community and the intent to help was serious, however raucously it was presented. Doc Murchison fished around in the heap of junk in the back of his battered 1984 Subaru station wagon and found a pair of dart guns. These he lent to Bingo, complete with darts loaded with sufficient Rompun to bring an 1,800-pound bull to blissful slumber without permanent damage, provided only that the dart was delivered to a major muscle, preferably the hip.

Try some fancy shot for the shoulder, or for the brisket if he's facing you, and you could wind up with a dart in his snoot or an eye or something like that. If it didn't get in a muscle it would be wasted and if it hit a bone, the skull or a rib, it could bounce right out before the sedative was delivered. Using these things isn't as easy as it sounds.

And figuring out the dosage is more art than science. You start out with the approximate weight of the animal, and any experienced stockman could look at Jake and come within 50 pounds, so you have a firm number there. But the amount it takes to bring him down when he's calm won't even touch him when he's excited and the adrenaline is pumping. So when you load the gun, you have to make certain assumptions as to what the animal's state of mind will be off there in the future when you actually pull the trigger. What you want to do is get the stuff into the bull and then hang back, leaving him alone, not disturbing him. If the dose is right he'll roar around some and then as he calms down, not seeing any threats around him, the sedative takes effect and after a time he'll go down. What it amounts to is you take a fact, the weight of the animal, add a couple of hunches, stir in about three guesses, and go for it.

Bingo kept one of the guns and gave the other to Stumpy. That put one of them down in South Woodbine and in good hands, just in case.

Now, on the second full day of Jake's freedom, the word was well spread and folks were checking their pastures and looking around carefully before they stepped away from their barns, and looking up every now and again from fence mending or garden planting to listen and look.

With so many eyes and ears on the job, Bingo figured Jake would be back in the barn by dark.

The problem was that in early June it's still pretty wet in the woods. Little seeps that would be dry by the end of the month were practically gushing. Streams that only existed during spring runoff still had plenty of water in them. What this meant was that Jake, once he ventured high on the side of Mount Harriet and found the irregular string of small meadows there, had no need to go down to the valley for water. And Mount Harriet, overlooking the golf course and totally undeveloped, got no regular human traffic at this time of year either.

So Jake spent a peaceful day grazing aimlessly where nobody was looking for him, meandering gradually south away from Woodbine.

Along towards noon Bingo got sick of waiting for the phone to ring and drove his truck up to the Brooking house. Flower beds needed some work before the wedding anyway. Working with the soft and moist soil was a comfort, as was the early summer sun on his back. Helped him calm down. And Milly knew where he was to get in touch if necessary.

Thaddeus Brookings was in the driveway, admiring his new Saab. Ousted from his own living room by a meeting of the Board of Directors of the Woodbine Area Canine-Equine-Feline Fellowship, to be followed by a luncheon, he was at loose ends.

"Cheerio, Mr. Reilly, cheerio," he chirped in the British manner he had so admired during his five years in the American consular service in Africa.

"Bit of all right, eh," he went on, flicking a bit of dust off the front fender.

"Yup," said Bingo, thinking about how much it cost.

"Mrs. Brookings tells me you've misplaced an animal, Mr. Reilly."

"Yup."

"Bull, I believe."

"Yup."

"Rotten luck, that."

"Yup."

"Good job you'll find him soon."

"Yup," said Bingo, wondering what that meant.

His Lordship was running out of small talk. Bingo had that effect on him. He decided to give it one more try.

"Too early for a little spot of something?"

"Nope," said Bingo, surprised, but ready.

Thaddeus led the way into the dim coolness of the potting shed off the back of the house. There, from under the potting bench, he retrieved his emergency bottle of Jack Daniels. The shelf above yielded paper cups, the pour was deft, and the two men faced one another over the day's first.

"To your beast," Thaddeus proclaimed, "and his successful retrieval."

"Mud'n your eye," said Bingo.

And they drank.

Cheered, Bingo outlined some of the practical difficulties of catching a young bull and returning him safely to the barn, first the problem of just locating the animal, then getting some kind of control over him, then managing transport, and finally into the pen.

Quite an undertaking, they both agreed.

"Calls for another little touch," Thad declared.

"By God you're right," said Bingo.

Later, after Thaddeus had driven off to get the mail and putter around the village, Bingo got around to looking at the flower beds. Truthfully, he had lost interest in them. Knowing where the emergency bottle was kept, he offered himself another application while he tried to think of a plausible reason to postpone the job. He was relieved when Laura Brookings called from the kitchen door.

"Mr. Reilly, there's something in the chimney. An animal or something."

He went in to take a look.

Through the perfect kitchen, with the Garland range, heavy pans hanging from a cast iron rack, hanging plants, skylight, windows overlooking the vegetable garden and fields beyond, Cuisinart food processor, and every other kitchen appliance known to man, including an electric bread maker that did all the kneading for you. Bingo, mindful of Laura Brookings's presence, resisted the temptation to pinch the ample bottom of Madge Kershaw, brought in to help out with the luncheon preparations, who was standing at the sink.

Through the dining room with its plate rail and absolutely authentic antique sideboard, dining table, and china closet.

Across the Sarouk that covered the broad entrance hall.

Into the living room, his boots sinking into the 9′ by 14′ Kirman centered on the old fieldstone fireplace and chimney.

Bingo was surprised to find the room heavily occupied.

The monthly meeting of the Board of Directors of the Woodbine Canine-Equine-Feline Fellowship was in suspension pending investigation of the rustling noise in the chimney. Eight ladies stood anxiously, teacups in hand, peering toward the fireplace.

The ladies, each carefully dressed by one of the two up-scale dress shops in Woodbine, were teetering on the edge of being ill at ease. This was the first meeting of the newly elected Board for the coming year. Some, including Laura, were new to the group, some were old-timers, and some were new last year. But things were still a bit up in the air, since the Chairperson, a no-nonsense horse owner from South Woodbine, had not yet established a pace for the Board, an animating attitude that would determine how things were done in the coming year, or even whether anything much was done at all.

There was also a certain tension over the yearly shift of power from dog people to horse people. It was assumed

that everybody was a cat person. The Board typically had
two horse people, two dog people, one or two whose sym-
pathies were uncritically extended to the entire animal
kingdom, and the rest new people who did the donkey
work of organizing the fund raising luncheons, saw to the
printing of bumper stickers, went around putting up home-
made posters, and generally did the public groveling for
donations.

That the incoming board members put up with this
arrangement hinged on one fact: it was the absolutely best
way to get yourself plugged into the upscale sector of the
community. A couple of years on the Board was usually
sufficient to guarantee access to the right tennis partners,
the desirable social gatherings, the circles of the well-to-do.

So this important get-acquainted, ice-breaking meeting
was bad enough; now there's something in the chimney
and that old scoundrel Bingo Reilly comes tromping into
the room, John Deere cap pulled down snug on his skull.

"Mornin' ladies," Bingo growled, thinking they were
all too skinny, no meat on them.

He listened at the fireplace and heard nothing. Whatever was up there was still. He fiddled with the damper and
thought about it.

"Easiest thing is start a fire," he said.

"Wouldn't that be cruel?" someone ventured. This is a
Fellowship meeting here, was the guilty thought.

"Wal, I could get up on the roof and poke it down,
but if it's bats you won't like it," Bingo answered.

The bats were persuasive. The fire was laid and set,
and they all stood watching, waiting for the chimney monster to appear.

"If it's bats I need a towel," Bingo remarked. Laura's
decision was immediate; no old worn out towel in front of

this bunch. So Bingo soon stood awaiting bat fallout with a brand new bath towel that was softer than his mattress at home and nearly as thick.

As the smoke of the new fire rose, the rustling in the chimney began again, growing to quite a hullabaloo. Then with a flibberty flap a bat panicked onto an unburning log, then to the side of the fire, then to the hearth stone where it was captured by Bingo's ponderous pounce. The ladies cheered and Bingo responded with an elaborate bow.

He carried the bat outside and released it, returning to see if there were any more.

"Can we offer you something, Mr. Reilly?" Laura asked.

"Don't mind if I do. Jack Daniels," Bingo replied, to everyone's astonishment. Good lord it wasn't noon yet.

"Help yourself in the cabinet there; I'll get some ice."

"Don't need none." He poured himself two fat fingers. "Mud 'n your eye," he said, hoisting his glass in the direction of the ladies and knocking it back in one swallow.

"Good stuff," he said, pouring a refill. "Never did like bats," he added.

Laura, who had so wanted the ladies to see her home ("She's done wonders with the old place," they were supposed to tell one another on the way home afterwards) despaired of salvaging anything from the day. She slipped out of the living room and called Milly from the kitchen phone.

"Mr. Reilly is in the living room with the Board of Directors of the Canine-Equine-Feline Fellowship," she began, wondering how to mention the Jack Daniels.

She needn't have worried.

"Is he into the bourbon?" Milly asked.

"Yes." She wondered if Thaddeus had had anything to do with that.

"Be right up."

When she got there eight minutes later Bingo's voice had risen to Grange Hall volume, booming amongst the delicate porcelain figures on the coffee table and the decorative dinner plates displayed on the south wall–Timothy Dwight, the Wellesley Chapel, Harvard Yard.

Milly could hear him as she stepped into the kitchen. She looked at Mrs. Brookings apprehensively and said, "Oh, oh," very softly. "Oh, oh," she said again. She looked at Madge Kershaw, who shrugged her shoulders slightly and rolled her eyes.

"Think we're too late?" asked Mrs. Brookings.

"Fraid so," said Milly. She went to the hall and had a look. The ladies stood listening, tea cups in hand, expressions varying from embarrassed to amused.

Bingo was well launched into a pretty good story.

" . . . lived down in there next to the old Jasper place 'n' kept some beef cows 'n' raised pigs 'n' I don't know what all. Wal, they caught a coyote live one day, been gettin' after the chickens, brought 'im in, they'd got 'im in some kind of homemade trap, and there he was in the yard.

"Wal, they got to drinkin,' and first thing you know they started thinkin' canny, thinkin' they'd outsmart this coyote and this coyote's whole family.

"Got a pitchfork through the bars and over his neck, and they fiddled around and one thing and another and got three sticks of dynamite strapped onto 'im. See, they figured they'd let 'im go and he'd run home quick and that'd take care of mama and the kits too.

"They got about a three minute fuse onto 'im, they knew he's denned up fairly close up on the sidehill, and they got to crowin' and talkin' to 'im and tellin' 'im he'd sure be glad to get home and such. And finally Harvey got a old kitchen match and lit the fuse and they turned him loose with a whoop."

Bingo paused and surveyed his audience. He had them in the palm of his hand, nice tennis-playing ladies who owned horses and golden retrievers and cats. The new country gentry. All silent now, waiting on his next word. He took another belt of the bourbon and spoke quietly, slowly, eyes intense on the group.

"That coyote run right under the truck."

The ladies gasped.

"Parked right there 'side the house, wan't but about three months old, bright red, four wheel drive, Harvey was proud as hell of it. Wal, the first thing they did, being half drunked up and not too smart to begin with, was run around in circles every whichaway. One of the boys run to the barn to get the pitchfork, which o'course was right where they'd been standin,' and another one run for the tool shed to get something with a handle to poke with and Harvey got down next to the truck and hollered at that critter to get the hell home where he belonged.

"That coyote wa'nt goin' no place. He was in the only dark place in that big bright yard and he was protected above and he wa'nt moving. The pitchfork was tangled up in the trap and they couldn't do much pokin' with the rake 'cause the critter kept movin' and snarlin' and Harvey was yellin' and gittin' red in the face. 'Thought the old man'd shit the bed right there,' the oldest boy told me later.

"Bout that time somebody said, 'How long was that goddam fuse?' and they all three run for the barn. They git

53

there and they're all peekin' around the door and waitin.' They probley had a minute and a half left; that's a long time to stand around waitin' for something to happen. Little while, Harvey's gittin' hopeful, donchaknow. 'Maybe it's gone out,' he sez."

Another dramatic pause. And a swallow of Black Jack to prepare the vocal chords.

"KABOOM!" Bingo roared.

"BLOWED THE GOD DAMNED TRUCK FOUR FOOT IN THE AIR! TOTALED THE SONUVABITCH!"

Bingo paused, enjoying himself. Served Harvey right, the whole affair, the damn fool.

"Broke every window in the house, knocked the old lady off the living room sofa where she's takin' a nap, busted half the dishes in the kitchen, pictures off the wall, the old lady thought the furnace blowed up and she's dead for sure, she ain't all that smart, it was July for Chrissakes.

"Harvey had an awful fight with the insurance company. 'We ain't payin' you to blow up your own god-damned house and truck' was what they said. The old lady was some ugly about the whole thing, too. The boy told me Harvey slept in the barn most of that summer."

"What about the poor coyote?" asked one of the ladies.

"Dead as a hammer," Bingo declared, "and if you ever seen three or four lambs all tore up and half et after a bunch of coyotes gets in the field, you wouldn't be worryin' about no coyote." Looking up, he spied Milly and Mrs. Brookings coming from the kitchen.

"WAAL," he said grandly, with a slight bow, "I'd like you lovely ladies to meet my wife Milly. Mebbe she don't look like much, but she sure can split wood."

———————

Bingo's afternoon didn't go so good.

For one thing, Milly was madder than $700 about the scene up to Brookings, although he had tried to explain he was only helping the lady out by getting the damn bat out of the chimney. It didn't help any that he fell asleep in his chair right after lunch, if you could call it lunch; the way Milly slapped that sandwich together you'd think he'd of planted the damned bat in the chimney himself.

Actually, Bingo and Thaddeus Brookings were faring about the same. Having buddied up to take on significant overloads of the pure and clear at an unusually early stage of the day, they had parted to further their intake. Bingo's venture into bat control culminated in Milly's cold fury. Thaddeus, at loose ends, wound up at the Country Club for lunch, fell gratefully in with questionable companions and, through a slight haze, happily lost $138 at gin rummy before doddering home to meet Laura's withering stare.

But the newspaper didn't call Thaddeus for an interview. That was the difference.

The telephone ring, set at top volume because Milly was often in the garden, jangled Bingo awake with a start. Groggy as always after a rare daytime sleep, he answered with dry voice and truculence.

"LO!" Blinking and squinting at the clock on the wall. Three in the afternoon.

"Are you Mr. Bingo Reilly?" Even tones, no nonsense please.

"SO WHAT!" Sleeping scrunched in the chair made his "tractor leg" act up. One summer back when he was in high school he had misjudged a side hill and rolled his father's tractor. Busted his right leg pretty bad, and although old Doc Bremerton set it the best he could, it healed just a couple of degrees off of plumb and had bothered him ever since. The accident did two things: it ended his career as a pretty good high school athlete and it kept him out of the Korean War. He flexed the leg, rubbing the thigh with his hand, working the ache out of it.

"This is Millicent Buchanan from *The Word of Woodbine*. Is it true that one of your bulls is loose?"

"THE ONLYEST BULL I GOT IS LOOSE."

"When do you expect to catch him?"

"HOW THE HELL DO I KNOW WHEN I'M GOIN' TO CATCH 'IM?"

"You do plan to catch him, don't you Mr. Reilly?"

Bingo took a deep breath, groping for patience. "Wal, first you gotta find 'im, you know, before you can catch 'im, and then you gotta be someplace you can load 'im easy, he ain't gonna jess tiptoe home, ya know."

"Mr. Reilly, I understand that this animal is dangerous."

"Course he's dangerous! What the hell'd ya think? This ain't no barn cat. This is a bull! God damned right he's dangerous."

"You sound very proud of this animal, Mr. Reilly."

"Oh yeah! He's a good'un."

"Well, what should people do if they meet him? Mr. Reilly."

"Stay the hell away from him is my advice, but he'd most likely run away from people than anything else."

"Well, when do you decide to shoot him?"

"SHOOT HIM? WHY THE HELL WOULD I SHOOT HIM?" Damnedest thing he'd ever heard.

"If you can't catch him and he's dangerous, there must be a time when you say we have to shoot him." Logical enough.

"AIN'T NOBODY SHOOTING JAKE!" That was definite. "We'll catch him."

"How much does this animal weigh Mr. Reilly?"

"Oh . . . mebbe eighteen hundred."

"Pounds?"

"O'COURSE POUNDS . . . WHATTA YOU THINK?" Jesus, what a dummy!

"Mr. Reilly, that's a monstrous animal to meet in the woods."

"The problem is gettin' to meet 'im, not the monster animal."

"Monstrous."

"That's what I said."

"Do you accept responsibility if this animal hurts someone?"

"AIN'T NOBODY GONNA GET HURT, DAMMIT!"

"That remains to be seen, doesn't it?" Millicent asked, "and do I have your name correct as Calvin Reilly?"

"BINGO REILLY'S MY NAME, BINGO REILLY!"

"Well, I have it right here from . . ."

"KEY-RIST!" Bingo hung up with a crash and went into the kitchen to get a drink of water.

Milly, coming in from the garden, asked who called.

"God damned girl reporter from the paper!" Bingo growled.

"And I bet you charmed the hell out of her."

"Charmed her? Can't charm somebody don't know nuthin,' fer Crissakes!"

57

Meanwhile, at the office of *The Word of Woodbine*, Ms. Millicent Buchanan, recent product of the University of Vermont Women's Studies Program, ever vigilant for signs of sexism in word, thought, deed, attitude, manner of dress and address, angle of eyebrow, tilt of chin, cant of hip and general intuitive bad vibes, set grimly to work on her story.

———————

Life in Woodbine went on this first day in June. Students were worried about final exams and summer jobs and college entrance. The movie theater announced that for the months of July and August there would be showings every night of the week instead of just on weekends. Lambs were weaned and chicks hatched. Gardens were planted, some of them doomed to be seas of weeds by the Fourth of July. Early June is an optimistic time of year in Vermont, that's the answer.

The town road crew swept the village gutters clean of the residue from winter sanding of the streets. Winter woolens went into cedar chests and short sleeved cottons appeared. Windows were flung open to the soft air, rugs were hung over tree limbs and beaten, and blankets flapped on clotheslines in the sun.

Plans were hatched for camping trips, visits to the beaches of Maine, and book sales on the Village Green to benefit this or that worthy cause. Piles of junk accumulated in a corner of nearly everyone's garage, to be offered to the gullible at yard sales. The Health Center treated three cases of severe sunburn as winter's white skin was overexposed to the welcome, luxurious warmth that was so long in coming, as it is long in coming every year. Skunks and porcupines ventured out and about, leaving their unmistakable presence with eager family dogs, some of whom should have known better.

Animals were fed and fences mended. Troths were plighted. The Woodbine Chamber of Commerce and the Woodbine Garden Club coordinated the annual window-box project, where downtown store owners filled their windowboxes with flowers. The South Woodbine Volunteer Fire Department announced that a Cow-Flop-Plop to raise funds would be held in tandem with the annual South Woodbine Community Picnic and Flea Market on the Fourth of July. The scene would be a corner of Horace Bakerfield's pasture, which is conveniently adjacent to the South Woodbine Fire Station where the Picnic would be held. The Reverend Hemmingway of the South Woodbine Universalist Church would be the judge and his decisions would be final, handed down from above, so to speak. The South Woodbine firemen themselves would see to the marking of the field, assuring contestants of every square being of equal size and therefore with an equal chance to be the repository of the winning Flop. The purse would be dependent on the handle. The crucial cow had not yet been selected. The Sons of South Woodbine, a barbershop quartet of local renown, would perform while the critter browsed the pasture reaching a decision.

Bert Grantham took to the woods after school for the second day in a row, searching for Jake, but today with the exquisite Beatrice English in tow. With a flash of inspiration he had convinced her that two searchers were better than one and, additionally, whoever was importantly involved in Jake's recapture would be mentioned in this week's *The Word of Woodbine* in terms of approval and admiration. Beatrice, who had fantasies of her own, was finally convinced when he mentioned the near certainty of front page photographs of the heroic searchers.

In truth, as they scrambled over the flank of Mount Harriet, Bert was doing very little searching for Jake. What he was searching for was a flat place that wasn't too wet, where he could suggest that they sit down and rest. When such a place appeared, the search for Jake ended abruptly, as Burt's limited powers of conversation with the opposite sex were put to the test. Coming down off the ridge before dinner with his fellow searcher after some 45 minutes of fairly uncomplicated smooching, Bert couldn't have told you what day it was, or if it was early or late.

——— ——— ———

Jake, as darkness approached, worked his way down off the ridge where he had taken an afternoon nap leaning against a tree, and refreshed himself at the brook that ran north through the length of the golf course and into the village. He was finding tender young grass here and there, but it didn't seem to fill him up the way he wanted to be filled up. He looked around impatiently and left the brush and trees along the brook, headed for the relative brightness of an open meadow. He was hungry, and therefore restless and a little grumpy.

Jake was missing his daily ration of grain, and he wasn't enjoying the sensation.

——— ——— ———

By the time Bingo sat down to supper at 6 p.m. he knew there was no way Jake was going to be back in the barn that day. It was not a cheery meal, what with Milly all pinchy-faced and the phone jangling every five minutes and the lingering effects of the midday Jack Daniels overload.

After supper he bowed to the inevitable and got on the phone with the Constables, organizing a Jake drive for the next day.

First they would try to figure out, from the early morning observations of as many people as possible, whether Jake was on Kirkridge or Mount Harriet, which formed the west and east sides of the valley in which the village, golf course and Bingo's place lay.

If they got a strong notion either way, they would start a line of folks working south along the ridge from the Woodbine end and another line of folks working north from the South Woodbine end. With any luck, they could flush him down into the valley where he could be dealt with.

Both sides of the road down the valley were sprinkled with gentlemen farms and horse farms and former farms, so there should be a barn within reach when Jake descended. At the least there would be some kind of a fenced-in area, even partially fenced-in, where he could be got to stand still long enough to take the dart. Someplace you could get to with a truck. Didn't need to be a big truck. You could get him home with a pickup truck by snapping a lead on his nose ring and leading him at a crawl. There isn't much you can't do with a pickup truck, one way or another.

Bingo's truck was a 1986 three-quarter ton Ford pickup that he was fond of describing as "the color of horseshit." The world he moved in was sharply divided into three groups: those who drove Fords, those who drove Chevies, and a smaller band of eccentrics who drove Dodges. Folks tended to be born into these groups, inheriting the preference for one or the other from their fathers and older brothers, defending their favorites with a passion and an astonishing range of arguments. "I'druther *push* a Ford than *drive* a Chevy," or vice versa, was a cliché along the bar at the Milk House. Anyone who drove a small truck, like a Toyota or one of the small Fords or Chevies, wasn't really driving an honest-to-God truck, and was not taken seriously.

Bingo's truck had 131,000 miles on it, most of them at 35 or below, although occasionally he kicked it up to 55 on the Interstate. He did most of the maintenance himself and it ran pretty good, but it had seen a lot of hard use. Off the road, hauling lumber, slam-banging up and down the gravel roads of the Woodbine area year round, plowing in the winter, hauling hay or firewood, whatever needed to get done, that truck did it.

There was a chain saw on the floor on the passenger side that Milly was always belly-aching about, and both an "ought-six" and a flyrod in the rack behind his head. The mud-caked chain in the back had hauled many a $40,000 luxury car out of snowbanks and one of the rear springs was broken. Bingo was keeping his eyes open for a buy; this one had seen better days.

———————

By the time Jake settled down in a small grove of cedar high on the flank of Kirkridge just before midnight, he had had an exciting evening.

Leaving the brook he had walked through a field towards a barn at the other end, moving around a corner of the building to come face to face with Miss Verity Hooseman taking out the garbage. Verity let out a screech like the noon whistle, threw the garbage bag in his face, and heaved her 245 pounds into a newsworthy gallop back to the house.

When she finally caught her breath, she got right on the phone to give the First Constable an unprintable earful, then dialed the Reilly residence to lodge her complaint personally, hollering at Bingo at maximum volume for several minutes.

Bingo, as was his custom, went on the offensive.

"Why dint ya tackle 'im and hold 'im, Verity? I coulda come right down with the truck and got 'im."

Verity, who, it was widely noted, "has a real mouth on her," was inspired by this remark to heights of vituperation that astonished even Bingo, referring to him in her peroration as "a loudmouth blowhard and a limpy-dicked cheapshit old fart."

Bingo hung up with a crash once more.

"How long you expect the phone to stand up to that treatment?" Milly wanted to know.

"By God, if she'd been here I'da knocked 'er on 'er ass."

"Don't go pickin' fist fights you ain't likely to win." Milly had the last word, delivering a shot not only to Bingo but also to Verity, whom she did not admire.

As Bingo headed for the back bedroom it occurred to him that he was tired, and that he had spent more time on the telephone over the last two days than in the previous two months.

Not too long after his encounter with the articulate Verity, Jake ventured across the South Road, only to be caught in the headlights of a BMW driven by Bartholomew Herbert, whose reactions had been slowed by the application of three martinis (extra extra bone dry Tanqueray rocks twist) at the elegant cocktail lounge of the Woodbine Inn, whence he had adjourned seeking solace after a disastrous misjudgment that afternoon in the area of palladium futures, which had put him some $26,000 down in the time it took to duck across the street from the office for a late lunch and return, no more than 40 minutes.

Although the brakes went on late, they went on full force, and the vehicle, wheel wrenched to the left, slid to a screeching rocking halt crosswise in the road, having missed Jake by a whisker. Despite having been a dangerous and near tragic encounter, the incident did both Jake and Bartholomew a world of good. It sharpened in Jake a wariness that he had not fully deployed before, an acquisition of street wisdom, and it put the day's financial reverse in perspective for Bartholomew.

"Hell with it," he mumbled as he straightened the car around, "as long as Nancy doesn't find out, it'll be camouflaged by the next quarterly check." Cheered by the thought, and delighted to have a personal encounter with Jake to brag about at the Country Club, he put the car in gear and went from 0 to 60 in less time than was prudent.

Sometime later, along towards midnight, Jake moved across a meadow, over a stone fence and onto a barely used side road, just off Rooster Road, along the flank of Kirkridge. There sat a pickup truck in the dark, engine giving an occasional small click as it cooled. Jake smelled grain from the truckbed and ambled over towards the vehicle.

Nearly there he stopped short, alerted by rustling and grunting from the truck. A head came up, sensing something, and looked three feet into Jake's rheumy eyes. A scream, a yell, a flapping blanket, coitus interruptus of the hastiest kind, Jake's reckless crashing departure through the brush, love's magic moment lost, at least for this night.

This encounter escaped historical notice, however, and neither the Constables' nor Bingo's sleep was disturbed by ringing phones, no exaggerated stories were retailed the following day at the Post Office about how close a thing it really was, no heroic feats written into the script. This was so because although the folks in the pickup truck were married, they were not, in fact, married to one another.

Thus, Jake's final encounter of the day went unreported.

WEDNESDAY

Wednesday morning, right after chores, Bingo scouted around the pasture on foot, hoping maybe Jake had found his way home. A vain hope, but worth the effort anyway, what with the damp coolness of the shade contrasting with the damp warmth of the early sun when you stepped out of the shade, not to mention the sight of mist coming off the brook.

Bingo felt recharged when his wet boots clomped across the back porch to the kitchen door, once more optimistic on catching Jake and ready to take a poke at anyone who gave him any guff whatsoever. People yelling on the telephone and damn Jake so elusive and Milly playing the deep freeze had got him down, but his early morning patrol got the blood pumping and restored his normal aggressive nature.

Golf! Who the hell played golf? Bunch of old potbellies in pink britches. Hit a ball with a stick and go hit it again. Damn silly thing for grown-ups to do, if you asked him, and too bad if their damn greenaway got hoof prints in it. Might stop some of them from hitting into the brook; always a bunch of them staring into the water, poking along the reeds with their sticks, looking for their golf balls. Jake might have helped them.

Back to the phone. No Jake anywhere yet.

It was late, nearly 8:30, before there was a report worth paying attention to. A flatlander named Herbert, bought the Anderson place on Otter Crick Road, claimed he almost run into Jake on the South Road last night and had to get out of the car and bravely chase him away in order to continue on his drive home. Said Jake run into the woods on the Mount Harriet side of the road between Bingo's place and South Woodbine.

That was the best intelligence they had heard and, what with time passing and men with work to do standing around waiting, and the South Woodbine Postmaster, who delivered the report, saying that Herbert didn't look as hung over as usual, all these considerations factored in, the decision was made to make the drive on Mount Harriet.

And so the morning was wasted, because Jake was across the way on Kirkridge. Bingo's decision was based on faulty intelligence and a general is only as good as his intelligence, as Hannibal or Rommel or Wellington could have told him if they'd been sitting in the parlor with him that morning.

Fidgeting around the house all morning clarified another difficulty encountered by generals. They don't get to do much but wait around to see what happens and Bingo wasn't really well-inclined to such active inactivity. By the time he got around to giving her helpful advice on how to make the pie crust she was working on, he had Milly going crazy.

"Go work on the damn fence," she said. "I'll call ya' if the phone rings."

It was the right prescription. Resetting fence posts was just the ticket. All his frustration went into swinging that six-pound maul and those fence posts were definitely reset.

After the fence work, Bingo went up the hill to Brookings' to do the flower planting that hadn't gotten done the day before. He hoped that Mrs. Brookings wasn't as mad about yesterday as Milly was. He'd just been trying to help out with the damn bat in the chimney.

There was no one in evidence around the house so he set right about the planting and checking the beds he had set out last week. He did a little watering but mostly worked on the beds since it was supposed to rain this afternoon or tonight, at least according to that damn fool disc jockey that woke him up every morning.

Although it was something of an embarrassment to Bingo since he considered it a sissy's game, the fact is he had always enjoyed working in flower gardens. A vegetable garden he could take or leave, but a flower garden, well, that was something.

The delicate petals, the blooms, the colors, the smells, all enchanted him well beyond what he would admit. Milly understood, and confined herself to the vegetable garden at home. The patch of the garden devoted to flowers was his domain.

His reputation as the owner of a green thumb had grown quietly over the years, although he never put himself forward as a gardener. Folks learned that you had to be careful how you went about approaching the subject with him. The best way, it was generally agreed, was to happen to meet him somewhere, maybe the supermarket, accidentally on purpose, and ask him by the way do you know of anyone who can help me out with the flower garden this year. Then if you're lucky, and he isn't building somebody a garage or something, and if he thinks he can get along with you, well then you might get that green thumb working on your behalf. "Waal, I might could he'p ya' out." At top dollar, of course.

He was working in the flower garden off to the left of the house when the Brookings new Saab pulled into the yard. Laura's wave was minimal, the wave of a person who is mad as hell and has every right to be mad as hell. His buddy Thad's wave was sheepish or resigned or browbeaten, Bingo couldn't decide which. All in all, best stay away from the house today.

Thaddeus Brookings would have been the first to agree with that judgment, but staying away was not one of the options open to him this morning. Laura had awakened him with a stabbing elbow, still furious over yesterday's events, with a list of errands to be accomplished today, and he, Thaddeus, was to be the chauffeur in "your brand new Saab, that we didn't really need, considering the Mercedes is running fine, but you just had to spend the money, didn't you."

After 26 years of marriage Thaddeus knew there was no way to deal with the situation except to let it blow over. Hell hath no fury sort of thing, it was, but combined with a low-grade headache and a less than tranquil stomach, it made for a tough morning.

No philanderer, and not a great one for playing poker with the boys or hanging out in saloons, Thaddeus had nonetheless thoroughly enjoyed yesterday, from the comradely imbibing with Bingo to his rusty attempt at gin rummy later on.

The truth was, he was more than a little bored with living in the country. He and Laura hadn't really spent enough time in Woodbine to make a lot of friends and he wasn't terribly enthusiastic about golf, so his days had settled into see to the horses, breakfast, into town for the mail and the paper, saddle up for the ride after lunch, and look forward to dinner and the outside world via the TV set.

They had been summering here for several years and now that the company was finally sold to West Texas Oil (A Tank of Texas Tickles Your Tach), just closed in March, he and Laura planned to live in Woodbine full time. Second thoughts were setting in, at least for Thaddeus. Pretty quiet up here, he was beginning to think.

He was 56 years old last January, the youngest of three children, all boys. His grandfather had opened a gas station outside of Philadelphia back before World War I, and by the time Thaddeus was born in 1937 the family was a power in the fuel business in the Philadelphia area. A chain of gas stations, tire and parts stores, and a network of home fuel distributors served great chunks of suburban Philadelphia and parts of the city itself.

He followed his two older brothers to Princeton but, to the astonishment of his father, joined the consular service after graduating instead of following them back to the family business. His years in Africa were happy ones but he found the work boring and the chances for advancement a matter more of politics than competence.

In 1961 his father died, and two years later the family business was in trouble; his brothers trying to do too much, business conditions bad, a couple of misjudgments come home to roost. Thaddeus left the Consular Service to help out.

It wasn't too bad. Downright interesting, in fact. Instead of the three of them trying to run everything, they split the company into divisions and each took one to manage. Thaddeus got the string of gas stations and did extremely well with them. He cleaned them up, kept them open 24 hours a day, and de-emphasized the car repair function. Then, inspired by running out of milk late one night, he put in coolers and racks of potato chips. Then candy bars. Then staples like bread. Then beer and soda. He practically invented the convenience store built around automobile service.

Thaddeus met Laura when she went to work for the company's in-house advertising division. She was from important Pittsburgh money that had faded a bit, due to mismanagement and a shortage of the work ethic. Bluntly: her father was a rich bum and would surely have reduced the family to poverty if he hadn't put himself and his wife and his Mercedes 250SL deep into the Monongahela River one night after a Christmas party.

Laura and Thad caught one another's eye and soon began finding it necessary to discuss packaging and media allocations and such over lunches which extended further and further into the afternoon. This led to drinks after work, which led to cocktail parties, which led to days at the beach, elegant dinners, gropings in the office, and even on one memorable occasion a coupling in a housekeeping storage closet at the Surf Vista Hotel in Virginia Beach at a 10:15 a.m. coffee break during the annual convention of the Pennsylvania Association of Petroleum Products Dealers Inc. To this day the Brookings attach special meaning to the phrase "Let's skip the coffee." Finding themselves a nice fit, they were married in a small ceremony, with just family members and a few acquaintances in attendance. They were among the fortunate who, when the heat dies down, turn out to be good friends.

Like his neighbor Bingo Reilly, Thad Brookings imagined himself to have chosen, pursued and triumphed. Like

Milly, Laura knew better. Kipling was right about the
Colonel's lady and Rosie O'Grady.

Laura liked to spend money, but she remembered her
father and knew the importance of prudence. From managing the family budget, which was ample, she gradually
took over their investments as well, doing her own re-
search, and making buy and sell decisions. At first, Thaddeus was in on the discussions, but he found investments a
dull subject and soon left it all to her. It was something she
could do while staying home with the kids and she took it
seriously. By the time they were 10 years married the rest of
the family were coming to her for advice. When West
Texas Oil came along to change the family from wealthy to
bloody rich, Laura devised and carried out the negotiation
strategy that resulted in the Texans paying about 30 percent more than the company was worth.

It was often remarked in the councils of the Brookings
family that "Laura is one smart cookie!"

Both children turned out quite well. Collier, the oldest, was flying in to Boston this afternoon from Chicago,
where he was in graduate school, and Kimberley, the apple
of Thad's eye, was now about to marry this young Boston
banker. Nice enough boy, and apparently smart enough,
but somehow not good enough for Kimmy, Thad thought.

He also thought the wedding was starting to get out of
hand. The small ceremony up in the country had grown to
the point that there were logistical problems. They had
ended up reserving 23 rooms and all 30 suites at the
Woodbine Inn. The phone was ringing off the hook with
Philadelphians and Bostonians and elsewheres asking
should we bring our overshoes? and even dumb things like
how do I get to Woodbine? What did you do with the
bloody map that went out with the bloody invitations? he

felt like saying, but he would go into his patient litany of routes and lefts and rights and blinking lights and such.

Kim had been here all this week, helping out, but it seemed to Thad that the level of giddiness was on the rise. Voices seemed to be pitched a note or so higher and volume seemed to be up a bit as well. Tomorrow, when the first of the bridesmaids moved into the attic bedroom, he expected both pitch and volume to reach painful levels. By the time the fourth and last of the girls in the wedding party arrived on Friday, he expected that exposure to the female residents of the house for longer than an hour or so would lead to permanent brain damage.

And his brothers would be arriving on Friday from Philadelphia, with their children, Kim's cousins, coming in from all over the country. And the UPS man was in the yard two or three times a day with packages. And the wedding consultant-caterer, a socially connected battleaxe that he couldn't stand but Laura thought was the last trump, was barging all over the house interfering, as Thad saw it, with the ordered routine of the country life he had looked forward to when he left Philadelphia. Things had gone from being a little too quiet to being much too hectic.

The wedding consultant even ordered Thad's favorite chair moved from the sunroom out into the potting shed for the week, describing it to Laura as "a bit on the dreary side, don't you think dear?" while Thad was actually sitting in it reading the paper. He hastily gathered the paper and stood up, watching this big burly kid from the village pick up his chair and carry it away. Meanwhile Laura and Mrs. Willoughby, that was her name Mrs. Bettina Willoughby, were going on as if he, Thad, were invisible or absent or something.

"Is there something a touch fetid in the air, dear?"

"No. Unless you mean Thad's pipes and tobacco."

A pause, just long enough to convey distaste.

"Oh." Another pause. "I had no idea you allowed smoking in this house."

"Well, only in this room." She could see that wasn't enough to mollify Mrs. Willoughby. "And only in the evening, after dinner." That was better.

"Even so, dear, I'd move that watercolor into the dining room." Another pause. "Bring in that humpty-dumpty English hunting scene reproduction from the upstairs hall; it's a better fit for this room and you're not risking anything to the cigar smoke."

"Pipes!" said Thad. "Just pipe tobacco."

"Yes, of course!" said Mrs. Willoughby. "Laura dear, if we could not have the smoking paraphernalia on the table we could get a lovely vase of something there, perfect spot, visible from the other room, maybe something pushy like jasmine or freesia, to counter the cigars."

"PIPES, GODDAMMIT!"

"Thad, please! If you can't offer any help you can at least be polite." A wifely reproof, gentle and sweet in tone, as Laura and Mrs. Willoughby swept from the room.

"I'm making a note, dear, that we have to get back to this room at some more convenient time," Thad heard as he began gathering up his pipes and tobacco cans to put them in a safe place. If he left it to that pair they'd wind up in the trash. He had passed through grumpy and was well into cranky when, with newspaper, pipes, and tobacco, he headed for the potting shed and his favorite chair. And a little touch of Black Jack. "To Mrs. Willoughby," he thought as he took his first taste of the day.

Jake had a quiet morning, munching his way along Kirkridge, headed north towards Woodbine. Pickings weren't all that great, it being so early in the season, but he was getting used to the change in diet and, with all the unaccustomed exercise over the past couple of days, he had lost about 50 pounds, fading to a svelte and businesslike 1750 or so.

You wouldn't go so far as to describe him as wild, but he was heading in that direction, becoming lean and mean and alert in attitude as well as body. It would be a fair statement to say that Jake's attitude closely resembled that of his owner: willing to live and let live, but requiring only minor stimuli to leap into full attack mode.

When he worked his way into Hiram Coughlan's upper meadow on this cool early morning, two doe with their fawns raised alert heads, noses testing the air, ready to bound into the safety of the woods at the slightest indication of threat. They stared at Jake and Jake stared at them. After a bit both sides concluded that no danger would proceed from the other and they resumed grazing. But keeping an eye on one another. "Trust everybody," said Mr. Dooley, "but cut the cards."

In the course of the morning, Jake encountered a fox, four wild turkey, a pair of eastern coyote, and three dogs running loose and looking for something to chase. The bravest of the dogs, or the dumbest, charged at Jake with a great threatening barking routine, got only a steady stare in reaction, and thought better of the project.

By mid-morning, Jake was just off Blueberry Road, grazing along the ditch, enjoying the quiet tranquillity of the day. Besides the natural sounds heard along the ridge, there had been only distant machinery noise off and on this morning.

And more coming right now, it sounded like. If Jake had been up on these things, he would have recognized the approach of a truck, probably an elderly one, with no muffler worth talking about. He might even have realized that the engine's loud complaint arose from a tired clutch trying to supplement exhausted brakes. If he had been a student of the local vehicle inventory, such as young Bert Grantham was, he might even have recognized the approaching noise as Steadfast Chapman's old International pickup.

———

Steadfast Chapman was by profession a better judge of cattle dead than cattle alive, being the knackerman for Woodbine and the surrounding area. He was 84 years old and touchy as hell about just nearly everything you could think of to talk about. He probably never got more than about 200 feet away from a loaded shotgun, and then only in the Grand Union or the Post Office when he had to park his truck far off, short visits both. So people treated him with considerable respect.

It was a delicious irony for those so inclined that his 140 acres was one of the nicest parcels in Woodbine, good-sized parcels that is. On a gravel road, little traffic, nice meadows and views across a narrow valley, five minutes from the village, the town plowed the road in the winter and graded it in the summer, school bus route, and–hold your nose–dead animals all over the yard, and the old house slumped up there on the knoll looking like it would fall down before the sun rose tomorrow.

The irony lay in the undeniable fact that Woodbine had gone from 51 working farms in 1950–defining working farm as one which produced over half of the family's

income-to three working farms in 1993; from an average
rural community to an upscale rural Vermont theme park,
and there was still a knackerman located right smack on a
piece of prime real estate. Surrounding towns were changing in the same direction, but not nearly to the degree that
Woodbine had changed, so the dead animals awaiting ren-
dering in his dooryard were mostly from other places. But
these corpses drew the attention not only of the neighbors
who could smell them but of others as well.

The Woodbine Listers knew all about them, because
some of Steadfast's neighbors came in every year to protest
their property assessments, citing his stock in trade as the
reason. The Health Department in Montpelier knew about
them, having grown accustomed to receiving imperious
phone calls from brand new, buttoned-down, just left the
metropolitan area, love the clean air and rural life but
didn't realize it had a stink to it, shopping around for a
beehive or two, Vermonters. The kind of people where the
wife's resume, when she applies for a vacancy on the
Woodbine Planning Board, has an entry about how she " .
. . was instrumental in securing passage of the Scoop The
Poop Law" in this or that suburb of New York or Boston.

Steadfast didn't pay much attention to any of this. He
considered himself a businessman and an asset to the
community, and pretty much retired anyway. Rich people
hire a vet and a back hoe and have a ceremony and cry and
bury their horses and cows, sometimes putting up a stone
with a mournful message to commemorate the spot. But
farmers want to be shut of their dead animals in the most
economical way and so welcome the knackerman and his
truck.

Anyway, here comes old Steadfast, in his 1976 International, picking up speed on a little downhill stretch of

the Kirkridge Road a couple of miles south of the village of Woodbine, dead horse in the back, beat up old workhorse from Thompson McKensie's place in South Bushville, and the brakes aren't really doing the job, what with the horse weighing too much for a 17-year-old vehicle with as much mileage on it as this one.

"WE AIN'T GONNA' MAKE IT, JENNY!" he bellowed at the nondescript little mongrel dog sitting in the passenger seat. "WHOA!" he roared at the truck, "WHOA, GODAMMIT!"

Worried about the final steep, half-mile stretch down into the village, Steadfast decided to cut his losses while the truck was still going a reasonable speed and yanked to the right onto Blueberry Road, a dead end gravel lane with a few houses on it. It was a question of turn around now and go by way of South Woodbine, or keep going and kamikaze down that last hill off Kirkridge onto the Village Green, by that time probably booking along at about 75 miles an hour and probably bump some stupid flatlander who wouldn't appreciate a dead old workhorse in his back seat.

The route change onto Blueberry Road was not that easy. It was a screeching, squealing, leaning, lurching, rocking, sluing, howling maneuver that put Jenny in his lap, shifted the load in the back to the point of two wheels off the ground for a second or two, and brought the truck face to face with Jake, minding his own business standing just off the road slurping from the shallow ditch.

He might not have made it even if Jake hadn't been there, but who knows?

Point is, he didn't make it! Jerked the wheel just too much, got a rear tire ("the off tire," he called it) down in the wet ditch, got to sluing and rocking and trying to stay upright, side-swiped a small tree, overcorrected, back in the ditch, really caught a wheel, yanked around, swerved off into the puckerbrush and WHUMPH!, up against a sugar maple that had taken root during the Spanish-American War.

It was *deja vu* for Jake, threatened by a vehicle just as he had been on the South Road last night, and he bolted for the woods without hesitation, on the move before the truck even came up against the tree. Good thing, too, because that quick reaction put him close to 300 feet off before Steadfast managed to get the shotgun into action.

Stumpy, who had seen the tail end of all this while driving slowly along Blueberry Road looking for some sign of Jake, stopped well down the road and counted the shots. He saw Jake heading for the ridge and figured he was out of danger. Steadfast was afflicted by what he called "the arthur-EYE-tis" and was known to be slowing down on the reload. When the count reached five there was a pause. It was common knowledge that the gun rack in old Steady's truck always carried a 12 gauge Remington pump, fully loaded, no plugs, plus an old double-barreled Winchester 12 gauge. So Stumpy waited until two more shots boomed, then drove quickly to the scene, jumped out of his truck and ran to Steadfast's door, grabbing at the shotgun barrel, which was hot. The trick with Steadfast was to get within 30 or 35 feet of him so he could see who you were. Beyond that everything was pretty blurry and he wasn't shy about shooting at blurs when he thought they'd done him wrong. But even when you got within Steadfast's circle of fairly good vision it didn't hurt to grab that shotgun barrel just in case, because when old Steady got his dander up you couldn't be too careful.

"HOLD IT THERE, STEADFAST, IT'S STUMPY!"
You had to yell pretty loud at old Steady because he didn't
hear too good anymore. "YOU ALL RIGHT?"

Well, it turned out he was all right and so was Jenny.
Truck had another nick in it, driver's side running board
and driver's side door banged some, but nothing that
Steadfast himself couldn't fix up. He'd whack the dents
out, more or less, with a mallet and a ballpeen hammer
and he'd fiddle with the door latch until it would stay shut;
window was only cracked, so that's all right, and it didn't
go up and down too good even before the accident anyway,
so nothing lost in the whole affair.

Except that Steadfast took offense at Bingo Reilly for
being such a damn fool as to let a bull get loose to run his
truck off the road when he was driving along minding his
own business, not a care in the world, and now everybody
was going to be saying well he's 84 years old and he run his
truck in the ditch and he shouldn't have a license anyway
and he's a threat to life and limb and he can't see good and
he's a menace to the community and it's high time he was
put out of business anyway and let's call the Board of
Health and who knows what all else.

Steadfast didn't have much to say at first, Stumpy reported later, just said he's all right and Jenny's all right,
and looked over the damage and they hooked up Stumpy's
come-along and after a lot of hullabaloo managed to get his
truck out of the ditch. And what a hullabaloo it was. First
they had to yank that old dead horse off the back of the
truck with the come-along, then pull the truck out on the
road, then get on Stumpy's CB radio and call Hiram
Coughlan to come down Kirkridge with his backhoe to
pull the horse up on the road and load him back in the
truck. All this while the horse was getting to the point

where you could smell him without even trying. Jenny seemed to enjoy the proceedings, running around barking and whatnot, but she was the only one who did.

Steadfast, never a loquacious sort, didn't say much throughout all this, although he seemed all right and helped in logical and direct ways. Stumpy had asked him first thing what all the shooting was about, to try to get a glimpse of his thinking, but didn't get much of an answer. Finally, just as he was ready to get the truck cranked up and on the move, Steadfast got to the heart of the matter.

"S'AT BINGO REILLY'S BULL I SEEN?"

"Yup," said Stumpy.

"I FIND'IM A'FORE YOU FIND'IM I'M SHOOTIN'IM!"

———————

"And he just might, too," Stumpy said an hour later at Bingo's house. They were drinking coffee in the sitting room, waiting for Milly to come in from the garden and suggest lunch. Then they would both act surprised and say is it that time already and oh you really needn't bother and all that, and then they would have one of Milly's special, just-for-company lunches.

And that's exactly what happened, except they didn't even have to be coy about it. Bingo went and looked out the kitchen window and spied Milly heading in from the garden at a kind of a half lope gait, holding the front of her dress out to make a basket.

"By God, Stumpy, I think the asparagus is ready," he said. That cheered him up some. Best thing that'd happened to him so far this week. He moved to the stove but she had already got the water boiling in the big spider.

Then Milly came busting in the door and pitched the asparagus, maybe three minutes picked, into the water, turned it down to a simmer, and cut two big fat slices of the bread she'd baked that morning. Not easy to cut properly, it being so fresh.

Bingo and Stumpy retreated to the living room door to watch the action; Milly didn't like people getting in her way when important cooking was in progress.

Bread cut and in the toaster, Milly turned to the now-blanched asparagus, poured off most of the water, threw a half stick of butter into the pan, and adjusted the burner so the delicate spears sautéed gently, filling the kitchen with the remarkable aroma of the first fresh asparagus of the season.

Bingo took three forks out of the kitchen drawer, along with three of the good paper napkins, and he and Stumpy stood and waited like a couple of schoolboys. Then plates on the table next to the stove, golden brown toast on the plates, tender spears arranged gently on the toast, and, the finishing touch, a little melted butter from the pan over the whole shebang.

The boys, being on their best behavior, hung back a bit.

"Go ahead 'n' eat," Milly said, "while it's warm."

Glad to.

They sat at the living room table and started in, while Milly toasted a piece of that bread for her own plate. The toaster's the bottleneck in any kitchen.

"Any good?" Milly called, fishing for praise. She knew damn well it was good.

"YEAH IT'S GOOD!" they answered together. They'd been too busy eating to remember their manners; you've got to stroke the cook. Milly joined them and the talk turned to the garden, especially tomatoes. Everybody has a variety of tomatoes they swear by; you can always get into an argument about tomatoes because there are so many variables. Growing time, color, flavor, size, hardiness, height of the bush, and that's just considering the tomato itself. You've got to add in such things as when the last frost is at your garden–and that could be two weeks different from the house just down the road–and how acid your soil, and how much sun you get, and what fertilizer and so on. If you're ever at a loss for words talking to somebody with a garden, bring up the subject of tomatoes. It made for a pleasurable time right on through the extra slices of fresh made bread, toasted and slathered with last fall's crabapple jelly, until finally the dishes were cleared and the problem of Jake was again taken up.

"Good thing the old coot can't see too good no more," Bingo remarked, getting back to old Steadfast.

"Well he told me he's gonna put his deer rifle in the truck," Stumpy said, "and, with his eyesight, that ain't good news for nobody. Half-blind old man, all pissed off, shootin' at anything that he thinks is Jake." They sat in silence, thinking about that.

"We better find him first," they decided.

Easy to say.

———————

After lunch, along about 1 o'clock, the reports started straggling in from Mount Harriet. People working from the Woodbine end were starting to join up with people working from the South Woodbine end and nobody had seen hide nor hair of Jake. And everybody who called had to be told that they had spent the morning on the wrong ridge and that Jake had just run old Steadfast into the ditch over where Blueberry Road runs into the Kirkridge Road.

Jake headed down towards South Woodbine full tilt, the sound of Steadfast's shotgun ringing in his ears. In fact, he busted right through Hiram Wickford's dooryard running flat out, with Hiram sitting on the porch with his jaw dropped in amazement. Hiram's log cabin was built right in the woods, so the chances are Jake didn't even realize that he had again brushed up against civilization.

Even Milly's company lunch didn't dispel the gloom in the Reilly front room. Another whole morning wasted, and Jake getting spookier by the minute, what with vehicle encounters, shotguns, and who knows what else.

Then, to top it off, it started to sprinkle. No surprise to Bingo; his tractor leg had been telling him all morning it was going to rain. Still, along with everything else, it was enough to make you feel a little down.

Bingo and Stumpy stood on the back porch and watched the sprinkle get heavy enough to be called rain. They could tell from the look of the clouds, the slant of the rain, the whispering sound it made on the early leaves, some damn lifetime instinct or other, that it was going to settle in and rain all afternoon and probably half the night. A miserable development, since in early June a rainy day is not just damp and miserable, but cold and damp and miserable, especially out in the woods with the damn water running down your neck and wet branches swatting you in the face and wet brush soaking your britches.

Another thing the rain did was fill up the Milk House right after lunch. Not too many carpenters; they were mostly still occupied with finishing up indoor jobs. Plenty of painters though, all a couple of weeks into outdoor work, it having been a particularly nice May. Also a scattering of masons, including all six of George Durkee's boys who were working on a three-fireplace log cabin being built by a 29-year-old software genius from Boston as a rustic retreat from the hurley-burley of megabytes and micromilliseconds.

Bingo and Stumpy arrived in mid-afternoon with the idea of working on their respective dart games to find a hubbub unusual for the time of day. A hubbub that unfortunately included the overly loud nasal tones of Wendell Coates.

"Wal if it ain't the great MATTIDOOR," he crowed. "We knew he's a bull thrower but we didn't know he couldn't catch one." Coates followed this with abrasive laughter, rather like the braying of a donkey.

The hair on the back of Bingo's neck tingled and his shoulders set in such a way that Stumpy stepped right in to put a stop to things before they went any further. "Now Wendy," he began, using Coates' least favorite nickname, "what would a city feller and a former ED-jucator like your ownself know about cattle? Can you look under their bellies and tell which one's a little boy and which one's a little girl? Best be sure ya' know the difference before ya' go to milkin,' by God." The hoots that greeted this sally effectively shifted the focus of talk onto safer ground and gave Bingo time to cool down.

Desmond Kiley slid two bottles of beer across the bar to Bingo and Stumpy.

"Savor the accouterments of an even temper, boys," he murmured mysteriously.

All three dart boards were going this afternoon, practice in progress for the up-coming tournament. Bingo and Stumpy took their turns, challenging, losing, challenging, winning, whiling away the afternoon, occasionally going to a window to peer out at the steady drumming rain, and hearing late reports on Jake, some coming in by telephone, some in person, some true, some false.

Along towards 5 o'clock Bingo called Milly and Stumpy called Sophie and they arranged to have the ladies come down to the Milk House and join them for supper. And later, over some nice fried chicken from the Milk House kitchen, it was Sophie who suggested putting the vamp on Jake with a cow in heat.

"By God, ya' could call it a stud fee," said Stumpy. "Must be somebody'd be glad to have a cow served by Jake, a fine bull like that."

But Bingo immediately rejected the idea of messing around with Jake's love life unless somebody came up with a proper cow, one of good breeding and conformation. None of his own cows were in season and he be damned, he declared, if he'd put Jake in with some goat-leggity, sway-backed, broken down old scut just to catch him.

The conversation wandered on, drawing on a lifetime in Woodbine of living and learning and wondering and wishing and gradually growing into the people they were, good honest people with flaws, Patsy Cline their Maria Callas, Hank Williams their Pavarotti.

"What landlord d'ya 'spose would take old Pluto fer a tenant?" Stumpy was the one who offered that one, for no particular reason. "Old codger like that, allus lived alone, set in his ways, ain't no landlord's dream, ya' know."

Bingo picked up the theme. "It'd sure take some kind of understandin' landlord." And, of course, a story went with it. "One time I'm coon huntin' alone down in Readin,' musta' been some time in November, and it got late and startin' ta snow, and I figgered to bunk in with Pluto." He took a swig of Donovan's, looking off pensively, remembering. "His shack, y'know, was way up in there near Skunk Pond and I remember he had the transmission from his Jeep right there on the kitchen table. We ate dinner around it.

"Wal, that's all right. But then I was rabbit huntin' a few months later, probley the end of March, and I looked in on 'im, make sure he's wintered o.k. and that damned transmission's still right there on the table." Bingo shook his head. "Ain't too many 'round Woodbine'd put up with that!"

"No wonder he's an old bachelor," Sophie said, "with a transmission on the dining room table."

"Well, he's a happy man," Bingo declared, "don't have to put up with no poutin' or crabbin' or nothing."

"There ain't nothin' in the world as useless as an old bachelor," Milly insisted, "and you can keep that old horse thief the hell away from our property, by God."

Which was where Bingo got the idea of moving old Pluto onto his place, maybe a swap or something, little piece of land along the brook, by golly might be able to work something out, but down the brook as far from the house as possible.

A mile and a half south of the fateful intersection of Blueberry Road and Kirkridge Road, Jake finally checked his flight to stop and listen.

Nothing, just forest noises. He went back to feeding off the land, going still and listening frequently, a little nervous at all the strangeness his life had encountered over the last few days. Quite a transition when you got thinking about it. Here all he knew was his pen in the barn and a not too big outside yard with strong fencing. Now over a period of days he'd been all over Woodbine, met an interesting variety of people and other critters, and discovered some new tastes and smells.

Now, in the early afternoon, he came on a well-kept six-acre hayfield just as it started to rain.

This hayfield belonged to Jack McGinty's place down on the South Road, about halfway between Bingo's and South Woodbine. McGinty's house and barn were down near the road and his very special stable of Morgan Horses were pastured down there too. But this hayfield way up on the ridge had been an unexpected and very pleasant dividend when he bought the place 15 years ago.

He didn't even know it was there for a couple of years. Then somebody mentioned it, maybe Stumpy, who was helping with the fence repair, and he went up the old road, just a track really, and there it was. It had a nice south, southeast exposure, but you could see it was in bad shape.

Good hay isn't just any old grass growing that you cut and put in the barn. It's a mixture of legumes, grasses, clovers and such, which are selected for their nutrient value to the animals that are expected to feed off the resultant hay. What we're saying here is that the best hay for cattle isn't the best hay for horses or sheep. And a hay field is like any other field; you have to take care of it. You have to reseed it now and then, and maybe run over it with a bog harrow, and lime it regular to sweeten up the soil, and fertilize it every few years, and make sure you trim the brush back that's always trying to work in from the tree line, and so on.

Jack McGinty pampered this hay field. Everybody said so. No big old truckloads of Canadian horse hay for him! No sir! He grows his own horse hay. And samples are always getting mailed off for this analysis or that analysis to make sure there was the proper amount of potassium or chromium or some other damn thing in the soil.

It was kind of expensive for the first couple of years because the field really needed a lot of work and it was unreachable until the spring rains had come and gone. But once established, it provided something like 1,200 bales at the first cutting in July and, most years anyway, a good second cutting in late August as well.

So when Jake came upon this marvelous hay field this rainy afternoon, he settled down to spend the rest of the day and most of the night right there, feeding on the delicate beginning growth of timothy, white and red clover, and who knows what other treats. There was water running off the ridge in a gully in the woods just off to the south. He had everything he needed and nobody to bother him. "Like bein' in the arms of Jesus," as Milly would say.

He would feed and rest and snooze and slurp from the run-off and feed some more all that afternoon in the rain and glowery misty weather, oblivious to the chill breeze moving from the trees across the field. It was his most restful period so far, most welcome because he was beginning to accept as normal the hullabaloo that seemed to move around with him.

He stayed in the field until about 3 o'clock the following morning, when a pack of three or four dogs made an uproar running a bunch of deer along the ridge. Every one of those dogs a house pet with a master who'd go to jail before he'd admit his dog would run deer.

The uproar woke Jake up and got him moving down the hill towards the South Road. The rain had just stopped and it was easy going since he followed Jack McGinty's road all the way down, past the barn, along the driveway and across the South Road to the Mount Harriet side, all before first light.

THURSDAY

This was the morning that Jake, through a lucky break, got some grain back in his diet. Only horse feed, to be sure; but a step up from eating just grass.

Wandering along the ridge of Mount Harriet just after dawn, he found a small patch of open meadow that was just right. Perhaps an acre or an acre and a half, it lay in front of a summer house that was only used a couple of weeks a year, with a few weekends thrown in. The meadow sloped slightly to the southwest, and this exposure to the sun guaranteed that it was the first patch of ground on the ridge to show in the spring. The owners, Massachusetts people, made a point of mowing the field each summer, so it was free of brush.

Jake had a breakfast of tender early grass shoots that was almost as good as last night's feed in Jack McGinty's hay field. He would have spent the morning in that meadow if he hadn't been spooked by the sound of a good-sized animal crashing through the dead brush up near the house.

After hurrying through the woods for two hundred yards, he stopped to listen, then went on more slowly, working north and down, looking for his morning slurp.

91

Presently he came to a fenced field and stopped, peering about near-sightedly.

It happened to be the Brookings' meadow and, with the barn undergoing preparations for the wedding Saturday, the horses were loose in the field, with an old equipment shed for shelter if needed. And, here's the real luck, the wooden hay feeder in the middle of the field had a grain tray as well, and Kimberly Brookings, the weekend's intended, had just trudged out with grain for the four horses who were now contentedly munching.

Jake walked through the fence, adding to the scratches on his brisket, and headed for the smell of grain. The horses scattered and Jake fell to, slobbering and snorting as he gobbled as fast as he could. Man or animal, to be street smart is to be a pessimist, and Jake had become a pessimist in his few short days of freedom. "Eat quickly and as much as you can" was his motto, and even though the horse grain wasn't up to his regular cattle feed, it beat the hell out of grass, especially in four-horse quantities.

Kimberly got back to the barn, hung up the grain bucket, and started for the house to get breakfast. And there were the horses, down by the gate. Puzzled that such avid grain hounds would abandon the day's first feeding, she stopped, and looking about, spied Jake.

And so with a shout and a yell Jake's breakfast was over, although he had pretty much cleaned up the grain anyway. Besides breakfast he had accomplished his first ruffled feelings of the day, which were to become even more ruffled as the damage to the back fence became apparent, and was responsible for the first phone call of the day to the Bingo Reilly residence.

"He's out feeding the stock," Milly said, "I'll go right out and tell him."

Bingo roared into action. Finally a positive identification, promptly received, and in an area he knew like the back of his hand. First thing tell Kimberly to stay away from him, don't spook him. Too late on that one, he's already spooked. O.K. which way did he go?

Second thing is quick get Stumpy and two or three others to see if Jake could be driven into range of the dart guns. Then, he hoped, Bingo!

"I don't give a damn if he's two miles off the road, we're bringing 'im down," Bingo told the group. "I'm gettin' sick of all this," he added.

"You think you're sick now, wait'll you read today's paper," Stumpy warned. He'd seen a copy first thing this morning at the South Woodbine store.

Into pickup trucks, out through fields and old logging roads, treacherous driving, things still too wet for such goings-on. Bingo buried his truck to the oil pan in a perfectly innocent looking patch of new grass, buried it deeper trying to get it out, hurt his foot and put his tractor leg to throbbing by kicking the front fender not to mention denting the fender, finally limped out to get help, and before they were through three trucks had been stuck at one time or another and they weren't all loose and on good gravel until Stumpy went and got his tractor to do the job.

Morning wasted, foot throbbing nicely (Milly said it served him right), Bingo was in a foul mood when he picked up *The Word of Woodbine* at the Mobil station just after lunch. Sitting in his truck, which was muddy to the windows, he looked at the front page. Jake was the sure enough lead story, three columns in the upper right hand corner:

Escaped Bull Terrorizes Woodbine;
"Extremely Dangerous" Owner Warns

By Millicent Buchanan

Residents of Woodbine have been terrorized this week by a bull which escaped from the farm of Calvin Reilly of South Woodbine last weekend and has been sighted throughout the area this week.

Diane "Muffin" Baker-Harden, Chairperson of the Woodbine School Board, expressed concern early this week for the safety of Woodbine students, noting that both the Elementary School and the High School are on the outskirts of the village, adjoining the wooded ridges where the beast has been most often reported.

The Woodbine Chamber of Commerce is also worried about the effect of the escaped animal on the tourist business. "Tourists don't want to have to face a raging bull," declared Chamber Executive Director Helen Ridsome, expressing fear that summer business could be hurt if the animal is not quickly captured or killed. "The bottom line is that it could adversely impact the area's economic profile in the near term," she explained. "That is, provided it's a done deal in terms of catching the beast ASAP," she clarified.

Authorities and the animal's owner urged residents to avoid the animal, although the owner, Mr. Reilly, discounted the danger to the general population from his beast. Asked about the danger to residents from the animal, First Constable Euclid Armstrong joked that he thought the bull in greater danger from the residents than the other way around.

Concerned parents who attended the regular Tuesday night meeting of the Board of Selectmen looking for answers were disappointed. Some two dozen anxious residents who showed up at the meeting demanding information were forced to sit through a two-hour discussion of damaged culverts and the prioritizing of their repair. Nine hardy people were still present when the problem of the escaped bull was taken up, only to be frustrated by the Selectmen's tabling the matter until next week's meeting pending more information.

"When I moved up here last year, I certainly didn't expect my child to be trampled by a raging bull," said Ms. Starlight Spotsworth, who was outraged at the Selectmen's action. She vowed further citizen's action and as we went to press was organizing a picket line in front of town hall.

Chalmers Peabody, Chairman of the Board of Selectmen, pointed out that Ms. Spotsworth is President of the local chapter of the Power to the Animals Collective and had opposed as cruel the use of an exterminating service when carpenter ants were discovered earlier this year in the basement of town hall.

Ms. Spotsworth denied any contradiction in her position, pointing out that the oppression of women in rural areas has historically been symbolized by images of bulls and at any rate the animals were of no use in the modern age since artificial insemination can meet the needs of cattle raisers. In addition she noted that the keeping of farm animals was a greater cruelty of national scope and part of a pattern perpetuating the domination and exploitation of women and female farm animals that she alleged is the salient characteristic of society in rural America.

There have been several reports of attacks by the animal in the South Woodbine area. In one report the bull threatened a BMW, but was driven off by the car's owner. In another incident, a woman narrowly escaped the animal by blinding him with a bag of garbage. The Word was unable to verify the several other attacks that have been reported, although property damage is mounting.

The Woodbine Country Club was the worst hit,
with extensive damage to a green and a tee. The annual mixed foursome event which kicks off the
Club's tournament schedule each year was set for
yesterday, but had to be canceled. It has been re-
scheduled for this coming Sunday, according to
Barbara "Babs" Smythe-Harrison, Chairperson of
the Club's Golf Committee.

As of press time Tuesday, the Vermont State Police had not been notified of the bull's escape. The
State Disaster Coordinating Committee, located in
Montpelier, has also been subject to what is apparently a local blackout of information. Local authorities are required by law to notify the Committee of
disasters, according to a spokesperson at the Montpelier office, who pointed out that in certain circumstances charges could be filed.

Two photographs accompanied the story, one a file
photo of what appeared to be an ox, the other, to Bingo's
surprise, featuring Bert and a skinny little girl from West
Woodbine over the caption:

TEENS PITCH IN–Bert Grantham and Beatrice
English, sophomores at Woodbine Union High
School were among those who volunteered to search
for the escaped bull. School officials warned students not to approach the animal if they located it
but to report its position immediately to the proper
authorities. The two young searchers reported hearing loud noises in the underbrush, probably from the
escaped animal, but were unable to visually verify
their belief. (The Word photo by Millicent Buchanan)

Bingo, moving his lips, read the whole thing through twice. Finished, he sat staring out the windshield, seeing nothing, wondering what the hell was happening in the world.

And that wasn't all; there was an editorial:

TOO MUCH BULL!

The news this week that South Road carpenter Calvin Reilly's pet bull had escaped emphasizes the importance of the revisions of the Zoning Regulations now being considered by the Town Planning Committee and the Town Zoning Board. The presence of such a dangerous animal only two miles from the village poses an unacceptable risk not only to the local population but also to visitors who come to admire the beauty and grace of Woodbine, and to enjoy themselves on our bike trails, golf courses, and tennis courts, and to feast on the beauty of our undeveloped ridge lines. We are not against agriculture, which is part of the uniqueness of Vermont as a tourist attraction. The sight of a group of cows grazing on a grassy hill is as Vermont as maple sugar and Ethan Allen. But it is time that the problem of dangerous farm animals was faced by this community. We think that sincere representatives of all segments of the community can sit down together and lick this problem. Let the selectmen, planners, store and boutique owners, hoteliers, zoning officials and other civic groups get together and work something out. It may require a little compromising by everyone, but we are confident that our town has the courage and vision to make the tough choices that are necessary to resolve the issue in a way that assures both public safety and the economic health of the Woodbine community.

"I'll compromise 'em, by God," Bingo growled. "I'll put Jake on a loose lead and walk 'im right through a couple o' them tourist bow-teeks, give 'em a good look at 'im."

He was addressing Desmond Kiley, who was presiding at the Milk House. Bingo, shaken by the newspaper report and at loose ends while awaiting a confirmed sighting of Jake, had dropped in to throw some darts. Big tournament coming up this Sunday and he hadn't hardly practiced in a week. Yesterday, during the rainy afternoon, was shooting darts, not practicing shooting darts. He needed to practice, all by himself, working on his rhythm and consistency.

"It might be an illumination of their experience, at that," Desmond remarked. He was given to weird configurations of speech that came across as Delphic wisdom in the Milk House, whose patrons generally got his drift no matter what he said. You had to watch what he did and how he looked at the same time as you listened to what he was saying, and, once you got the hang of it, you could usually figure out what he meant.

Well, some things were obvious. Like when he said: "You have o'er weened your arrival." That meant you had overstayed your welcome and if you didn't get out quick you would be physically thrown out just as quick. Maybe even quicker.

Bingo was concentrating on his stroke, looking to attain the smooth and fluid motion that had made him a top-five finisher in every tournament that past winter, including the Christmas match, which he won. This record was second only to that of Wendell Coates, also a consistent top-five finisher, but a two-time winner.

Wendell Coates, whose braying tones had caused Bingo to bristle yesterday afternoon here in the Milk House.

This Coates was a brash and loud youngster of 30 or so, jeering in victory and full of excuses in defeat. Whether it was the tone or the manner, or both, he got under Bingo's skin. A carpenter, he had worked for several small builders who found his work satisfactory but his presence on the job disruptive.

As for Bingo, beating Coates was more important than winning the tournament, even considering the money. Well, prit'near.

So he worked on his game, starting with the 20 and working down to 1, then back up to 20 again, concentrating on delivering the darts with smooth, sure strokes.

The game played at the Milk House was Cricket, sometimes called American Cricket. The boards were standard size, round, divided into 20 pie-shaped sections extending out from a double bull. The pies were numbered one through 20, and each had a narrow "treble ring" midway between the bull and the edge of the playing area. The edge of the playing area was formed by the "double ring." The rest of the pie counted as singles. So a dart in the triple ring of the 14, for example, counted for 42 points, a dart in the double ring for 28 and a dart elsewhere in the pie for 14. It comes as a surprise to most beginners that the bull is over twice the size of the double area of a given number. The smallest target on the board is the triple ring of a given number.

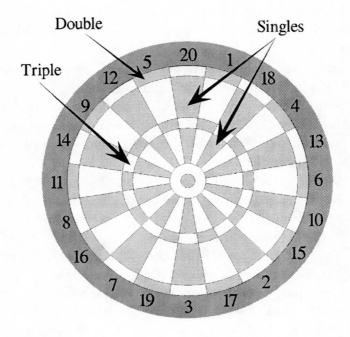

In American Cricket, a player must bring a number alive by hitting it three times. Any subsequent dart into that number by that player scores the value of the number, or double or triple the value as the case may be. Three darts into the number by the opponent and the number is dead, out of the game for good.

A game of strategy, best played by two people of approximately equal talent. The question is always how much effort to devote to defense by killing an opponent's numbers and how much to offense by developing live numbers of your own. One dart in the triple can bring a number alive or kill it. Most shooters go for the 20 right off, but you can use any number to start; no need to go in order.

Like Coates and the other leading players, Bingo had a
personal set of darts. He had paid "sixty-five damned dollars" for them up in Burlington, as he complained to anyone who would listen. He really had nothing to complain
about, since he had won probably a truckload of Donovan's Downtown Stout with them. They had a nice heft to
them, perfect weight and balance, the barrel nicely tar-
nished where his fingers gripped, and there were spare
points and flights in the box. The feathers on the tail end
of a dart are called "flights." Coates had a perfectly
matched set as well, which he kept in a wooden box lined
in silk. All personal darts were kept on a shelf behind the
bar. A dozen or so of the better dart players had such personal sets, but Coates' were the only ones in a box with a
lock and key. To prevent tampering, he said.

"Humpf," Bingo humpfed, just thinking about the
effrontery of it.

Desmond thought the subject was still the center village merchants.

"They viccisitudinize themselves before ever the woes
unleash," he declared.

"You got that right," Bingo replied. He had learned a
long time ago it was better to puzzle out the drift of Desmond's difficult pronouncements because his clarifications
tended to make things worse.

Then the phone rang, the First Constable looking for
Bingo.

"Jake just stuck his head through the back window of
the South Woodbine Post Office," he said, "and scairt the
b'jesus out of Harry Muldoon." Muldoon was the Postmaster at South Woodbine, a small station, really just a couple
of rooms stuck on the side of the South Woodbine Store.
"Must've come out of the woods behind the place. Prob'ley

after some tomato plants Harry's got started, had 'em in the sun right by the window."

"Know where he is now?"

"No, but get ready to add to the bill because when Harry turned around from selling a stamp to old lady Marigot, he seen Jake and give a helluva yell." He paused for breath. "Jake yanked back and near took the window out of the frame, busted the glass, gave a big ugly yodel and run right across the damn road to the South Woodbine Inn, across the lawn, round the back and almost run over Angelina Bertoni and the fella that drives the fish truck. He's delivering some fish and Jake run right between 'em."

"Anybody hurt?" Bingo was starting to lose sympathy for Jake.

"Nope, but Angelina says she's gonna' start keeping her deer rifle by the kitchen door and the fish man is shaking like a leaf." He paused. "Bingo, you better catch that critter, he's crazier'n a shithouse rat."

"Any idea where he's at now?" Bingo asked.

"Heard about three different stories so far. When he's roarin' around everybody's lookin' for a tree to climb and by the time he's gone, one's convinced he's gone south and the next one's sure he's gone north." He paused. "Harry's pissed about his tomato plants."

"Wal, he's prob'ley so spooked now he won't even start slowin' down till after supper. We're setting up a big drive for tomorrow morning and we'll get 'im then, by God, or I'll shoot the sonuvabitch." Bingo didn't add that the morning drive would be on both ridges, with speed and mobility heretofore lacking in the Jake chase. Off-road motorbikes, "hou017da's" Bingo called them, would supply the difference.

But he and Stumpy, who had assumed the role of second in command, had agreed to keep mum about the "hounda's" so as not to take the chance of getting the local environmentalists all steamed up about irreparable damage to some damned weed or other. He'd about decided that environmentalists would picket a cure for cancer to keep dandelions from being plucked.

Hanging up, he related Jake's latest adventures to Desmond.

"He ricochets the ruction through the week," Desmond observed.

Bingo sure had to agree with that, he thought, as he drove along the South Road towards home, he surely had to agree with that.

Thinking to finish up the flower beds and accomplish something besides getting stuck and shooting darts for the day, Bingo rattled up the hill in his mud-caked truck in mid-afternoon to the Brookings house, where everything was abustle. Saturday was the big day and things were starting to fall together. Three men were organizing the ropes that would support the tents which were laid out on the lawn. The portable wooden dance floor was being unloaded from a truck. The caterer's large gas grills were standing near the barn. Boxes of plates, silverware, racks of glasses (no tacky plastic at this wedding, thank you very much), were stacked about awaiting attention.

Bingo set to work finishing up his gardening work. Wasn't too much could be done, really, first week of June. Make things look ready; freshly turned, neat, maybe set out some of the hardier plants, but there still could be a late frost, especially with the full moon due tomorrow night.

Along around 4 p.m. he went up to the house, figuring to call Milly for the latest news on Jake, or as he was beginning to think of him, goddamjake.

The Brookings family stood in the driveway talking to The Reverend Hoskins, who was still a bit cool about not having a church wedding although there were enough heavy hitters on the guest list to keep him from getting too huffy. He was being very fussy about the setup instead. The sun would be right up there over the barn and the shadows would be falling that way and the people would be right there and the photographer must be over here on this side and under no condition would photographs be allowed during the ceremony and so on and so forth.

Bingo went to look at the horses, not wanting to have to listen to the pompous old windbag. Then he checked the flower beds again, which looked good still. Finally he drifted back to the driveway where Laura, Thad, The Reverend, and what he later described to Stumpy as "a sneery looking, over-the-hill, golfie woman" were just finishing up. Kimberly had gone to saddle up for an afternoon ride with her intended, who would be arriving from Woodbine any minute.

"Well, Mr. Reilly, what have we to say for ourselves this fine afternoon?" boomed the Reverend, glad of the chance to exhibit his fine baritone in ritual mode, not only to impress the Brookings but also to test the acoustics of the lawn area. He hoped it wouldn't be windy on Saturday. At high volume his voice sometimes developed a little squeak, like a poorly adjusted microphone.

"Howdy, folks," Bingo greeted all.

"Have we taken the bull by the horns yet?" the Reverend asked with a chuckle, enjoying his little joke. He didn't approve of Bingo Reilly from what he heard of him, besides which Bingo didn't represent even one nickel to him. All eyes turned to Bingo, Laura and Thad expecting the worst, Mrs. Willoughby not hiding her alarm at being so close to a person wearing a Caterpillar cap, the Reverend congratulating himself, prematurely, on his rapier-like wit.

"Mebby could use yer help, Reverend," Bingo said. "Heard yer quite a expert on bull."

Don't mess with Bingo Reilly.

"Well," Laura filled the breach with a nervous laugh, "I'm sure it will all work out."

The jumpy silence was broken by the arrival of Kimberly leading her saddled horse, a nine-year-old mare named Veronica who was a bit skittish from lack of riding.

Small talk, with awkward gaps, lurched along.

Even Bingo felt the strain and was about to take himself off when the horse, moving restlessly, put her backside against the electric fence along the driveway. It was a temporary fence, there to protect the lawn from deer droppings and the reception paraphernalia from midnight raccoon ruckuses and such. It was to be removed before the wedding on Saturday.

Veronica started with a snorting leap, a sudden clenching of musculature, an explosive lunge that loudly overtaxed her sphincter.

"WHOA!" yelled Kim, hanging on the bridle.

"My Lord!" said the Reverend.

"Good heavens!" exclaimed Mrs. Willoughby.

"Oh dear!" said Laura.

"Quite so!" said Thad.

"A FAHTING HORSE WILL NEVER TIRE,

'N' A FAHTING MAN'S THE MAN TO HIRE," quoth Bingo Reilly at the top of his lungs, pleased he could contribute.

———————

Bingo spent what was left of the afternoon and most of the evening in the front room with Stumpy, making lists and phoning people, getting the "hounda" drive organized for Friday morning.

The operation was set up in four divisions, a north-bound and a south-bound division for both Kirkridge and Mt. Harriet. According to the plan, Jake would be moved to a position about halfway between Woodbine and South Woodbine, regardless of which ridge he happened to be on. And if he could be forced down off the ridge to the South Road, he should be fairly close to his home grain bin because Bingo's place lay close to the halfway point. And, the plan was, Jake, upon reaching the South Road, would encounter Bingo, Stumpy, Wilbur Foster and Hyacinth Spencer, who seemed to have a calming effect on cattle, for some reason. She had a way of half cooing, half humming to them that seemed to mesmerize the fiercest of beasts.

The manpower came from the very cultural roots of the Woodbine-born-and-raised community. All the 35 men on the list of participants were members of at least one of the following organizations: The Woodbine Volunteer Fire Department, the South Woodbine Volunteer Fire Department, the Woodbine Valley Rifle & Pistol Society, or the South Woodbine Fast Beef & Venison Association. The only function of the last group was to organize two big venison cookouts to benefit the South Woodbine Volunteer Fire Department. The October affair, which occurred during Bow Season, was called a Venison Cookout. The June edition, however, being out of deer season, was billed as a Fast Beef Cookout. Just kidding, they told the Game Warden when he inquired, it's last November's kill that we froze. And how could you even suggest wrong-doing on our part, they added, looking wounded, how could you? Of the eight women on the list, five were married to members of the above organizations, two were themselves members of the Rifle & Pistol Society, and the last was Verity Hooseman, who defied classification. All members of the four groups making the drive had off-road bikes or four-wheelers of some description and every old logging road and track would be covered.

The Fire Department members came complete with two-way radios hanging from their belts, so communications should be no problem. Stumpy, as First Assistant Chief of the South Woodbine Fire Department, had a two-way radio as well. He and the others with Bingo made up the strike force. They would be at Bingo's place, eating Milly's fresh donuts, ready to pounce on Jake wherever along the road he made his appearance. Then WAP with the dart gun and the job would be finished.

So went the script.

———————

When the members of the Woodbine Zoning Board straggled into Town Hall for their regular first-Thursday-of-the-month meeting that evening they were forced to negotiate a picket line composed of members of the Woodbine Power to the Animals Collective and the Woodbine delegation to the Windsor County Chapter of the Worldwide Organization of Women, known as WOW.

Millicent Buchanan wore a sandwich board sign which said "NO MORE BULL" on the front and "DOWN WITH BRUTES" on the back. Besides the opportunity of simultaneously sharing two consciousness-raising thoughts with the public, the sign had the additional advantage of leaving her hands free to take notes, since she was covering the event for The Word.

Starlight was dressed in a gorilla suit and carried a sign saying "WOMEN REJECT BRUTE FORCE," while her five-year-old daughter Carotene was dressed as Little Red Riding Hood. This complex multi-media message confused all upon whom it fell, including her companions on the picket line. Indeed, by the time the meeting was called to order at 7 p.m., the two picket line factions had begun to distance themselves from one another and, filing into the meeting room, gravitated to opposite sides of the aisle.

This beginning split in the activist ranks was nipped in the bud by Millicent Buchanan's trenchant 800-word analysis in the following week's *The Word of Woodbine* of the symbolic significance of the gorilla suit, the main point of confusion, and the entente between the Collective and WOW was saved for a few months at least. The rupture would become wide, deep, and irreparable in November when the Collective launched an all-out campaign on behalf of the rights of turkeys. The opening salvo was fired at the local Grand Union, with Starlight and her followers screaming threats and imprecations at departing shoppers. What happened was that the young zealots of the Collective got all steamed up and went after the North Tamarack Senior Citizens' Van with such fervor that by the time Officer Harkness got there they had it rocking pretty close to tipping it over.

"THERE'S FIVE VICTIMS ON THIS BUS," they screamed at Officer Harkness, referring to fresh turkeys. "THERE'S SEVEN!" he roared back, referring to people. The officer's call for back-up was heard by approximately 165 scanners around Woodbine and the disturbance immediately drew so many spectators that the First Constable, trying to respond, couldn't get through the traffic to get there.

Well Good Lord, the WOW people couldn't support an attack on the Senior Citizens' Van, not when five of those on the bus were women over the age of 75. Starlight's claim that her group had been provoked by the old codgers was dismissed out of hand, even though there were witnesses who saw old Minnie Hoffbinder bop a demonstrator with her only purchase, a loaf of French bread. Minnie didn't really need any groceries that day, she was just making the trip for the company and the latest gossip. It was generally agreed that the demonstrator got off easy, since Minnie carried a pistol in her huge handbag. Devouring the crime stories in the Rutland Herald, she had become convinced that rape and torture were imminent, and took to practicing every day with a worn 38 revolver, shooting from the back porch at an old Redman Chewing Tobacco sign painted on her barn. "Barn oughtta be prit'near dead by now," someone remarked after a few months of it.

Minnie was better than a fair shot but the day of the demonstration her weapon was buried in the bottom of her bag with old shopping lists and hairpins, combs, $13 worth of change, a magnifying glass, a pair of soft slippers in case her bunions got acting up, and who knows whatall, and she didn't have time to dig it out. The experience taught her a couple of valuable lessons. One was that French bread may startle an assailant but it lacks stopping power. The other was that you might as well not have a weapon if you can't get it into action quickly. Which is why she had her son drive her to Harry's Guns & Ammo over White River Junction way the following day to buy a shoulder holster. When they finally went to court on the bus-rocking charge, Starlight made Minnie a prominent feature of her fiery plea for a total, nation-wide ban on guns.

That brought up another problem, since although the WOW folks were in favor of gun control as well, they had so much time and energy and money tied up in the campaign against the leghold trap that they didn't want to dilute the effort with a second issue. As for Minnie, she spent a lot of time practicing her draw. And she never missed a trip on the Senior Citizens' Van, riding shotgun, hoping she'd get another try at "those little twits," as she referred to the Collective. But that all came later. Now, in the first week of June at the Zoning Board Meeting, the fragile coalition of the Collective and WOW was still intact.

And so the meeting was called to order by Chairperson Alexis Lexington, a new lawyer in town who hoped someday to be Governor. From Connecticut, she had looked around after getting out of law school and spied this little state to the north whose whole population wasn't much more than Hartford or Bridgeport. So she hotfooted up Interstate 91, passed the Bar Exam, opened an office in Woodbine, and tippy-toed right across the village green to Town Hall to volunteer for anything that needed to be done. Now it is a fact of village life that there is ALWAYS an opening on some board or commission whose only requirement is the stamina to sit through meetings so irretrievably boring that only a very few good-government junkies can meet the test. But she had done it; and now, two years later, she was chairperson and getting ready to run for the Legislature on the progressive ticket.

She looked the room over and did some rapid figuring. There were three variances up for consideration this evening and, if necessary, she could make them last until 4 in the morning, by which time everybody would have gone home. Her chair was padded; the ones out in front weren't. And she knew by the Mammy Yokum boots sticking out of the gorilla suit that the wacko Spotsworth was inside, which meant an unintelligible harangue was all but unavoidable. On the other hand there sat that fanatic little snip Millicent Buchanan, and the support of *The Word of Woodbine* would be crucial to Alexis' elevation to the Legislature. The calculations didn't take long.

"It seems to me that an important issue is to be raised here tonight," she began, looking statespersonlike. "So perhaps we should move New Business to the head of our agenda." This with a sweeping 180 degree nod of her head signifying both consultation with her colleagues on the Board and her assumption of their approval.

"Perhaps we could hear from a spokesperson from the floor?" she continued, and when the gorilla leaped to its feet, " . . . ah, Ms. Starlight Spotsworth, welcome to the Woodbine Zoning Board. You have the floor."

Starlight was taken by surprise. She wasn't used to getting the floor so easily. In fact, she was all set to launch into disruption Plan A in order to be heard, and had a Plan B ready if the first one didn't work. There was a Plan C as well, which never worked except to get her arrested, which, in some ways was just as good as getting the floor. So she was a little flustered at this easy first success. Nobody noticed, owing to the fact that even under the best of conditions, such as reading from a prepared text, her presentations were not what you would call well organized.

Taking off the gorilla head as she got to her feet, she wondered how Alexis had recognized her.

Then, feeling the rush of exhilaration that swept over her whenever she had an audience, she launched into her very difficult consciousness-raising talk, in which she condemned the practice of farming, called for better conditions in barns the world over, defended the rights of baby seals, presented the case for asparagus, lashed out at skin cancer, recommended the ingestion of only natural foods like milk, decried the lot of chickens, called for the elimination of horseback riding, endorsed 10-speeds as both healthful and ecologically benevolent, urged that the entire third grade academic year be devoted to the instruction of recycling techniques and other environmental truths, called for banning vehicular traffic in Woodbine on weekdays, and, in peroration, offered for signatures a number of petitions, one banning inheritances of any kind, another making the operation of a slaughterhouse a felony, and the last requiring bulls to wear electronic identification devices like parolees so that they could be monitored by the State Police Barracks at Bethel.

She lost most of the crowd early on and, in fact, stirred some spirited opposition.

"MY NAME IS JERROD," came a voice from the rear of the room, "AND I THINK YOU'RE FULL OF SHIT!" The man was on his feet, looking pugnacious. "CHICKENS GET TREATED GOOD, BY GOD, AND ANYWAY THEY'S THE DUMBEST DAMN ANIMAL IN THE BARNYARD AND DON'T KNOW NO BETTER!"

Alexis felt the meeting slipping away. "Let's have some order, here," she said, "I didn't recognize you, sir." The man was medium-sized, needed a shave, could have been 40 or 60, wearing a bright new flannel shirt. Never could tell. Didn't recognize him, but he might be some eccentric, rich and important.

"SOME O' THE BEST FOLKS I KNOW IS CHICKEN FARMERS, DAMN IT!"

Starlight was leaping to her feet, the other members of the Collective were aghast at the presence of such ignorance and intolerance and lack of empathy for the poor chickens of the world, and the chairperson realized that if she didn't stop it now, she never would regain control.

"Quite so, sir, I'm sure," Alexis declared, banging her gavel and without a pause adding, "the Board will now go into executive session." The gavel banged again and the seven board members trooped out of the room into the Town Manager's office down the hall, while general hubbub ensued and the Constables and Officer Harkness walked around creaking their leather outfits.

"Jeez, Alexis, what took you so long?" asked Jonathan Abercrombe, who could be talked into anything and so was a valuable member of the Board.

"Jon, you have got to let these people blow off some steam and get their names in the paper. I bet they go quietly now; that crazy girl bored even her own people." An afterthought. "By the way, who was that last guy?" Nobody knew.

In 10 minutes they had caught their breath, planned their moves, and were ready to face the grassroots of Woodbine once more. Into the hall, through the crowd, back into the meeting room. On the way Alexis came upon the chicken farmers' champion, under fire now for smoking a Camel in Town Hall, which under Vermont law is practically a capital offense. Alexis pushed through the irate clump of Starlight's followers that surrounded him.

"This young lady is right, sir, this is a no smoking area," she offered.

"Good meeting tonight," said Jerrod, ignoring his antagonists, ". . . lively."

"I'm afraid I don't know your name," Alexis said.

"Jerrod."

"Jerrod what?"

"We ain't supposed to give but Jerrod."

"I don't understand."

"Well, ain't this the AA meeting?" Jerrod asked. "When they give me the pass they said it's up on the green where all the cars is parked."

As the truth dawned on Alexis he added: "Somebody's got to stamp my pass I sure enough come to the meeting or they'll never let me out for another one."

"It's across the way at St. Thomas Church," Alexis said to Jerrod's blank stare, "The AA meeting is across the way at St. Thomas Church." And after a pause she fished a card out of her pocket and gave it to him. "If they give you a hard time back at the Jail, I'll vouch for you." So much for rich, eccentric, generous, important strangers.

"You sure this ain't the AA meeting?" Jerrod asked plaintively. He was disappointed. Best one he'd ever been to.

Gavel in hand once more, Alexis decided she had had just about enough of this crap.

"The Board has agreed to consider the matters brought to our attention by you good folk," she soothed, "and although it may be necessary to consult the Secretary of State as to the authority of the Zoning Board in some of your areas of concern there is no doubt that this is a sincere and wonderful demonstration of the Town Meeting spirit of Vermont and the willingness of our citizens to stand up and be counted on matters dear to their hearts, no matter how controversial they may seem at the time. One of the pleasures of public service in this unique State is the constant reminder that hands-on democracy is alive and well in the Green Mountains. The Board joins me in thanking all you folks for taking the time and making the effort to come here tonight to let us know your concerns for the future of Woodbine. Thank you. . . now, in the matter of Henry Whittaker's application for a variance of the 25-foot setback requirement for construction of a storage shed . . ."

The grassroots of Woodbine got up and filed out, pleased with their accomplishments, while the Zoning Board got down to the long-winded and surreptitiously pleasant task of saying no to Henry Whittaker's request, not least because nobody liked the grouchy old bastard.

———————

Jake, like the Woodbine Zoning Board, had a long evening. No further encounters with people or machines, but a series of near encounters that kept him jumpy and unsettled. He'd find a place that seemed peaceful and, the first thing you know, a door would slam just through the trees or a vehicle would roar by right over there a little ways. He couldn't seem to settle down and zonk out, as was his after dark custom.

Yanking his head back out of the Post Office window had been an easy thing, but it shook him too, since the window took him in the back of the head and he considered that he had been attacked from behind. Something he didn't see coming. Something to puzzle over. Reason for suspicion.

Working along Kirkridge heading north, he came onto the same old track he had used that morning while descending from Jack McGinty's hay field. The only place he'd found any peace and quiet for the last four days. He turned up the hill, heading for that fond remembrance.

Jake wasn't the only one seeking respite this Thursday evening. Thaddeus Brookings was beginning to wonder if he would make it through the weekend without punching Mrs. Willoughby right in the snoot. It seemed as if every time he settled down someplace to read the paper, here she came, issuing commands, ordering furniture moved from here to there, and generally being a pain in the neck. A pain in the neck with an irritating way about her, Thad thought.

The potting shed seemed to be the only refuge from the commotion, although even there he could occasionally hear the strident tones that now seemed to be tormenting him at every turn. Thad had even rigged a light in the potting shed, since the window was a small one. This morning on his trip into town for the mail and the newspaper, he had popped into the State Liquor Store specifically to bulk up his potting shed reserve.

By noon he was home again and, after making himself a sandwich, repaired to the potting shed with a bucket of ice, his sandwich and newspaper, and every hope that the rest of the household would forget about his existence.

Sandwich eaten, paper read, soul soothed by the Black Jack, he soon slipped into a relaxed snooze in his favorite chair, rousing at 3:30 in time to be on hand for the performance by The Reverend Hoskins. Bingo's arrival and timely delivery of an old country adage cheered him up even more than the nap. He had to pretend to a fit of coughing to stifle the raucous guffaws that would otherwise have sounded the wrong note with the Reverend.

By this time Sunday afternoon, just three short days from now, this whole blasted thing will be over, he consoled himself. And he held that thought through dinner, ignoring Laura's efforts to continue the guilt trip over his priming Bingo Reilly with Black Jack on Tuesday, which evidently had tainted the Board of Directors luncheon that followed. He retained his natural buoyancy through a dull and tiresome conversation about the possibility of rain on Saturday. He even kept his rediscovered good humor when he was reminded that the Rehearsal Dinner tomorrow evening would be vegetarian in character, owing to the peculiar dietary habits of the family whose name Kimberley would take on Saturday.

But gloom returned when he was informed that he was meeting a plane at Bradley Field near Hartford, Connecticut the following day at 7 a.m. That meant that he would have to leave at 4:30 a.m. or thereabouts, meet the plane, and then drive back north through the morning rush hour traffic of the Hartford-Springfield-Holyoke area. Besides the traffic and the five hours of driving, which he hated, the return trip would be polluted by the insipid cacophonies of the bridesmaid he was picking up, whom even the other girls of the wedding party referred to as "the dippy one."

So Thad went to bed grumpy in spite of his late afternoon rally. He determined just before falling asleep to resist getting up in the middle of the night. He would, he

decided, fall back to sleep enough times that Laura would
have to get up and, fully awake and too hyper to go back to
bed, would make him coffee so he wouldn't fall asleep at
the wheel in the pre-dawn murk.

Misery loves company, he thought, and if I have to get
up at that god-awful hour, so will Laura.

FRIDAY

N either Thad nor Jake found the peace and rest they sought; both spending restless nights, uneasy periods of sleep broken by uncomfortable awakenings, movements and tossings. A branch scratching against the side of the house where never a branch had scratched. Three deer bursting out of the trees followed by two howling dogs. And a breeze was up, causing dark and mysterious rustlings and clackings just out of sight, uncertain movements of animal or vegetable, it was enough to give anyone the willies.

Jake, feeling himself surrounded by enemies, moved to the northern edge of Jack McGinty's hayfield at just about the same time that Thad gave up trying to sleep and got up to make coffee. By the time the first streaks of morning light touched the sky, Thad was fully coffeed and starting the Saab, and Jake was grazing along the western edge of the field, gradually working south. Later he moved into the trees and off the ridge down toward the South Road, unwittingly putting himself in practically the only position where it would be possible to evade the net that the "hounda" brigade would begin closing in an hour's time. A bit of luck for Jake. Proved the old saying that lucky beats smart any time.

Of course there's two kinds of luck. So the "hounda" groups would have a wonderful time roaring around the ridges and high pastures of Kirkridge and Mount Harriet, flinging mud, scaring the deer herd, and generally carrying on in such a way as to inflame not only the upper-middle Forever Wild crowd but also the middle-upper-middle un-shaved legs faction, both of which would be well repre-sented in the Letters to the Editor section of next week's *The Word of Woodbine*. But they would not accomplish the flushing of Jake.

Meanwhile Thad, as he accelerated smoothly up the ramp onto the Interstate, was brooding about the screwball family that Kim was about to marry herself into. A weird bunch, the Callanans, for sure. In fact, Ronan, the one she was marrying, along with his brother Quinlan, seemed to be the only sane ones in the family.

Ronan's father, Patrick James Callanan, Jr., was the son of a prosperous and well-connected Boston contractor. Old P.J., Ronan's grandfather, who would be arriving to-night in his Lincoln Town Car for the wedding, had not always been prosperous and in his climb from a South Bos-ton tenement he had operated on the premise that as long as you never missed Mass and got to confession once a month, the ratio of sand to cement would not be noted in the hereafter. So Patrick grew up in the kind of house where there was usually a priest or two for dinner on Sun-day. As the Callanans prospered, the parish priests were replaced by bishops at the table.

After Boston College and Georgetown Law, Patrick married Mary Catherine Dugan from across the street and joined a proper law firm downtown. Eighteen years later,

Patrick and Mary Catherine found themselves unhappy and, passing up the parish priest, went to a marriage counselor who recommended Yoga. At Yoga class they became acquainted with a couple who had adopted Buddhism and they became enthusiastic converts.

With stacks of money from the law practice, an investment portfolio that rivaled Harvard's, and a major inheritance awaiting only some archbishop or other to perform extreme unction on old P.J., the rejuvenated couple went completely round the bend. Leaving the law firm, Patrick and his Mary Catherine became nominal vegetarians and traveled the world to various Buddhist shrines and holy places seeking peace and tranquillity.

Being a devout Buddhist is as much work and inconvenience as being a devout Catholic, so as prudent modern up-scale Americans, they selected what seemed to apply to late 20th Century suburban Boston and let the rest go. It's one thing to have quiet time every day; it's something entirely different to sit on a mountaintop for three months with your legs crossed, staring into the east.

So they had arrived at a comfortable mix of quasi-religious weirdness that was enjoyable and socially acceptable, while preserving capital and taking full advantage of tax-free municipals. They were also in wonderful physical condition, owing to the yoga and their version of a vegetarian diet. In fact, their practical American approach to the ritual and practice of the Indian sub-continent allowed for a porterhouse every week or so, not to mention an occasional rib roast. "It works for us," Patrick said, and you couldn't argue with that.

Their bizarre enthusiasms required little sacrifice on their part. They traveled, which was great fun, slept until noon on Sunday, which was deliciously evil, and sought converts, which was uplifting. Their lives became sectionalized, as they mingled with different groups of zealots and fanatical believers on different days. The total package to which they dedicated their lives was an incomprehensible porridge of radical environmentalism, dietary old wives tales, preposterous biorhythmic calculations, superficial meditational exercises, public gestures of love for mankind, Socialist hallucinations, recipes for the preparation of obscure vegetables, world peace, racial harmony, massive doses of vitamins for this and that, reverence for the life values of little-known spiders and beetles, and occasional chats with a 4,500-year-old witchdoctor who assured them she was in favor of abortion and against child pornography.

Their two boys were 17 and 16 when the first yoga lesson occurred, and by the time their parents' conversion really took hold they were in college and pretty much out of danger. Now they were both fledgling bankers, Ronan in Boston and Quinlan, the younger boy, in Syracuse. Their eyes had a tendency to glaze over when their parents were present and in declamatory mode.

The Rehearsal Dinner this evening, Patrick had explained over the telephone, was to be dedicated to the wedding party, the wedding guests, the future children of the perfect couple, and world peace, as well as a means of calling attention to the plight of some whale that was reported under attack by the Norwegian Navy. "We've got to stop the wanton killing and engender in man a respect for all living creatures," he explained.

He then described the menu in enthusiastic detail.

It was during that telephone conversation last week that Thad realized the full implications of the Callanans' enthusiasms. The rehearsal dinner would be vegetarian.

(4)(4)

Period. No steaks for non-vegetarians. Not even fish. Not even an omelette. Seeds and berries and vegetables nobody had ever heard of.

"And no booze," Laura added.

"WHAT?" roared Thad.

"I don't think any of those eastern religions permit drinking." She was groping back to A *Survey of World Religions*, sophomore year, but the only thing she could remember was that she had gotten a B+ on the final.

"WELL I'M NOT GOING!"

"You certainly are going and that's all there is to that!"

Thad knew she was right, but sustained a pro-forma grumbling, mumbling, hard-fought and bogus retreat to acquiescence over the rest of the afternoon. He was somewhat mollified by the news that several wines would accompany the meal, although he figured they would be from some off-beat vintner, down at the heels in Bulgaria or some such place, probably located right next to a leaky oil refinery or maybe a broken nuclear power station.

And that was what he had to look forward to this evening. Tofu or some such ridiculous thing for dinner, and no Jack Daniels. Now, at 4:45 a.m. on the Interstate, that dinner seemed a long way away. Thad settled the needle on 75 and punched the cruise control. State cops shouldn't be a problem at this hour.

———

Bingo, with the chores all done by the time first light streaked the sky, peered anxiously out the kitchen window, looking for Stumpy's truck. He had a sense of urgency this morning, a feeling that the search for Jake was slipping out of his hands, getting away from him. Changing in ways he

couldn't make out until they were all over, the way Woodbine had changed without his really noticing at the time.
One day he woke up and said, "Hey! I don't know what
happened but this isn't my town anymore."

In the old days in Woodbine, taxes went to the
schools and the roads, with a little left over for the constables and the fire department. The town budget fit on two
pieces of paper and everybody had a fair idea of what went
where and who paid what.

But over the years things changed little by little, without people taking much notice of it. Pretty soon there's a
board of this and a commission of that and a committee
for something else, and the town and school budgets together weigh two pounds. And then one day you wake up
and you can't even build a damned shed on your own
damned property that you pay the damned property taxes
on, like Henry Whittaker got turned down last night.

Bingo was to have built the shed in July, but where
Henry wanted it was too close to the property line so they
wouldn't let him do it. Even when Thompson McKensie,
the neighbor whose property was too near, testified that he
didn't give a damn if it was built right snug against the
line, they still wouldn't approve it. Bad precedent, she said;
that female lawyer that's always in the newspaper.

Henry called Bingo right after the hearing last night to
tell him and he was some pissed. He was an old grouch,
but Bingo got along with him well enough. Last night he
was sputtering about pickets and god damned flatlanders
and how the Zoning Committee or the Planning Commission or something was going to get after Jake somehow.
Bingo didn't get it all straight over the phone but he didn't
doubt the general drift; things had changed more over the

years than anybody realized until they came right up against it some way.

So it was in something of a siege state of mind that Bingo watched Hyacinth Spencer pull into the yard in her old Jeep. Hyacinth was stirring her coffee and chatting with Milly when Stumpy rolled in, with Wilbur Foster beside him in the truck. Wilbur was along to provide muscle-power, if it were needed. His IQ was not significantly higher than Jake's–his brother Reuben once remarked that Wilbur burnt his fingers every time he struck a match–but he represented some 75 percent of the foursome's lifting power. Might come in handy dealing with Jake.

Wilbur looked up to Bingo with something close to awe, which annoyed Bingo.

"Want some coffee, Wilbur?" Milly asked.

"I dunno."

"Wal, do ya' or don't ya'?" snapped Bingo.

"Why?" Wilbur was getting flustered, with everybody looking at him and all.

"Wilbur, come over here 'n' gitcher coffee." Stumpy knew how to deal with Wilbur. Tell him firmly what to do and he'll do it. Just don't give him any tough choices. Don't give him any choices at all. They're all tough for Wilbur.

The "hounda drive" did not go well.

Strategically impeccable, the operation encountered tactical problems that doomed it from the start.

On the Mt. Harriet side of the valley, things went smoothly enough, both parties moving pretty much according to schedule, covering the terrain well, one from Woodbine moving to the south, the other from South Woodbine moving north. The two groups met towards mid-morning near the Brookings place, just as planned.

And they didn't see hide nor hair of Jake. In fact, what they did was roar down the Brookings Road to the pavement, hurry down to South Woodbine, and join the hullabaloo on the south end of Kirkridge.

Things had started out in good order on the Kirkridge side of the valley. And if they had stayed that way, the drive would have flushed Jake out onto the South Road by nine a.m. But what happened was that Telford Abernathy got going too fast on an old logging road, now really nothing but a track, hit a soft spot and lost it, somersaulting over the bank like a stuntman and seriously injuring himself in the process. Telford was hurt in several ways: when he ricocheted off the tree trunk, when he landed on the rocks in the brook, and when the bike landed on top of him.

It happened shortly before 8 a.m., but it was nearly 8:30 before the gap in the skirmish line was noticed, the country being not only fairly rough but also mostly wooded down at that end of the ridge.

Finally Verity Hooseman, coming to where Blueberry Hill Road peters out by the old cellarhole that used to be the Dominic Farm before it burned, looked around and was surprised to see Orestes Rundell on her right where Telford should have been.

Well, they got looking around and checking by radio and nobody could raise Telford. The reason was that Telford was down by the brook with a badly broken leg. He'd managed to drag himself out of the water–good thing, the water temperature being what it is during the first week in June–but his two-way was still in the water, taped to the bike. He was in a lot of pain, too; he'd pass out from it, then the cold would wake him up, then after a while he'd pass out again.

They said afterwards at the hospital that the only reason he made it was he was such a strong young guy. He was in the woods on a pretty typical early morning in the first week of June, down in a gully on damp, even soggy, ground right alongside the brook, little sun to warm him down in there, soaking wet from falling in the water, and all banged up and bleeding into his thigh.

Once they realized Telford was missing, the South Woodbine end of the Kirkridge operation broke off and started looking for him. Since there was then no point in the northern group continuing the drive, they broke off and sped south to help look.

Time they found him and got the ambulance down from Woodbine and as close as they could, and then got the ambulance free from being stuck in the mud, and got in there with a traction splint and a backboard, hauled him the quarter mile back to the ambulance, with three or four people doing the work and everybody else running around in circles, and yelling, and yakking back and forth on the radio like a flock of blue jays, the drive for Jake was definitely over for the day.

One of the South Woodbine group actually was within 100 yards of Jack McGinty's hayfield, where Jake had spent the night, when he broke off to join the hunt for Telford. And Jake had just left, hadn't even reached the South Road yet.

The fortunes of war, so to speak. What if Major Reno had done this or that instead of what he did? Would Custer and his men have survived the fray? Speculate in vain at what might have been, Jake was off the hook for the moment, at least.

——— ———

After standing very still and listening, partway down the ridge, Jake decided to move along. There was too much movement and sound in the area, not too close but close enough to cause a vague concern, set the nerves on edge, to frequently go still and listen, to bring on an unfocused apprehension.

So Jake moved furtively down the hill, Jack McGinty's horses raising their heads alertly as he moved along the edge of their pasture. He drank in the ditch along the South Road, then crossed the road and disappeared into the woods on the flank of Mt. Harriet, moving into an area that had been declared Jake-free by the "hounda drive" just 30 minutes previously.

If Jake was a general, they'd be calling him Swampfox or Old Crafty or some such. But he was just lucky. Which is all right. Generals called Swampfox or Old Crafty are mostly just lucky too.

——— ———

By noon Thad was back in his kitchen, standing at the counter eating a hot dog fresh out of the microwave. "The dippy one" had lived up to advanced billing, babbling enthusiastic inanities from baggage room through the trip north right into the driveway.

But if anything, being home was worse. Final preparations were underway. The phone was ringing off the hook. Laura was off at the hairdresser. Mrs. Willoughby was rushing from one detail to the next, micromanaging everyone to distraction.

The Callanans were in town, just called, and were on their way to the house to say hello. Then they would be off for a last minute check on the arrangements for the Rehearsal Dinner. They had been up to Vermont a month ago to select the site and plan the menu with the chef; now they would get to taste, verify the wine selections and approve the setting.

The UPS man had spent so much time in the Brookings' yard of late that he now knew both dogs and the cat by name. He also knew to stay out of Mrs. Willoughby's way.

The six girls had adjusted the pitch and volume of their voices to a level that registered somewhere between a jet engine and a police siren.

Everywhere he went in the house Thad came upon people he didn't know, had never seen before. And these people were without exception busy doing things with just enough urgency that he could tell there was a deadline involved, he knew that someone had delivered orders ending in the phrase "or else!"

It was actually a relief for Thad to officiate at the Callanans' courtesy call. Laura wasn't back yet, so he offered refreshments, conducted a tour of the place, explained the tents and what not. The Callanans appeared to have adopted a fairly normal middle American configuration for the weekend, a courtesy to their son perhaps. A pleasant surprise and a hopeful development.

When the Callanans had gone Thad took over the phone detail, stationing himself in his and Laura's bedroom where it was fairly quiet, and using the intercom to locate Mrs. Willoughby, whom most of the calls were for. When Laura came back from the beauty parlor, she and

the girls and the seamstress began making final adjustments on their gowns.

At that point, Thad went off to his potting shed with
his newspaper. He had the crossword puzzle nearly finished
by the time he slipped into a mid-afternoon snooze.

The clans gathered.

At the Woodbine Inn, old P.J. Callanan and his
"three normal sons," as he referred to them, strode into
the taproom and took up positions along the polished mahogany bar. They weren't just Irish; they were Boston Irish,
right out of Southy. Not the slick suburban Irish that dress
up like Harvard professors and never set foot in the old
neighborhood once they leave it. Not the grinning Irish
politicians who never tire of pointing their faces at the
nearest camera lens. Old P.J. was good old-fashioned,
what's in it for me, up at the communion rail every Sunday, knows who to call at City Hall, well-connected Boston
Irish.

P.J. went to the end of the bar, turned a stool sideways
and sat down. The three "boys," ranging in age from 44 to
51, stayed on their feet, clustered protectively around the
old man, craning their necks, checking out the room like
some kind of Secret Service detail. Each of the four put a
$50 bill on the polished bar. Four pairs of eyes sized up the
bartender; looked like he might even be Irish.

When the drinks were in front of them, P.J. pushed
his 50 out. "Take it outta' here," he growled. The bartender was definitely on probation. The Callanans were
well-versed in Boston saloon etiquette and regarded any
variation from that strict canon with suspicion and disap-

proval. This guy was going to have to prove himself. If he were smart he'd get right at it; there'd be a hell of a tip in it for him.

But the bartender was young Jimmy Elmendorf, recently promoted from doorman at his own request so he could "interact more with the guests and help to enrich their vacation experience at the Woodbine Inn."

Naturally, young Jimmy hit the wrong note. "Hi fellas," he bubbled, "going to be staying with us long?" It was the kind of thing that the golfers and tennis players loved.

There was no answer from the Callanan clan to his sally. The four simply looked at him and then dismissed him forever from their consciousness. Jimmy never knew that. When he was relieved 45 minutes later by Harpy Flannigan he went off with what he thought was a wonderful tip. Another group of satisfied customers, he thought.

Harpy, on the other hand, had been in some saloons in his day, and he could see what he had at the bar as soon as he walked in the door. He set about exploiting it immediately. The Callanans watched with appreciation and approval. This is more like it; here's a real barkeep.

Money in the cash drawer, he looked around and complained about Jimmy. "Don't never cut no limes; kid couldn't get hisself locked up."

He got out a small cutting board, a knife and a half dozen limes, and proceeded to cut some limes on the bar directly in front of his audience. He was very good with the knife, the limes cut in attractive shapes, not too small and not too large. Just right, he knew, and a demonstration of a small professional skill that these saloon guys would appreciate.

Next he iced the cake with a comment on the Red Sox pitching staff, although he'd have done just as well with the Celts or the Bruins. The Callanans relaxed. This place isn't too bad after all.

———————

Thad and Laura were the last ones to leave the house for the Rehearsal Dinner, Laura having organized transport like the top sergeant at a motor pool. They were silent as the Mercedes bumped down the hill toward the South Road with Thad steering carefully around great potholes, mud patches and through a deep furrow in the road where a clogged culvert had diverted the spring rains across the gravel.

"They ought to do something about this road," Laura said as they swooped across the brook and up onto the pavement, "You should call them."

"They will, dear, when they get to it. They can't do all the roads at once." This exchange occurred every time they drove down the road together at this time of year, the phrasing always exactly the same, as if it were some complicated password sequence necessary to get them off the gravel and onto the pavement.

Turning right, toward Woodbine, they passed the Reilly house, with Bingo visible through the uncurtained front window sitting in his big chair reading, looking odd without his John Deere cap.

The car hummed quietly into the village, past the speed trap which paid for the police cruiser, around the Village Green, where either exquisite old homes or drafty old arks stood in line, depending on whether your focus was early 19th century New England architecture or the fuel oil bill. Across the Green the lights of Brannigan's Saloon gleamed invitingly.

Thad was thinking glumly about rice, bean sprouts and tofu as the car accelerated across the village line onto the highway and one of those sudden highway crises arose that no driver is ever prepared for. Aubrey Jenkins, janitor at the Elementary School, brooding about whether he had locked the door leaving work and with his saloon capacities reduced by a bout with the flu, made about a six-beer swing onto the highway from the Milk House parking lot, although he had in fact only consumed his usual three beers after work. Aubrey's maneuver caused Patience Hargrove to swerve her brand new Ford 150 four-wheel drive bright yellow truck across the center line to avoid the oblivious Aubrey, and to come radiator to radiator with Thad and Laura. Thad's automatic response was to jam on the brakes and yank the wheel to the right, which action put the Mercedes to bumping along in the ditch until, just before stopping, it nudged into a culvert with a tinkle followed by a brief silence, followed by a trickling noise from the radiator.

No injuries were sustained in this brief skitter of lives entangling and parting again. Indeed the preoccupied Aubrey was unaware of anything untoward having happened and continued on his way back to the school to check on the door.

Patience was unscathed as was her new truck. For Thad and Laura she had sympathy in enormous quantity, hope you're not hurt, my goodness what a scare, goodness gracious, heaven' sakes, there ought to be a law, and similar flutterings. For Aubrey, she had even more sympathy, telling the Constable when he arrived that she didn't recognize the other vehicle, that it came out of nowhere, and how come there was never a cop around when something happened.

Constable Armstrong, known neither for his debating skills nor his reasoning power, was thus deftly maneuvered into delivering a long explanation of why he had not been a witness to the accident. To Thad the message was clear: Tough luck Thad.

One good thing, he thought, was that Laura was not the hysterical type. There the Mercedes lay with its snoot jammed into a culvert, weeping engine coolant into the ditch, and she stood calmly at the side of the road, new shoes covered with mud, inspecting all east-bound cars looking for one that was headed to the Rehearsal Dinner.

Since the Constable had parked his cruiser in such a way as to nearly block traffic, blue lights whippity-whanging around irritating the hell out of everybody, Laura was able to peer into each crawling vehicle with ease and soon had a ride with a pair of young ushers on their way to the tofu. Although Thad assured her that he would be along as soon as he saw to the towing and accident report, they both knew that he had in fact been delivered beyond his wildest hope. He was off the hook, for sure.

"I'll drum up a ride somewhere and come along as soon as I can," he lied.

"O.K. I'll see you there," she lied back. "We won't wait dinner for you," she added, telling the truth.

"Then again maybe I'll just go out in the yard and dine off the bird feeder," he muttered when the car was safely pulling away.

An hour later, the Mercedes hanging by the chin from a tow truck, statement recorded, suddenly at loose ends, Thad turned down the offer of a ride and walked, with a jauntier step then one would have expected, across the parking lot to the discretely lighted entrance of the Milk

House. Not only did he have a thirst; with the accident, he had a good excuse for it.

———————

Bingo finished the newspaper, stretched, burped, and thought about dinner.

"What's fer dinner?" he hollered.

"Fix yer own god damned dinner!" Milly hollered back.

Bingo sat staring at the opposite wall, eyes wide and jaw dropped in astonishment. "What the hell's a'matter with you?"

No answer.

He got out of his chair and went into the kitchen. Milly sat at the table eating a big piece of chocolate cake, his favorite.

"Dessert first?"

"No, I et before."

"What about dinner?" He still couldn't figure it out.

"I toldja, getcher own damn dinner." She forked up the last morsel of cake, rose and put the dirty dish and fork in the sink, and stomped into the front room.

Bingo stared after her with amazement and growing anger. He had his mouth open to say something corrosive when the TV came on at higher than normal volume. Puzzled and disgusted, he slammed out of the back door and into his truck, careening out of the yard with a growl of gravel, headed for the Milk House.

———————

It was nearly 7 p.m. when Thad Brookings stepped through the door of the Milk House and looked around. It was his first time in the place, although he had heard the food was very good, if somewhat unassuming and the menu subject to little change.

The late afternoon rush was over, the bulk of the callused crowd gone. The dining room off to the left was sparsely filled but there was a nice moderate hum to it. Taking a seat at the bar, he noted the three dartboards in the room to the right, which seemed to contain little else. Four men in work clothes occupied the dart room, two playing a match, each of the others practicing by himself. The wall facing the dartboards had a long shelf of dark polished wood upon which the shooters parked their beer glasses. There wasn't a lot of talk; darts appeared to be serious business at the Milk House.

The bearded giant behind the bar approached, looking him over, performing the preliminary psychological frisking that is automatic with the experienced bartender, tentatively connecting him with the hubbub in the ditch across the road.

"Jack Daniels, rocks, with a little water on the side please," Thad said.

When the drink was set before him on a paper napkin, the bartender spoke.

"Repair should be preferred to reparation, at any season."

"I beg your pardon."

"My name is Desmond," said the giant, "good brakes infatuate the soul." He returned to the waiters' station at the other end of the bar, leaving Thad baffled and staring.

He was thinking about looking at a menu when his neighbor walked in the door, looking truculent.

"Well, Mr. Reilly, what a pleasure!"

"'Lo,'" said Bingo, startled at finding Thad in the Milk House. "What's up?"

The accident was described in great detail. Desmond planted a bottle of Donovan's Downtown Stout in front of Bingo and remained, listening to the tale. As Thad was describing the additional damage to the Mercedes that was inflicted by Horace McAlbee's brutal and poorly planned towing technique, he became aware of another listener at his right elbow. Glancing over he was surprised to see a slender little man dressed in maroon sweats, white socks, bedroom slippers and wearing a bright yellow Caterpillar cap pulled down as tight on his head as it would go. He might have been bald underneath it or he might have a full head of hair; it was hard to tell.

"That there's Patchy Flaxon," Bingo said, "he's the town drunk." Now that he was remembering his manners, he added, "This here's Desmond Kiley; owns the place." After a pause. "My neighbor Tad Brookings."

"Pleased to meetcha," said Patchy. Despite his direct and unblinking stare, there was a certain furtiveness about him, as if he had something in his pocket he didn't want you to see.

Desmond nodded his huge bison head. "Exacerbated, I'm sure," he rumbled.

"Wendell Coates is sayin' he's gonna beat the shit outta you," Patchy told Bingo seriously. "In the tournament," he added.

"Well he ain't gonna," said Bingo, "and that's that."

Thirty minutes later, having switched to Donovan's Downtown Stout at Bingo's urging, Thad was pegging away at the largest roast beef sandwich he had ever seen outside his own kitchen and getting filled in on the Patchy Flaxon story.

"Patchy's a guy never did no harm, speak of, turned up around here mebbe 20 years ago, worked here 'n' there, in restaurants, on farms, he's pretty good with horses, did some janitor jobs, don't steal or nothin,' but he drinks to where he's no good to work, yu' know.

"Then when that happens, he lays drunk for a couple weeks and then gets sick and they put 'im in the jailhouse for a while till they let em out and he starts the whole thing all over again, and he allus swears he's done that for the last time and never again, and he for certain means it this time and all the rest of it.

"Well last time he pops out of the can he's in here havin' a welcome back beer–beer don't seem to hurt 'im like the liquor does–and Desmond give 'im a job with one condition that he can't drink on duty and he can't drink no liquor at all anytime. And along with the job he give 'im a home, which he ain't had in a long time. Before he kinda lived around, you know, which ain't so bad in the summer but it's the shits the rest of the year. Like one summer he lived in a ole abandoned Buick back of Henry Tefner's barn on the Owl Crick Road, or he moves into somebody's hayloft or a huntin' camp or someplace.

"Winter's different. One year he started out in the cellar of the drugstore but their insurance company got nervous about it and they put 'im out. Then he lived in the basement at Town Hall for a while till some of the better Christians in town caught wind of it, and he had a place in a dairy barn for a while but he allus got booted for one thing or another, one thing he's got a real mouth on 'im when he's tuned, especially when he's tuned on whiskey.

'Nother thing he stinks, or usedta, specially when he gets into the booze.

"So here's Desmond givin' 'im a job and a cot in the furnace room downstairs but with conditions. No liquor atall, clean the bar and dining rooms ever' day minimum wage, two free beers a day, can have a third if he pays fer it, no exceptions. He's got the furnace room fixed up real homey, he took me down to show me one day, neat as a pin.

"After a couple months Desmond put a shower in down there fer 'im, there wa'nt no cellar in the original Milk House but the dining rooms was built on with cellar below and that's where Patchy lives for three, four years now I guess, and no relapse to the booze. He can shoot some darts, too."

Patchy was indeed shooting darts as they spoke, zinging them into the first board with a crisp authority surprising in such a nondescript little man. Bingo and Thad watched him as he finished his throws, strode to the board to retrieve his darts, and returned to the hockey, a doormat precisely matched to the edge of a black line on the floor, the line itself precisely seven feet, nine and one-quarter inches from the front surface of the dart board.

The board itself was the best; a heavy duty, inch and one half thick "bristle," that produced a solid and comfortable "thud" when struck by a well-thrown dart. The center of the bull's eye was exactly five feet, eight inches above the doormat hockey, putting the little yellow button on top of Patchy's Caterpillar cap two inches below the bull's eye.

"He ain't got but three changes of clothes, all of 'em sweatsuits, different colors, the gray one he cleans in, the blue one and the red one are for dress, yuh know, and the bedroom slippers and some sneakers he wears when he ain't workin.' The bedroom slippers is for like now when he's off duty. He's got a old army overcoat comes down to his ankles he wears if it's cold out."

Patchy was in his red outfit this evening, although Thad would have called it burgundy.

"It's got to where Desmond'd have trouble gittin' along without 'im, he takes all deliveries and checks make sure there's three hams when there's 'sposed to be three hams, counts the empties, orders the booze, all that stuff. He don't go on a tear pretty soon he'll lose the job of town drunk."

"If somebody's taking applications perhaps I could submit a resume," said Thad, wondering, "Who's in charge of hiring?"

They finished their sandwiches, watching Patchy practice his triples starting with the 20 and working down to 10. Patchy was devoting particular attention to the 14 and 11 "pies" on the left side of the board and the 15 and 10 "pies" on the right side, which seemed to be giving him some trouble.

"Still having trouble with the triple 15?" Bingo yelled to him.

"Nope," Patchy declared, "Got it right down to pat."

The three boards along the back side of the dart room were mounted in hand-rubbed walnut cabinets built some years ago by a Haitian cabinetmaker who drifted into Woodbine one frosty October morning, having strayed from an apple-picking job over above Vergennes near Lake Champlain. Desmond took him on as a dishwasher and when his cabinetmaking talents were mentioned, put him to work for the winter around the Milk House. By the time it warmed up enough so Francois dared to go outdoors again the following May, he had redone the back bar, extended and replaced the bar itself, framed a bunch of Desmond's old maps, installed a plate rail around the dining room, and built the three dartboard cabinets that were admired by even the most particular finish carpenters who saw them.

In the first place the dartboards were firmly, precisely installed. The dark polished beauty of the walnut itself lent a certain dignity and importance to any dart game of which they were a part, and when the two cabinet doors were swung open for play, the back of each door was revealed as a scoreboard, a smooth slate in a beveled frame with a channel along the bottom to hold pieces of chalk. There was plenty of room around the boards for misses. Anyone who missed wide enough to nick the cabinet was expected to make a point of explaining to Desmond why it happened, what circumstances had led to the violation of Francoise's handiwork. Those lacking a proper excuse–and saying you were plastered was not considered a proper excuse–could find themselves banned from the dart room entirely for up to a month, depending on the circumstances. Across the bottom of each cabinet was a drawer, with antique cut-glass pulls from Desmond's grandmother's old dresser. Here were kept the house darts, chalk, and erasers.

"Played a little darts myself at the Club in Nairobi," Thad remarked.

"Why'n'cha enter the tournament?" Bingo inquired. "Desmond, got a big dart player here," he called down the bar. "Wants to git in the tournament, he says."

"No, I was never that good at it." Wrap modesty like a protective cloak about you, his Mother always said.

"Git the ten big ones up on the bar," Bingo commanded, turning on his stool, "Patchy, git over here and sign this man up for the tournament; the more money in the pool, the better."

Bingo had a sudden thought. "You know how to play cricket?" he inquired. "Darts cricket?" Without waiting for an answer he described the rules, talking right along, leaving no space for interruption, coaxing the $10 bill out of the pocket and up on the bar and into the pool before letting a silence occur.

Listening, while coughing up what he considered a $10 donation, Thad recognized the game that had been known as Sweaty Betty back in Kenya. He hadn't been half-bad at it, he recalled, and the competition had been tough, straight from the pubs of London.

So it was done. And Thad decided he'd better throw a couple darts for the first time in 25 years. So they adjourned to the dart room for a "spot of practice, old boy," taking their Donovan's along with them.

By 8:30 the two lads had accomplished the difficult transition to the easy use of first names, although in Bingo's case he had slightly altered his neighbor's to where he felt more comfortable with it. He'd never known anyone named Thad, or even heard of anyone named Thad, and the TH sound bothered him. When he was younger he'd known a Theodore out in North Bridgewater, but everybody had called him Teddy so the problem really never presented itself. Of course there were plenty of Thomases around but in that case the H just sat there on paper and had nothing to do with how you said the name. He thought Thad was a sissy name and he felt like a sissy calling anybody Thad, so he had settled on Tad, which soon alternated with Taddy.

Thaddeus Brookings, on the other hand, had negotiated his adult life through and behind a dignified and courtly, one could almost say old fashioned, manner. Outside the circle of his family he was generally considered too cool, too austere for the latter half of the 20th Century. More like a patrician of the 1920s and 1930s.

So it was understandably difficult for him to address another human being, an adult human being at that, using the name Bingo. After a few tries, however, and given the strobish personality of his companion, the name rolled easily off his tongue.

"Say ain't you 'sposed to be at some dinner or sumpin'?" Bingo looked at his neighbor with sudden concern. "Want a ride or sumpin'?"

Thad, well into his third Donovan's, and feeling among friends for the first time since his pipe tobacco moved to the potting shed, launched into a malicious and fictitious description of the vegetarian delight that he was missing, dwelling incredulously on the absurdity that any sane person could even momentarily entertain the idea of designing an elegant celebratory feast around sliced beets and steamed turnips and the like.

"RUTABAGAS, MY GOOD MAN!" he roared, drawing a raised eyebrow and a measuring look from Desmond at the other end of the bar.

Over the next few minutes Desmond paid close attention, without seeming to, to the two men at the end of the bar. After placing two fresh stouts in front of them, he sent downstairs for Patchy. "Disassociate Bingo's keys," he told him, "and relegate them accordingly." Patchy, who was adept at interpreting Desmond's difficult style, went out to the parking lot, took Bingo's keys from the ignition, and brought them back to the bar. Just before dropping them in the open till, Desmond looked down at Bingo and jiggled the keychain.

Bingo's head snapped around; every key chain has its own jingle and he recognized his own. There was the truck key, of course, which never got used except in the ignition. And there was a key to the tool box in the truck bed just back of the cab. Funny thing, but true; nobody would even think of touching that "ought-six" on the gun rack but there's plenty who'd dive into that tool box and grab anything by Mikita. Then there were the keys from three different houses that Bingo took care of in the winter while their owners played golf somewhere else than Vermont, and the key to the gasoline tank that sat alongside the barn, vehicle fuel for farm use selling for less in bulk than at the Mobil station. There was the key to the strong box on the closet shelf, which contained nothing of any importance, and there was the key to the strong box out in the barn that you had to go through Jake's pen to reach, where the important stuff was kept. And finally there was the key that looked important as hell but he couldn't remember what in the damn world it went to.

Anyway, when those keys clunked into the till, Bingo, conditioned by years of experience at the Milk House, accepted that transportation arrangements were now in Desmond's hands. First time in quite a while, by God. Kind of a relaxed feeling came over him, cheering him up, making him appreciate his good friend Taddy all the more, to hell with Milly and her damn disposition, Waylon was on the jukebox singing about "lovable losers, no account boozers and honky-tonk heroes like me," he hadn't thought of Jake all evening, and he was warm and full of strength and among friends.

"Lemme tell ya' sumpin' Taddy, women's the damnedest creatures God put on this earth, worse'n fisher-cats," he began and, as Thad nodded in agreement, the

144

lads commenced to share their current woman problems. Desmond, doing little chores behind the bar as the dining rooms quieted down, settled in to learn more about his fellow men in general and the difficulties faced by these two fellow men in particular.

By quarter past nine Taddy and Bingo had moved on to reminiscences of women long ago.

"They all talk about Paris, my dear fellow, but I'll take London any time, when it comes to gorgeous, complaisant women the British lead the league. I've always thought it had something to do with British men." Two men of the world here, conveniently forgetting the tough spots.

Later on it was Bingo's turn to take the floor with a 40-year-old tale of conquest and surrender, an evening's campaign retold with embellishments. This was a Rutland girl who turned up at a dance in Starksboro one night long ago. A story retold from first acquaintance at the ticket window through dancing, walking in the moonlight, and finally the back of Bingo's pick-up truck. "RIGHT FLAT ON 'ER BACK, NOTHIN' FANCY!" he concluded. Then in confidential tones, "Some of 'em like ya to nibble on 'em ya know."

Desmond closed his eyes and shook his head slightly. After that he gave Patchy the liquor order for next day, then went into the back room and came back carrying three cases of beer, setting them down on the duckboards and starting to pack the coolers for the next day. None of this business of wait till morning at the Milk House. Come in here 11 a.m. and you get a nice cold one, not one that's only been in the cooler 20 minutes since the day man came on.

Between the Donovan's and the unexpected camara-derie with his neighbor, Bingo was relaxed for the first time since Jake left home. The tensions of the week–Jake's odyssey, whatever was ailing Milly, the attention of all the various Woodbine communities focused on him–had bothered Bingo more than he realized.

Feeling suddenly confident and unbeatable, he began poking around for information.

"How ya' gittin' along with your neighbor up there?" he asked.

"Hickham?" Thad considered the question a moment. He knew enough about the two of them to be sure they wouldn't get along. "Not my cup of tea, actually," he said, thinking back to when Hickham has first bought the property above his. He had floated the claim that nine acres of the Brookings' property, including a nice seven-acre meadow, was actually his. Hickham had withdrawn his claim in the face of Thad's survey and the very thorough title search which went with it. Thad and Laura had concluded that Hickham was just routinely probing, sizing up his new neighbors, looking for advantage, on the hunt and addicted to acquisition.

"Truth be known, I don't trust the baah-stid," he added, showing his Donovan's.

"TWO OF A KIND, BY GOD," Bingo roared, "and time fer another Donovan's."

By ten they were into personal exploits, some of them true.

"It's September, see, and we's up to Stumpy's uncle's deer camp bird huntin' and drinkin' beer and raisin' hell and we come out in the morning and there's a big goddam buck right in the meadow actin' like he owns the place, Stumpy's got his ought-six right in his hand carryin' it and he ups and BOOM we got us a helluva deer. Only thing is, it's wrong time of year fer it. Well Stumpy had a ol' Plymouth station wagon, kinda beat up, and we quick stuffed that buck in the back and throwed a blanket on 'im and headed fer his uncle's farm to dress the damn thing. We hadda go through Woodbine and Stumpy's low on gas so we stop at Basil Stockwood's to git gas, Basil used to have a gas station there next to the brook where all them BOW-tiques is now, and Basil's standin' there pumping gas and we're standin' there watchin' 'im and we see that blanket give a helluva twitch and there's a damn antler stickin' out."

"My God," said Taddy, while Bingo stopped for breath.

"'That'll do it for gas, Basil,' says ol' Stumpy, 'cause Basil was quite a snitch, yu' see, and we figgered he'd have the Game Warden after us in a minute, he was allus sniffin' around tryin' to catch us doin' something. 'Well lemme bring it to two dollars, boys,' sez ol' Basil, looking at the gas pump all the time, 'and I wouldn't mind a steak or two my own self,' he sez. 'Count on it,' we sez, jumpin' back in that station wagon whilst he's puttin' the cap on, 'Count on it!'"

"That ain't all of it. Stumpy no sooner got 'er movin' and we look back and the goddam thing is tryin' to stand up. Right there on Main Street! God! Horns clackin' around, it's a wonder we didn't git a eye poked out or sumpin,' Stumpy quick ducked onto Oak Street, ya know by the church, and that thing is really thrashin' around now so it's gittin' dangerous, ya know, and I dug through the glove compartment there and grabbed this old 38 re-volver Stumpy had for varmint shootin' and put a couple of rounds into his brisket and that took care of it. Then we're lookin' around to see if anybody's seen anything or heard the damn gun go off, scared shitless, we broke every law the state had that morning, firin' a gun in the village and shootin' a deer out of season, and whathaveyou." He paused, remembering. "And I never heard nothin' quite so loud as that damn pistol goin' off in that damn little car. Thought my ears was busted; couldn't hear nothin' fer the rest o' the mornin'."

"Well done, my good fellow," Taddy declared, his accent more British by the minute. "Never hunted, old boy, but I must say it sounds amusing," said ol' Taddy, "but I guess you grew up with it."

"Got a deer a year for 41 years," Bingo declared. "A minimum of one deer a year," he amended. He paused, looking into the distance. "Course one year I hadda hunt clear to December 29 to do it."

My Youth Dodging The Game Warden was followed by Exciting Victories on the Tennis Court, a detailed description of a tennis tournament in Nairobi which settled the question of who was the best player in Kenya for that year and the three years that followed, putting that arrogant limey in his place for good and introducing the local aficionados of the game to the quiet, unassuming modesty of the new club champion from Philadelphia. "The rally difficult thing was getting used to the hard courts when I returned to this country after all those yaws on the grass in East Africa," His Lordship concluded.

Shortly before 11, lights out in the dining room, waitresses cashed out and gone, Desmond perched on a stool behind the bar after the long day of standing, and the Taddy & Bingo show reached the singing stage.

By the time Thad knew the words to three verses of The Winnipeg Whore, Desmond had gone off to call Stumpy, raising him from a deep sleep.

"Bingo exonerates pretensions," Desmond declared. Stumpy couldn't make head nor tail of that but he could hear Bingo's voice in the background, now punishing *Brennan on the Moor* at full volume. Right away he knew the keys were in the till and he was the designated driver. He got up and dressed, taking his time, knowing there was no need to hurry. If Bingo was still in the raucous Irish spit-in-your-eye stage, he had a ways to go. He wouldn't be amenable to leaving until well into the upcountry love song stage.

Meanwhile, the Donovan's was flowing and the old timbers of the Milk House ceiling suffered through their first ever rendition of *Lili Marlene*, delivered off-key in an English accent.

Dinner, to the profound astonishment of nearly all who attended, was wonderful. Given the ecumenical quality of the occasion–Catholic Boston, Protestant Philadelphia, and new age, quasi-mysterious-East, wackawackawacka California, all cheek by jowl–the unusual and remarkably delicious dinner was the perfect icebreaker.

The Callanans were at their best, charming, perfect hosts, circulating, introducing people when necessary, talk of chunneling put aside for the moment. Only old P.J. made a fuss, demanding "a goddamn piece of red meat" in tones usually reserved for OSHA zealots and others of the unbaptized.

The Tamarack Inn was beautifully decorated with cut flowers, the grounds already impeccably groomed. Built as a getaway by a wealthy industrialist and politician early in the century, the Inn had 26 rooms, fourteen fireplaces, a library, a study, a den which was now a lounge, a dining room and a magnificent central living room 40 feet by 40 feet with a monumental fireplace on the back wall and French doors all along the front which opened onto a patio, which overlooked the pool, lawn and flower gardens.

Arriving guests were offered a choice of Chateau Trimbach Pinot Blanc or Chateau Trimbach Gewürztraminer as they entered, wines selected to go with the hors d'oeuvres of Mushroom and Herb Terrine and Stripped Vegatable Terrine. "The earthy, delicate flavor of the mushrooms is not only complimented by the Pinot Blanc but literally wrapped in the wine's own additional delicate flavors of peaches, toast and earth," the groom's father explained, "while the Gewürztraminer, with its spicy pear, peach and lemony flavors with almond-like overtones will not contradict the flavors of the Stripped Vegetable Terrine, the sweetness and rich flavors of the carrots and sweet peppers, the nuttiness of the fava beans and the unusual spiciness of nutmeg."

There turned out to be a dozen wine enthusiasts in the group, including the Reverend Hoskins, so the hum of conversation was assured; no silences when that many viewpoints are available for ventilation on one subject, however boring the subject. The clever selection of Carrot and Ginger Soup, which called for the same wine characteristics as the Terrines, allowed guests to carry their hors d'oeuvres wine to the table and tackle the soup without irreparable damage to the palate. Opinion varied as to which ingredient of the Vegetable Kabob demanded the most consideration in selecting the accompanying wine, some plumping for the apricots and raisins, with a strong minority stressing the pine nuts and rosemary. Sentiment was split among Chardonnay, Dry Riesling and Beaujolais, but there was no criticism of Patrick Callanan's selection of a silky smooth William Hill Gold Label Chardonnay, with its "harmonious balance of honey, pear, apple, pineapple and butterscotch flavors," in the words of the Reverend Hoskins.

The party spilled out of the huge living room onto the patio, the weather being just right at the 6 p.m. arrival time, and then gradually moved back indoors as the evening chilled. Conversation grew to a pleasant hubbub, stopping just short of the shrill din of the average cocktail party. Perfect.

Hors d'oeuvres
Mushroom and Herb Terrine, with Melba Toast
Striped Vegetable Terrine, with Melba Toast
Crudité

Chateau Trimbach Pinot Blanc
or
Chateau Trimbach Gewurztraminer

Soup
Carrot and Ginger Soup

Main Course
Vegetable Kabob with Rosemary, served with
Brown Rice Pilaf with Apricots, Raisins, and
Pinenuts
Tomatoes with Spicy Stuffing
William Hill Gold Label Chardonnay, California
or
Beaujolais Grand Cru, St. Amour, France

Salad
Bibb Lettuce with French Dressing

Dessert
Pithiviers: Almond Tart with Vanilla Ice Cream,
topped with Whipped Cream
Country Apple Pie with Vanilla Ice Cream,
topped with Whipped Cream
Robert Pecota Trockenbeerenauslese
or
Sweet Andrea, California
or
Inniskillin Ice Wine, Ontario, Canada

Coffee or Tea
Havana cigars illegally smuggled in from Canada,
and mints
Remy Martin V.S.O.P.

The toasts were cleverly worded and brief. The hum of the crowd good hearted and happy. Laura found the accident a helpful conversation piece with one and all. "Poor Thad! He's missing all this," they said.

"Sure he is!" she thought.

When all was said and done, last cheek pecked, last dainty hand shaken, and the wedding party safely away for the evening, the groom and the ushers in the taproom at the Woodbine Inn getting stupid on WooWoos and the bridesmaids in the Brookings living room telling college stories and squealing together for perhaps the last time, Laura made midnight chocolate sundaes for herself and the girls and wished that Thad had been at the dinner. Surely he would have enjoyed it more than some dour cheeseburger at the village sandwich shop, she thought.

When Stumpy stepped into the Milk House it was just midnight. Only the bar was still lighted. Thad Brookings sat blinking towards the door, trying to focus on the newcomer. Bingo's voice, raised in raucous song, sounded faintly from the hallway beyond the bar where the restrooms were located. He was roaring *The Irish Rover*, badly off key, the verse describing the cargo.

We had one million bags
Of the best Sligo rags,
We had two million barrels of bone.
We had three million bales of old nanny goats' tails,
We had four million barrels of stone.
We had five million hogs
And six million dogs
And seven million barrels of porter.
We had eight million sides of old blind horses' hides
IN THE HOLD OF THE *IRISH ROVER*!

He finished with a whoop as he reappeared from the hallway. Catching sight of Stumpy he stopped and growled "Whuddyou doin' here?"

"Couldn't sleep. Thought I'd have a stout." Stumpy understood that Bingo wasn't yet ready to leave and was wary about anybody trying to talk him into leaving before he was damn good and ready to.

That cleared up, Bingo greeted Stumpy with a pat on the back and an introduction. "This here's my pal Taddy from up the hill," he said. "Shake hands with Stumpy Parker," he ordered.

"Howdy," said Stumpy.

"Charmed, old boy, charmed," mumbled Thad. He was running out of gas, having risen from his bed almost exactly 20 hours ago, spent about seven hours driving, endured Mrs. Willoughby yapping at his heels in the afternoon, and finally driven his car into a culvert. He felt wonderful.

"Extricate a well-chilled Donovan's for young Stumpy here," Thad called. "On my bill, of course, old shoe," he added.

"The delineation matriculates eastward," Desmond grumbled as he placed a stout in front of Stumpy, who nodded in agreement with he knew not what. Bingo and Thad meanwhile were hard at work merging their slightly different versions of *O'Reilly's Daughter*, which merger required negotiations as complicated as those the School Board had with the teachers' union up to the High School.

Done with *O'Reilly's Daughter*, they continued exploring Bingo's repertoire which, while not extensive was loud and satisfactorily rude.

Taddy knew a few late evening songs himself, now that he thought about it.

> Oh, dear, what can the matter be?
> Seven old ladies locked in the lavetree,
> They were there from Monday 'till Saturdee,
> Nobody knew they were there.

Bingo kind'a liked that one, so they went through all seven verses.

> The first to come in
> Was old Mrs. Quinn,
> Prided herself on bein' so thin
> When she sat down
> She continued on in,
> And nobody knew she was there!

154

Stumpy was too far behind to find Bingo and Thad amusing, so he wandered into the dart room to watch Patchy, who was still practicing.

"Gettin' them darts sighted in, Patchy?" he inquired.

"Got them threes right down to pat, Stumpy," the little man replied. "Got 'em right down to pat."

> The last to come in,
> Was old Mrs. Wickle,
> She hurdled the door
> Cause she hadn't a nickel.
> Caught her foot in the bowl
> What a terrible pickle,
> And nobody knew she was there.

Bingo was humming along with the verses ("Sounded like a pig caught under a fence," Stumpy reported the next day) but by the time they got to old Mrs. Wickle, he was pitching in pretty good on the chorus.

> OH! DEAR! WHAT CAN THE MATTER BE?
> SEVEN OL' LADIES LOCKED IN THE LAVATREE!
> THEY WAS THERE FROM MOND'Y TO SATURD'Y!
> NOBODY KNEW THEY WAS THERE!

Judging by the slurred words and sour notes, both troubadours were losing steam rapidly, Stumpy thought, wishing they'd get it over with so he could get them and himself home and get some sleep. He looked in Desmond's direction, hoping for the beginning of the end of the evening, but leaving it all up to the burly giant, whose sense of timing in these matters was impeccable.

Back at the bar Bingo was hard at work on *Mick McGilligan's Daughter Mary Ann:*

> She's my darlin'
> My daisy,
> Cross-eyed and lazy,

With hairs upon her chest like any man.
And you know she's on the rocks
When she's wearin' cotton socks,
Mick McGilligan's daughter Mary Ann!

Then, in an abrupt reversal, he was segueing into *Amanda* in his best Waylon imitation.

Stumpy took this as a promising sign, a halting first step into the realm of maudlin sentiment which would lead, probably around 1 a.m., to a consensual departure for home by Bingo and his new buddy.

"AMANDA-AH, LIGHT OF MY LIFE," howled Bingo, throwing his arms wide like Tony Bennett on some stage in Las Vegas, one arm spilling Taddy's stout over the bar.

"Bingo's tuned pretty good," observed Patchy.

"Yep," said Stumpy, and after a pause, "Well, I've been there." But by God, he thought, I hope I don't sound that bad. He settled back to nurse his Donovan's and wait for the high sign from Desmond, which would indicate that it was time to ease the boys out the door and pack them into the truck. On the way home he would decide whether to deliver Bingo to the house or the barn. A delicate decision, arrived at through sensitive interpretation of the prevailing winds in the Reilly marriage. Cold and from the north at the moment, he judged, which made the barn the tentative first choice. He didn't have a clue what to do with the flatlander, but from what he'd seen cleaning the barn up there last Monday, Stumpy figured that classy looking wife of his could be hell on wheels. I'll just dump him on the lawn and beat it, he figured; don't want no part of her.

When he heard Bingo trail off into silence, Stumpy knew the wait was almost over. "Won't be long now," he said, moving back toward the soloist and his rapt audience. A new song began, but trailed off as the words got jumbled up.

And sure enough, along about one o'clock the magic moment arrived.

"The hours increasingly accentuate particularity," said Desmond firmly, slapping tabs down in front of both men at once.

"Catchittommorrow," said Bingo, trying to read the clock.

"Quite so, old shoe, quite so," Thad said, speaking slowly, enunciating each syllable carefully as he fumbled with his wallet, finally extracting some bills and squinting at them. But squint though he might, he couldn't make out the numbers in the now-darkened bar.

"This ought to cover it, Old Chap," he said grandly, tossing the bills on the bar and lurching off after Bingo Reilly, who was warbling his way to the door with an arm around Stumpy. "Sailed along the northern shore," Bingo wailed, and Thad continued: "Otherwise known as the Winnipeg whore, ho, ho."

Patchy locked the door behind them and headed for the cellar stairs and his cot. Desmond looked at the money on the bar–seven $100 bills–collected Thad's bill from one of them and put the change along with the other six hundred in an envelope, wrote Bingo Friend on it and threw it in the register. Bingo's bill he threw on top of the register. He'd pay next time in; Bingo didn't like owing people. Then Desmond lumbered off to his apartment in the back of the building and went to bed.

When the old grandfather's clock in the living room struck one, Laura stifled a yawn and decided it was time for bed. Gathering the ice cream dishes, she took them to the kitchen and loaded the dishwasher. Partway up the stairs she turned to call back to Kim.

"Turn off the lights when you come up and be sure to see if the cat's at the back door." Very few things irritated her more than to be awakened by the cat scratching at the window in the middle of the night. Occupied doing the Lord knows what when Laura went to bed, the cat would climb a tree, jump on the kitchen roof and come scratching on the bedroom window. It presented no alternative. The only way to stop the scratching was to get up and let the wretched thing in. The scratching never woke Thad.

Speaking of whom, Laura moved quietly into their room, which ran from front to back on one end of the house, undressing in the dark so as not to wake him. Well, there was plenty of light as her eyes adjusted, since the strawberry moon sat right over the pasture. She was thinking that the poor fellow had had a long day, getting up so early and driving to Hartford and back, when she became aware that she was alone in the room, the bed still neatly made and dressed with frilly pillows.

She stood motionless in her slip, thinking about that. Where was he? She moved to the window on the back side of the house, looking to see if there might be a light in the potting shed, Thad's retreat of late.

She was wondering if she should pull on some clothes and check the potting shed, the poor lamb might have fallen asleep in his chair, when she heard a vehicle coming up the hill. A noisy vehicle, at that. She moved to the front window and watched a pickup truck pull into the driveway.

"PULL'ER RIGHT UP ON THE LAWN THERE, STUMPY, WE'LL LAY 'IM OUT ON THE PORCH!" Bingo was trying to whisper quietly, but all that Donovan's Downtown Stout had disabled his volume control. Anyway Stumpy wasn't going to pull up on any lawn, not with a wedding on that same lawn tomorrow morning and, most particularly, not a lawn that's all cluttered up with equipment, folded chairs, boxes of this and that, and tables and what not.

The truck stopped in the driveway behind the three cars parked there and the engine chuff-chuffed into silence. Bingo flung open the passenger door, half jumped and half fell out of the truck, stumbled, windmilling to catch his balance, lurched into the same electric fence that had so discomfited Kim's horse the day before, and fell into a tangle of hot wires, cold moist grass and a good-sized rock that banged his tractor leg. The connection broke quickly though, because the fence was temporary, just up for the wedding to keep the lawn free of dogs and horses and deer and anything else that came along. But not before he got a nasty shot from the fence. His roar of pain, chagrin and outrage was probably audible in Rutland, some 35 miles away and over the mountain to boot.

Startled by the profane howls coming from the other side of the truck, Stumpy quickly jumped out the drivers side and ran around to see what was going on. His first thought was the Bingo had been set upon by a dog or something. The snoring Thad, with Stumpy's supporting shoulder suddenly removed, fell sideways across the driver's seat and, twisting in his sleep to get comfortable, ended up on the floor with his feet on the passenger side and his head next to the clutch pedal.

"GOD DAMNED FENCE," Bingo roared.

"Shhhhhh," said Stumpy, looking over his shoulder at the house just as the front door opened and a bunch of young girls came out. "Oh shit, now ya' done it," he groaned.

"DONE WHAT, GOD DAMN IT?"

"Hello out there, is something wrong?" It was Kim.

"NOPE! WE WAS JUS' CHECKIN' ON THE HORSES 'N' LOOKIN' FER JAKE." Bingo was getting crafty. Have to look out for his pal Taddy.

"Okay." Kim recognized Mr. Reilly's voice.

By God it's working, he thought. "STUMPY! LET'S GIT!"

Too late. A slender figure in a long dressing gown was striding across the lawn. No getting out of this one.

"Is Thad there, Mr. Reilly?"

Bingo, on his feet at last, peered into the truck. "BY GOD IF HE AIN'T!" He tried to sound surprised.

"Perhaps you two gentlemen could help him to the potting shed." Even tones, very cool. Icy, in fact. This lady is some pissed, Stumpy thought.

Bingo tried another angle. "SEEMS LIKE OLD TADDY ET SUMPIN' DIDN'T SET TOO GOOD." That was it; should have thought of this in the first place. "COME RIGHT BACK UP ON 'IM, BY GOD!" Got a sick and pitiful case on our hands here. Bingo hiccuped.

Stumpy spoke up before things got any worse. "Any way I can get the truck nearer, Ma'am?"

Recognizing that she was hearing from someone sober, Laura directed him between the tables and stacks of chairs and around the end of the house. She had stopped a good 20 feet from the truck and was unable to see a third person in the cab. Maybe, she thought, he's passed out in the back. She knew he was there some place; she could hear him snoring.

"Put him in his chair out there; I'll send out a couple of blankets." Laura turned and walked stiffly back to the house, up the front steps, past the gaping girls, into the house and upstairs. Nobody said anything. Nobody dared.

Stumpy was sure glad when she left. That way she didn't have to watch him and Bingo yanking old Taddy around to get him up off the floor so Stumpy could operate the pedals to drive the damn truck around back of the house. Then there was a big hassle getting him out of the truck, with Bingo fog-horning around issuing commands and being damn little help. By the time they got old Taddy in the shed, there were two folded blankets setting on the chair. Stumpy tucked him in and turned to find Bingo rooting around looking for "the 'mergency Black Jack."

Shooing him back to the truck, Stumpy rattled down the hill planning to drop Bingo halfway between house and barn and let him make his own damn decision. He'd about had enough of Bingo Reilly for one night.

Approaching the bottom of the hill, Bingo spoke.

"BY GOD, I THINK SHE BOUGHT IT!"

"Bought what?"

"ABOUT TADDY EATIN' SUMPIN' 'N' GITTIN' SICK."

Stumpy looked at him in astonishment. I'll have to thank Desmond for picking me to call, he thought. He stopped the truck at the driveway and let Bingo out. Tomorrow would be time enough to talk. Pulling away, he could see Bingo in the rear view mirror, weaving like a blade of grass in the wind, waving his arms and yelling something after the truck. Let him decide for himself whether to sleep in the house or the barn.

161

SATURDAY

S tumpy was back in his own bed and asleep by 2:30 a.m. Just about the time his eyes closed, Jake's eyes snapped open. Standing under a tree high on the shoulder of Mt. Harriet, snoozing peacefully, his serene world was split by the squawk and frantic uproar associated with the sudden death of a nesting wild turkey at the hands of, or claws and teeth of, a fishercat.

It was over quickly, but Jake, startled and uncertain just what had happened off in the dark, was fully awake and on the move by the time silence returned to the stand of cedars where he had been snoozing. He moved off along the ridge, heading nowhere in particular, looking for something to eat in grown over pastures and long abandoned tracks, the full moon so bright it was casting sharp shadows, sometimes heading down, sometimes up, going where his snoot happened to take him.

Which happened to be in the general direction of the Brookings house, with all its tensions and expectations.

———————

When Thad came awake at around five a.m. he simultaneously experienced so many negative feelings and im-

162

pulses that it was hard to sort out which one had the high-est priority. Was it the dry mouth and throat with the foul-tasting tongue plopped down in the middle of it like a caked mudpie? Was it the stiff neck and the aching ribs from sleeping cocked over the arm of the chair? Was it the numb arm, deprived of proper circulation for hours while his weight lay upon it? Was it the need to pee? Was it the dismay of realizing that he must have made an ass of him-self last night? Was it the early morning chill that seemed to penetrate clear to his bones?

It was none of these.

All were secondary to the overwhelming, swelling, rising, unstoppable, look out here it comes, necessity to vomit. Lurching to his feet, he executed a stumbling lunge towards the door, hanging on to the work table, limping and shuffling and hooching along against the aches and stiffness of his body, attaching great importance to not barfing in his crude hideaway, letting it go just as he threw himself out the open door into the barely tinged begin-nings of dawn.

Right smack into the left side ribcage of Jacob Mulli-gan's Meticulous Rumpus the Third, who, preoccupied with the tender shoots of the lilac bushes that had been planted to shield and disguise the potting shed, had no inkling that another being was so near, much less one who would venture an all-out head butt on him.

The week thus far had taught Jake to run from what he did not immediately understand. That's what had been working for him so far, and that's what he did when Thad barreled into his side.

He bolted in the direction he was facing, which was toward the house. The house caused him to cut sharp left. He raced to the end of the building and was then steered towards the front lawn by a big stack of folding chairs covered with a tarp. He was immediately faced with the band tent, which was next to the big tent where the dancing would be.

By this time he was up to speed and there was no stopping, especially with Jake's rather sluggish decision-making apparatus. The tent sides would be rolled up later in the morning; now they were down to keep out the damp, but with a flap opened a bit by the breeze. Jake went for the opening and, finding himself in the blackness inside, tried to stop, skidded across the wood flooring, lost his footing and fell with a thunderous crash, landing heavily on his side.

Through the opposite side of the tent and into the dance floor tent slid Jake and all that was before him: amplifiers, speakers, chairs, a spider's nightmare of wiring, clips, connectors, music stands, dinner plates, cups and saucers, salad plates and four racks of highball glasses that the caterer had stuck in there just for the night. Most of the band tent came with him and what he collected along the way, his nearly a ton at full momentum snapping the center tent post and taking out two of the corner posts as well.

All this amid a great smashing, crashing, shattering, cacophonous din; a screeching rending of metal, a roar, a startling earth-shaking dissonance, the first Battle of Bull Run, so to speak.

When Jake slid off the floor of the band tent, he dropped the two feet to the dance floor, and spun to a halt; a great rattling bundle of junk and broken glass and miscellaneous debris, wrapped in part of a canvas tent.

There was a brief moment of silence, God catching His breath. Just long enough so that everybody in the house with a window on the front side could get into position. Just long enough so Thad, fluttery stomach forgotten for the moment, could poke his head around the house. Just long enough for Jake to decide he'd had just about enough of hassle, and he wasn't putting up with any more of it.

He struggled to his feet, throwing his head this way and that, horns tearing at the canvas. And he bellowed. An ear-splitting, outraged, angry son-of-a-bitch of a bellow. A bellow that lasted awhile, with a beginning and a middle and an end, Wagnerian in scope and intensity, nuanced in tone and pitch, an anguished appeal and complaint and threat in one, a declaration of implacable hostilities, of an insufferable frustration, a head-thrown-back "WHY ME?" and a "LEAVE ME BE!" and a "COME AND GET ME!" in one great misery-laden arching parabola of sound.

Lunging off the edge of the dance floor, he ran for the road trailing canvas and tent ropes and wires, getting a nasty gash where his right front leg joined his brisket when he ricocheted off the Saab, running off down the road towards Bingo's house and the South Road.

Of course he didn't just run the whole mile down the road and knock on the barn door and ask to be let in. No such luck. He went only to the end of the Brookings pasture fence, maybe a hundred yards, and then turned into the woods, occasionally bawling his frustration, leaving his audience awed and astonished. Very few people are ever in their lives as close to an angry bull as the Brookings and the bridesmaids were that morning. The experience left them feeling diminished.

The telephone woke Milly, Mrs. Brookings reporting the sighting of Jake. She got up, put on her bathrobe and a pair of chore boots, and went out to the barn to rouse Bingo. The road went off the South Road right by the Reilly place, so she had heard all the back and forth early this morning, had recognized the failing muffler on Stumpy's old pickup, and had heard her beloved shout after it: "DON'T DO NOTHIN' YA' WOULDN'T SLEEP IN, STUMP!"

He must have been really tuned if he went to the barn, she thought, sliding open the big door and setting the animals all in a hullabaloo. The creature that raised its head from the loose hay in the spare stall resembled her husband, she thought, or what he would look like in another 20 years.

"Jake's just up to Brookings raisin' hell," she declared, "and gone back in the woods."

"Wha'?" growled her hero.

"JAKE," she yelled, "BROKE LOTS OF STUFF UP TO BROOKINGS'!" Every syllable was a piercing blade of pain into his brain, and since he was trying to do two things at the same time–make sense of what Milly was saying and get his eyes to stay open without allowing the gelatin inside his eyeballs to boil–he didn't get very far with either one.

Milly stepped back and gave him a measuring look, suspecting that he hadn't registered her message. She stepped over to the feed storage area. The cattle feed and the horse feed were kept in metal 50-gallon drums with flat tops. The goose feed and the chicken feed were kept in ordinary metal garbage cans, with handles on the tops. It was important to keep food in metal containers to discour-

age rats and raccoons and other varmints as well as to prevent contamination and spoilage from dampness.

Grabbing the tops of the goose feed can and the
chicken feed can Milly spread her arms wide and clanged
them powerfully together like cymbals, 1812 Overture
style, putting Bingo right back down in the hay and practically out cold. Pleased with the effect, she gave them another humongous clang, then tossed them in the general
direction of the feed storage area, turned on her heel and
marched back to the house feeling better than she had all
week. Behind her she could hear the complaints of the
various animals demanding to be fed, wondering what the
unusual clanging was all about, and generally setting up for
a fractious morning feeding. She could hear Bingo too, just
a low mumbling growl, not intelligible at a distance, but
surely the sounds of a suffering man.

———

If you were to buy an old house and bring it from the
1870s up to the 1990s, as the Brookings had, and if the
water supply for that house was a pipe from a surface
spring further up the hill, as theirs was, one of your first
moves would be to go dicker with old Raleigh Starkweather
for a well-drilling, as the Brookings had done. A driven
well is a strong guarantee that water will be available even
during very dry years, it greatly reduces the possibility of
casual contamination by a dead squirrel or some such, and,
unless you have extremely bad luck, the well pump will
provide better pressure than is obtained by water just running down the hill through the force of gravity.

Furthermore, if this house of yours were located at
approximately 43° 37′ north of the equator and 72° 32′

west of Greenwich, England, more or less, not only would the water be coming out of your showerhead at 12 gallons per minute, it would be coming out of the ground at about 46° Fahrenheit.

Thaddeus Brookings stood with his mug pushed up towards the showerhead and let the terrible cold of the water restore him to useful consciousness, taking the time to thank the Lord for Jake's appearance.

The brief shattering elemental violence of Jake's passage this morning had neutralized Thad's misdeeds, turning all those who witnessed the event into dazed and disbelieving people, like the poor souls shown on the 6 p.m. news right after the tornado hits the trailer park.

They all went out and looked, the girls and Laura wandering around in their nightgowns and bathrobes, Thad in his dishevelment not saying much, taken aback by the menace and power they had witnessed and which was confirmed by the wreckage. Full light had developed while they experienced the first shock of assessing the damage. Their feet scuffed meandering tracks in the dew on the lawn as they wandered about in wonderment.

Thad rose to the occasion. "I'm taking a quick shower; be right down. Get some breakfast and start making a list. We'll get on the phone right away and have this place squared away in plenty of time." He was looking at his wife's face, plenty of things going wrong this week and this the worst, the possible demolition of the wedding. She looked stricken. "Really, Laura, it'll work out." She was tough and resilient. He knew she'd be all right as soon as they got calling, improvising, cajoling, and generally raising hell to repair the damage before the guests started arriving at noon.

Just before reaching the point of hypothermia, Thad turned off the shower and stepped out of the stall. Scrubbing himself dry, he was astonished to find himself feeling pretty good; probably a good thing he barfed this morning, although he had no plans to share the details with anyone, preferring to allow Jake's swath of destruction stand as an act of God rather than a response to an unintentional head butt.

Imagine trying to explain such a thing. He shaved quickly, without cutting himself, dressed and hurried downstairs to take command. He felt wonderful and he couldn't get over it. How could this be?

By 7:30 a.m. this beautiful Saturday morning most of Woodbine was up and about, maturing their plans for the day. Starlight Spotsworth, for example, was making picket signs with a thick black magic marker in the kitchen of her apartment. Bingo Reilly, back in touch with his friends and loved ones after plunging his head in the brook and holding it there as long as he could, was finishing breakfast and preparing, with some trepidation, to drive up the hill and help out at the Brookings in answer to his old buddy Taddy's phone request. Actually, he was waiting for Stumpy, who would give him a lift to the Milk House to get his truck. Then they could go up to the Brookings' together; neither one wanted to arrive alone and have to look Laura Brookings in the eye.

In the parking lot of the Woodbine Inn, one Manfred Livingstone flicked a speck of dust off the left front fender of his gleaming light tan 1935 Aston Martin MK11 Long Chassis Tourer, preparing to ensconce himself in the recently reupholstered leather seat for a drive out amongst the common people. Mrs. Livingstone would be along soon to accompany him, having stopped off at the Front Desk to lodge a complaint about the jam served in the coffee shop. It had come to her attention that it was not imported from England and she wanted to know why and she wouldn't be satisfied until she spoke to someone in authority who could give her a reasonable answer. The Livingstones were part of the Central Connecticut Antique Automobile Society, in Woodbine for their first rally of the season.

In the huge kitchen of the Woodbine Inn, Busboy Douglas Monahan, working the early morning room service shift, blinked as he wrote down the breakfast order for Suite 318. Two orders of scrambled eggs, English muffins, bacon, toast, coffee, sweet rolls, and two double shots of Bushmills. As he punched the order into the computer the name came up on the screen. Suite 318 was occupied by Mr. & Mrs. P.J. Callanan, Sr. Terrific tipper, according to the grapevine. "That's the way to live," he remarked to the breakfast cook when he relayed the order, "that's the way to live."

Down towards the village line, at the parts store, the usual talk of plugs and filters and shocks and carburetors was leavened with the latest news of Jake and the so far unsuccessful attempts to locate and capture him. The "hounda drive" was on everybody's lips, as were the injuries to Telford Abernathy. And, the word was, Jake had cut quite a swath through the wedding preparations up to the old Chester place this morning. Truth be known, the local folk of Woodbine were beginning to take it personally; Jake at large was starting to reflect on them all. Pretty soon every stuck-up flatlander golfing prissy-britches in town would be looking down his nose and saying if you folks are such great country people how come you can't catch 'im? And a bunch of little skinny-flanked, stringy-haired women running around saying shoot the beast, he's emblematic of oppression, whatever the hell that meant.

It was coming to seem like catching Jake had something to do with upholding the honor of the working man and insuring the continued existence of the family farm, home-made apple pie, fresh strawberries (which ought to be elegant this year the way the weather's been), and the value of a high school education.

———————

It was a frantic few hours. More chairs and three good-sized tables were borrowed from the parish hall at the Catholic Church. Glassware for 197 expected guests was rented from the Woodbine Inn, sent through the dishwasher in the Inn's kitchen, and transported down the South Road and up the hill to the Brookings house in the Inn's van. "They're not doing us any favors," Thad pointed out, "since we're responsible for about 60 percent of their business this weekend."

The unsalvageable wreckage on the lawn was thrown into the back of Stumpy's pickup. The salvageable but not today wreckage was tossed into the back of Bingo's pickup. The just has to be cleaned and wiped off wreckage that could still play a part in the day's activities was put in one place for the cleaning and wiping.

The band was apprised of their loss, assured of its replacement, and sent scurrying about begging and borrowing replacement equipment. The guitar player had a son on the High School baseball team who, along with the first baseman and the entire outfield, was enlisted for high speed cleanup work at $10 per hour, pretty good money.

When the heavy debris had been cleared, the baseball team picked the big chunks of broken glass off the lawn. Then the Woodbine Inn's big vacuum machine that was used to pick up leaves in the fall was trundled off the Inn's van, complete with two men to operate it, and started making a huge racket sucking up the shards that were too small to pick by hand.

The phone's din was constant.

Mrs. Willoughby was the first person Thad called, and she turned out to be the key to the morning's rapid recovery. Having put the operation together so meticulously, she instantly recognized where it was compromised, who would be affected by the dislocations and how they would be affected. Her rearrangements in scheduling, placement of incoming supplies, and timing changes enabled the revised set-up to proceed with a minimum of confusion and loss of time.

"My hat's off to you, Mrs. Willoughby, you know your business," said Thad at 11:30, just as he ducked up the stairs to get dressed.

Laura looked delicious standing in front of the full-length mirror, tugging at her dress so it hung just right, patting the perfect hairdo, picking an imaginary bit of lint off a shoulder, generally preparing for the fray; it was take a deep breath time.

Thad, buoyed by the morning's excitement, was relaxed and untouched by stage fright. All he had to do was march down the aisle with Kim and hand her over. Nothing to it. "You look fetching," he said to his wife, who didn't even hear him, so engrossed was she in the creature in the mirror.

"Thaddy dear, please be on your best behavior today, will you?" A certain conciliatory tone in the delivery cheered him up even more. Now that the moment was at hand, the strains of the last weeks of planning and worrying seemed to fall away, returning a certain lilt and skeptical good humor to her voice. Music to his ears.

"You betcha!" said Thad, adding, "Pick me out a tie for the blue suit, will you?" God's in his heaven, he thought, all's right with the world. And not a minute too soon.

———————

Stumpy's truck, full of wreckage bound for the dump, was parked down by Bingo's barn. He had grabbed a ride back up the hill with one of the musicians and was now, as the upper pasture accumulated out-of-state cars, standing with Bingo in the Brookings' enormous barn next to a bar, not yet open, which was one of three that would be going all out shortly after the ceremony concluded.

One bar was just behind the dance floor tent. The idea was that it would be hidden until after the ceremony when, assuming favorable weather, the sides of the tent would be raised and there it would be, with Murdock Fletcher at the controls and wearing a necktie for the first time since he himself was wed in the Rutland Town Hall 13 years before. The morning's toil had gotten the tent top and one of the sides back in place, so Murdock was sheltered from the thirsty throng as planned.

Not so lucky was Winifred Morrison, whose station was to have been completely set up, ready to go, and disguised by a six panel screen on the edge of the lawn down near the flower beds. None of the blue suits and new dresses, none of the subtle hints of pearls and solid gold tiepins, none of the $800 cordovans and three carat emeralds were supposed to be aware of a bar until after the solemn ceremony. But the schedule change caused by the cleanup efforts left poor Winifred still stacking glasses and hauling ice as the guests arrived, and she had to spend a lot of time telling people what they could see for themselves: she wasn't ready to open for business. By the time the wedding was ready to begin, she had met just about all the male guests. Some of them wandered over to her station out of thirst, looking for a drink; some of them just went over for a closer look at her impressive physical attributes.

In the barn, Bingo went to work on young Roscoe Lintelmark.

"You got any Donovan's in them coolers?"

"What if I did have?"

"Wal if ya' did have, you'd oughta' know enough to respect yer elders 'n' snap one of 'em open fer yer old friends and comrades Bingo Reilly 'n' Stumpy Parker; that's what!"

"I ain't sposed ta . . ."

"Hear that, Stumpy, the boy's loyal and true from hoof ta helmet, by God." The sweat was running down Bingo's nose and dripping off the end, although it was a perfect day with a light breeze and a temperature of just over 70.

"By God he's a good'un!" Stumpy agreed, feeling a bit of a thirst himself.

"And ain't we all workin' for the same blessed wedding?" Bingo's arms flung wide dramatically as he posed the rhetorical question. "Ain't we, Roscoe?"

"Guess so, but . . ."

"And ain't we dropped ever our own chores ta run ta the aid and comfort of our good neighbor Taddy that I et supper with jest last night and now he's in the darts tournament and by God wouldn't he be pissed if he knowed you's argyin' with us over a lousy Donovan's that's been slavin' like a cupla' God damned 'dentured servants here all mornin' . . ." Bingo moved to the row of ice-filled coolers against the barn wall as he spoke, yanking two Donovans out of one of them.

"Now Roscoe," he purred as he tossed one of the bottles to Stumpy and twisted the cap off the other, "ya' sure don't wanna' be sloppin' beer while yer on duty or I'd git one fer you too." He and Stumpy walked to the Dutch door of the barn, leaning on the closed bottom halves, and watched the proceedings in the yard.

"Winifred seems to be drawin' flies over there," Stumpy observed. A cluster of the younger guests were around her station, offering to help with the lifting, trying out their charming faces on the busty beauty. None of them seemed to be getting anywhere.

"I'll tell ya what!" Bingo declared, recovery well enough along that he could once more appreciate what he sometimes referred to as the "femy-NINE" sex. "She'd make a ol' hound dog bust his chain!" That first long, cool swig of Donovan's hit bottom, and by golly, things weren't so bad after all.

————————

At precisely noon, Ms. Starlight Spotsworth and seven other ladies met on the village Green with every intention of breaking whatever local ordinances, state statutes, and federal laws that happened to come along. Their cause this fine June Saturday was to urge upon the community the implementation and meticulous enforcement of a recent proclamation from the National Secretariat of the Power to the Animals Collective suggesting the adoption of a schedule of fines starting at $250 for the crime of road killing.

Her colleagues included an 85-year-old widow who liked to meet new people and "had a soft spot in my heart for animals all my life," three WOW members who were trading picketing chores today for a guarantee of three Collective pickets at the equal rights rally scheduled for the Fourth of July, and three true believers of the Power to the Animals Collective.

Millicent Buchanan was on hand to cover the event, but as a matter of principle abstained from active participation. Susan B., absolutely the best cat she had ever been associated with, had disappeared just two weeks ago while on an evening hunting expedition and Millicent's dark suspicions had settled on a family of raccoons living near her as the responsible parties. After several days of agonized soul-searching she had decided that lending her support to the potential road kill population, some 40 percent of which was raccoon in nature, would be hypocritical.

The protesters' signs carried cryptic messages misunderstood by most motorists. It was kind of hard to get the whole rationale of the proclamation across on just a picket sign. But they had pamphlets as well, and when folks slowed down, squinting to interpret the signs, a pamphlet was thrust at them for their education. Dangerous work, though, because so many vehicles are air-conditioned these days and Starlight had to keep jumping in front of them to get them to roll down a window so she could pitch the propaganda into their laps.

The Collective's picketing permit, issued along with a stern warning against traffic disruption by the Selectmen, was for Starlight nothing more than a departure point. Any attempts to limit her activities she regarded as an attack on the Constitution and an infringement of her rights to life, liberty, and the pursuit of happiness. The right of a person to drive through the village unimpeded she dismissed as subservient to the desperate plight of all the potential roadkill currently innocently strewing garbage about back porches, gnawing wires in attics, burrowing holes in foundations, killing chickens, and generally doing what road kill does before it ends up as road kill.

ROAD KILL SHAME! said one sign. DON'T MAKE ORPHANS! said another. CARS KILL INNOCENTS! said a third.

Starlight, as usual, got carried away and after a few angry objections from motorists, stopped regarding them as potential sympathizers and began considering them as implacable enemies. Soon it was a combination of hand-to-hand combat, bull-fighting, and dodgeball, as she challenged vehicles, slipped to the side and felt them brush her stylishly baggy slacks, slapped a pamphlet into an outstretched hand or flipped it past a yelling face.

Officer Harkness, who dreaded his encounters with Starlight, kept himself and the police cruiser down at the South Road speed trap, hoping that, just this once, he could get through a weekend without having to deal with her. No telling what she would do. Especially when she got all steamed up about something. He even ignored the Dispatcher yelling over the radio that there's some kind of problem up at the Green and go see what it is. The Town Manager had to go looking for him to finally get him to respond.

That's why he was too late to witness the confrontation between Starlight Spotsworth and Mr. & Mrs. Manfred Livingstone.

Starlight's strenuous challenging of the motoring public had worked her into a state of high excitement, a testy and combative exhilaration that she achieved only in the pitch of battle. So the sight of the Aston Martin triggered her easily-triggered "to the guillotine" reflex. The driver of such an automobile just had to be an evil captain of industry, a corporate raider feasting on the meager savings of widows and orphans, an exploiter of the working class and a cruel producer of corrupt and corrupting products.

So BONK! Starlight slammed her picket sign across the hood of the Aston Martin, eliciting an agonized howl from Manfred, who screeched to a halt and jumped out of his pride and joy to inspect the damage. Starlight assumed he was on the attack–in his shoes she would have been– and nailed him with the sign on the backswing. She then gave a great screech, as if she were the one who had gotten bopped, and the melee was on. The other picketers rushed to her aid, signs slashing about and screaming heroic last words. Manfred realized he was in trouble and, jumping back in the car, stalled and flooded it trying for a fast getaway

Officer Harkness had his hands full when he arrived at the Green, as he explained to the Judge later that afternoon.

———————

The finishing touches were completed on the Brookings' front lawn just as the first guests began to arrive. They would never have known of the violent disruption at dawn

178

had it not been for the fact that the Brookings and the bridesmaids and the band and everybody else who participated in the crash recovery effort could talk of nothing else.

So Jake was further enshrined as some dark legend, lurking half-seen in the obscuring brush, malevolent eyes staring, impatient to be on the attack, sinister and dangerous. The city folk, hearing the story and inspecting the dent Jake had left in the Saab, had a tendency to glance at the woods bordering the pasture from time to time, looking perhaps for a hint of movement or straining to hear the snapping of branches.

Thad was flawless in his duty as Father of the Bride, which consisted in getting down the porch steps and across the lawn to where the Reverend Hoskins was situated, and then a few feet back to a folding chair, without falling down. Few knew he had gotten tangled up with Bingo Reilly the night before; that had happened in another Woodbine, a Woodbine from a parallel universe. Several of the people working on the grounds that morning knew about it, but none of the wedding guests did, even those who lived in Woodbine. A close observer might, however, have noticed that his eyes seemed just a shade too moist, evidence of the eye drops that had removed the bloodshot effects that still remained after the cold shower. Or perhaps it was the emotional impact of the occasion.

Laura was charming and lovely, the perfect hostess, making it look easy. Between her and Mrs. Willoughby, the wedding struck just the intended note: elegant and casual, relaxed but formal enough so that some ten percent of the female guests had guessed wrong and felt underdressed.

Not only a wedding, it was a meeting of two clans and their formal introduction to one another, for good or ill.

Protocol was observed. When Colin, one of old P.J.'s "normal sons," started getting a bit loud, due to a combination of single-malt scotch and an empty stomach, he was swiftly squelched by the other members of the family. The Brookings and the Callanans would get along all right; it wasn't as if they would see each other every day anyway. Still it took some getting used to. There were measurements to be taken, judgments to be formulated, labels to be applied, niches to be filled. Lifelong prejudices demanded satisfaction and adjustment.

Old P.J. took up a position and stayed there, approachable but surrounded by his hierarchy of sons, grandsons, and sons-in-law. Daughters and granddaughters and such were around as well, but they didn't count for that much with P.J. Asked to describe his family, he would reply that he had "four boys and two other children."

So the liquor flowed and the Brookings and the Callanans mingled with careful restraint, testing the limits of this new alliance, getting used to adjustments of religion and attitude, making cultural allowances for their new acquaintances. It was a wedding, a happy occasion; but it might as well have been a meeting held at dawn on a mist-covered highland crag to work out some Celtic boundary dispute.

———————

At the Milk House, Desmond Kiley posted Patchy Flaxon behind the bar to handle the lunch trade, while he took a table in the dining room to spread out his charts and lists and try to make some sense of the Darts Tournament, which had attracted 138 entrants, some from as far away as Randolph and Claremont.

Business was sparse on this beautiful first Saturday in June; it was just too nice to spend time indoors. Still Patchy, looking spruce in his blue sweats, did a fair lunch business, a sandwich here, an order of lasagna there. And usually a beer to go along with it. Not many lingered, however; eat and run was the cry. Too much work around home this time of year.

Patchy enjoyed tending bar. There was always backup; Desmond left the building from 9:30 to 10:30 every weekday morning to go the bank and the library. Otherwise he was on the premises.

And the working men of the Woodbine area were good tippers. In a tourist town, even those who had never worked in a tipped job knew plenty of people who did, or had a son or daughter who did. So Patchy made out pretty well behind the bar, besides getting to jabber at everybody and generally act like he was in on important secrets. Patchy liked to visit and a big secret of visiting with folks is not telling all you know. "Take in more than you give out," was Patchy's motto.

In the dining room Desmond, always a bit uncomfortable with his dominant role in the darts tournament, was having his problems.

There would be six divisions of 23 players each. He decided to pick what were in his opinion the 12 best players and seed them, two to a division. But he came up with 15 players that were without question good enough to be seeded, so he had to expand the list of the best to 18, providing three to a division.

Lunch was over by the time he finished picking the 18, and Mildred Tapinger, who cooked on weekends, was leaning on the end of the bar in her apron watching Patchy fill a pitcher with Tinker Mountain Amber Ale, the color

181

of honey and with a head like fresh whipped cream. It was to make beer batter, if anyone asked her, but in truth it would end up in Mildred before she was finished cleaning up and making things shipshape for the night cook.

Desmond showed the list to Mildred, looking for a second opinion. She wasn't a bad darts player, knew the local players pretty well, and was nothing if not blunt.

"What's old Holcomb Pettibone doin' on this list?" she asked in a loud voice, fully aware that Holcomb was 15 feet away practicing at Board #1. "He couldn't get a dart into his own foot if he squatted and used a hammer!"

"Circumstances alienated the inevitable consequences," Desmond declared firmly, thinking that making out that list would probably do as much harm to his bar business over the next two months as the tournament would help his bar business over the next 10 days.

There were 15 players who deserved to be on the list, another three who weren't far behind, and another six or seven who deserved to be on it as much as the last three did. The last three were the problem, not the top 15.

Patchy had the list in his hand now, looking at it. "This thing in alphabet order?" he asked, frowning at his own name towards the bottom.

"Peevish symbolism is ebulliently illustrated," Desmond replied, taking the list back and beginning to fill out his charts. He set Patchy to writing names on pieces of paper. When they were all done, they would throw them into a soup kettle and fill in the tournament divisions. There would be some grumbling from the usual quarters, but he didn't care who won and everybody knew that and respected his integrity, so it wouldn't take too long to blow over.

Still, setting up the tournament was a heavy responsibility, especially since he was also the ultimate court of appeal for problems which arose during the competition. If they couldn't be thrashed out informally, they landed in his ample lap.

"Admonish me a Donovan's Downtown Stout," he said, to Patchy's amazement. Desmond only took a drink three or four times a year. And every now and then–maybe three years, maybe four years apart–he really got into the Donovan's. If this was one of those times, Patchy knew he'd be behind the bar at least until four the next morning, and a busy bar it would be. When word got out that Desmond was taking on the Donovan's, the local folks would be coming from miles around. The last time he'd done so was when he turned 50 and he'd finished off two cases and was two bottles into the third, one beer per year, when he finally stood up from the bar, issued a thunderous belch, and marched off to his apartment and bed, "stiff as a little tin sol'jer" as Patchy noted at the time.

As he snapped the cap off the Donovan's, Patchy was trying to remember just when that last toot had occurred. Was it two years ago or three? One thing, he remembered it'd been in the fall of the year because Agnes O'Toole from South Pineheart had showed up with a bushel of Northern Spys for pies and she had sat right down next to Desmond and started matching him Donovan for Donovan. Time she fell by the wayside she had the women's record, with 22 bottles, but Charley Chiverton had to drive her home laid out flat in the back of her own pickup. Probably was October, because Agnes had been telling people for 20 years that a Northern Spy was best left on the tree until after a good solid frost.

Patchy put a napkin in front of Desmond and placed the bottle carefully on the napkin; no glass, Desmond drank right out of the bottle.

"Plentitudinous preparation confounds the fickleness of surging demand," Desmond declared, taking a long pull on the bottle.

Oh-oh, Patchy thought to himself as he went to check on the Donovan's supply. Good thing the beer truck came yesterday with that big pre-tournament order.

———

Jake spent the morning meandering around aimlessly, never getting more than a couple of miles from where he had been attacked by the tents and the automobile and all the other stuff he had destroyed. He grazed some and browsed some and he spent some time standing in Daring Brook up to his shoulders, letting the cold water soothe his aching brisket where he had banged into the car.

He had come to the brook thirsty and when he stepped into it to get a drink it dropped off quickly and he found himself doing the medically proper thing: chilling the injury to reduce swelling and pain. It goes without saying that this serendipitous outcome was occasioned by luck rather than any brainwork on Jake's part.

At about three in the afternoon he found himself in the trees just west of the Brookings horse pasture, looking across the sweep of tender new green grass to the barn where a great feast was now in progress ("First decent looking piece of beef I've seen since we crossed the Charles River," old P.J. was saying at the time.), wondering at the noise from the band and the wedding guests, who had been working the bartenders hard since right after the ceremony.

It struck him that he had gotten some grain from that wooden feeder in the middle of the pasture earlier in the week, and he was about to move toward it when he heard the distant bellow of a cow, at least it sounded to him like a cow.

Jake went motionless, still as a stopped clock, and listened, cocking his head a bit, straining to pick up some sound besides the breeze. After a bit, it sounded again, and he turned south towards the sound and set off, stopping now and again to listen.

———————

Bingo and Stumpy maintained their position in the barn until after the wedding ceremony was over, browbeating another round of Donovan's out of the grumbling Roscoe. "I'm gonna' tell old Taddy what a helluva job yer doin,' Roscoe m'boy," Bingo assured him. "Don't worry 'bout nuthin'."

They observed the proceedings across the road with interest, commenting when appropriate.

"That Kimmy's a pretty girl."

"Old Taddy didn't look so bad this mornin' as I 'spected."

"Y'know, the missus ain't such a bad lookin' woman neither."

"Listen to that old windbag Hoskins."

When the knot was tied, the Reverend Hoskins' operatic delivery a footnote to the history of two families, and the champagne corks were starting to pop, Bingo and Stumpy enjoyed one last Donovan's each before slipping out of the barn to mount Bingo's truck and ease unobtrusively down the hill.

Bingo, ever slyly alert and pleased to keep Roscoe as confused as possible, noted that the Callanans, led by old P.J. were on the lawn moving toward the bar in the barn. As Bingo headed for the back door he confided to Roscoe: "I told them Boston folks you's the best there is when it comes to keepin' bar, and an orphan besides, Roscoe; now don't be shamin' me."

Roscoe was just as glad to see them go; he always felt 15 years old when dealing with them, especially Bingo. The fact that old P.J. chose his bar as the "Callanan bar" would send him home that evening with his pockets bulging with Boston money, convinced, as Bingo hoped he would be, that it was all Bingo's doing.

The two drove slowly down the hill, parked Bingo's truck in the yard and switched to Stumpy's truck, which was full of unsalvageable junk. They drove to Homer Jefferson's junkyard in East Barnhill, dickered with Homer, who figured that everything was salvageable one way or another, long enough to drive away with $30 in beer money, and headed right for the Milk House to spend it. Have to find out the darts schedule, too, they told one another gravely. Thirst had nothing to do with it.

Their travels touched paved main roads and thaw-ravaged gravel roads and everything in between and the truck never got above 35 miles per hour. Slouched in their seats, they kept their eyes peeled for Jake, noted how such and such a farmer's hayfield looked, and where the culvert was about to wash out, and ventured opinions on such subjects as how the apple crop would be this fall on the basis of the looks of the trees right then in the first week of June.

And when the cars piled up behind the truck on the roads where passing was impossible, they ignored them. Let 'em be impatient, let 'em tailgate, let 'em honk, let 'em hang out over the white line wantin' to pass, let 'em go straight to hell in a hand basket.

Jake, moving purposefully toward the siren bawl, was crashing his way south along the flank of Mt. Harriet, angling down somewhat toward the South Road and the hamlet of South Woodbine. It was mostly wooded, with patches of overgrown pasture, abandoned fertile fields now gone to blackberries and fast-growing junk trees.

Loping off the ridge onto the valley floor, he came up against a split-rail fence just as he heard another bawl, surprisingly loud and near. He bulked right through the fence, hardly noticing it and put his own croaking bellow on the breeze.

And who should come stomping out of the small shed in the corner of the field but Hernando, a rather tattered looking burro whose recent rescue from certain starvation and ignominy in some Republican state or other out west of the Missouri River by Mrs. Magda Billington Smithers was the talk of the Country Club. Billi, as she was known, had responded from the heart and the pocketbook to an advertisement showing sorry-looking animals starving to death on the desert sands of the western U.S. And soon a crate arrived with Hernando in it.

Although she enjoyed the celebrity and was exploiting it to the hilt in an effort to achieve unofficial recognition as a truly concerned animal lover while avoiding the usual initiation fee of several years drudgery as a foot soldier of the Woodbine Canine-Equine-Feline Fellowship, Billi, in truth, was pretty much fed up with Hernando.

The burro had arrived named "No. 168." Billi had already decided to call him Hernando, after a croupier in the casino of her hotel, who had added a great deal to her vacation in Puerto Rico.

The day he arrived, when he was out of the crate and into the field, she had no sooner offered him a carrot when he bit her and took the carrot too. Next day he ran her right out of the shed, according to old Stanford Lamphere, and nipped her again "right in the backside" Stanford said. Stanford had been called in by Billi to teach her how to care for her little burro, she being under the impression that he knew something about animal husbandry because he looked like an old farmer and swamped out the stalls at the South Woodbine Stables. In fact he was a retired bus driver from Cleveland who had moved to the area to be near his daughter and her family. He worked at the stables now and then just for something to do. Well he figured he'd go over and have a look anyway, kind of flattered by the invitation, and after just a few minutes hanging on the fence watching Hernando he came up with the right conclusion despite his lifetime lack of animal-raising experience. Truth be known, Hernando was a nasty little critter, and any damn fool could figure it out by just looking.

He was about the size of a Saint Bernard dog, maybe a little taller. His coat was shaggy, uneven in texture and color, being about four different shades of gray. He'd never really been in danger of starving, as many of his fellow burros were. But it was true enough that out west he had been considered something of a useless mouth to feed, a low-priority boarder, and had been pretty much left to make his own rough and tumble arrangements with the other denizens of the barnyard.

The result was this cute looking, charming little disheveled creature that wasn't afraid of anything and didn't trust anything or anybody and would just as soon bite you or kick you as have you scratch his nose.

This is the creature who walked boldly up to Jake, bawling, well braying really, and threatening. Jake stood there and watched him come, confused that it wasn't a cow, as he had expected, but certainly not afraid of anything. The two met, snuffled their snoots together, and, in one of those inexplicable connections that are usually reported only in the check-out counter press, each decided the other was all right. Twenty minutes later the two of them were well up on the flank of Mt. Harriet grazing along a seasonal brook now alive with the rains of spring.

The calming effect of a companion animal is a well-known phenomenon; many a high-strung race horse settles down only in the company of a companion goat or some such. But there are very few examples of another animal having that effect on a mature bull. Another first for Jake.

By the time Stumpy, with Bingo slouched in the passenger seat, eased his truck into the parking lot at the Milk House, it was mid-afternoon and getting on towards the time when business would begin to pick up along the dark, polished mahogany bar.

Pushing in the door, their eyes went past the four customers to Desmond, perched on a bar stool looking like an elephant sitting on a bicycle seat, a Donovan's open in front of him. "Predominate some Donovan's in the hap-

penstance of them two," he instructed Patchy, who understood that the boss was buying a beer for the newcomers.

"You're buying them one; how come you didn't buy us
all one?" It was the unmistakable nasal bray of Wendell
Coates trying to sound as if he were joking, and it moved
him immediately from Category D (jury's still out) to Category F (definitely a loser) in Desmond's mental rolodex of
his customers. It was a good deal easier to lose ground in
Desmond's rankings than it was to gain, and Coates had
been a bit shaky even in D, which explains the skip right
over Category E (good qualities about equal drawbacks).

Desmond, with his great height and girth and coal-
black beard and piercing eyes, had a habit of just ignoring
effronteries such as Coates,' although Bingo piped up
quickly:

"'Cause the sun don't shine on the same dog's ass
ever' day," he snapped, "and today ain't yer day." That
about covered it for everybody, and even Coates shut up.

Patchy had a yellow pad where he was keeping track of
Desmond's bottle count, plus, as a double check, he had a
beer carton just for Desmond's empties. Can't be too careful when you're dealing with a record that may stand for
years to come.

Stumpy wandered over to study the charts showing the
matchings for the darts tournament, and Bingo, after paying Patchy for last night's bill, followed.

Each of the six divisions consisted of three seeded
players and 20 others. Starting at noon tomorrow Divisions I, II, and III would play down to six survivors, one
loss and out. A week from tomorrow Divisions IV, V, and
VI would do the same. The following evening, a Monday,
the survivors in Divisions I, II, and III would play, double

elimination, until each Division had a winner, and the next day Divisions IV, V, VI would do the same.

The following night, on a Wednesday, the six Division winners would play, double elimination, for the Championship and summer-long bragging rights.

The total purse was $1,800. Division winners received $100, the Champion got an additional $800 and the runner-up an additional $400. Heavy money, indeed. Worth doing a little practicing for.

Bingo was in Division V, another week before the action started, and Stumpy was in Division II, playing tomorrow. Old Taddy was in Division III, as was Wendell Coates.

As the afternoon wore on, the cluster of darts hopefuls around the charts grew and shrunk and grew and shrunk again, like crows on road kill. The pairings were essentially fair, no division markedly easier than another, although there was a bad break here and there, such as Roscoe Lintelmark, a pretty fair thrower but easily rattled, having to open against Verity Hooseman, who was no better a thrower but never shut her mouth and was not above wearing something low-cut in the front to bring her enormous breasts into the equation. Poor Roscoe might as well concede right now, Stumpy snorted.

"Rehabilitate the guitar's efflorescent ariosity *a la* Waylon," ordered Desmond, showing off his French. Patchy took some quarters from the till and gave them to Agatha Hanneford, who had just come in from the kitchen. Agatha was forty-something, by general consensus "a pretty good looker," and a long-time waitress in the Dining Room. In her 20s she had been married to a handsome fellow from New Hampshire, but she divorced him after a couple of years, sick of paying his bar bills. Then her father died and she moved back home to take care of her mother, who didn't get around too well, and there she stayed, even after her mother died. A hard worker, Agatha, and reliable, she now had 11 years in as a waitress at the Milk House.

She was also Desmond's girl friend. Both of them pretended that nobody knew about it. In other words, although she sometimes went to bed at the Milk House, she always slept at home. But of course when a place closes before midnight and the lights go out, and the head waitress's truck doesn't pull out of the parking lot until just before dawn, well, in a small community that's the sort of thing that people notice.

A nice girl, Agatha; most everybody liked her, although every now and then one of the ladies at the Senior Center, where she helped out one day a week, would let it be known in some oblique way or other that Agatha would do well to take the bull by the horns and drag him to the altar, him being a successful businessman and having considerable assets and all.

Actually, both she and Desmond liked the situation as it was. She was happy to get out of there every day to go home to her own things and the peace and quiet of the house she grew up in. Desmond left the building only for his trip to the bank and library. He read a great deal and liked his solitary routine. They got all the sex they wanted, which was plenty, and the shared confidences, while keeping their public lives intact, unmerged. It worked out pretty good, especially since he gave her a few shares of stock in the corporation every Christmas, along with the lingerie that came in a plain brown wrapper. What it came down to was: She ran the dining room and he ran the bar and they both stuck their noses in the kitchen.

Anyway, Patchy gave her the quarters. "Boss wants some music," he mumbled. He was silently in love with Agatha and took to mumbling and stuttering when she was around. He never had said anything about it to anyone, and was under the impression that nobody knew, although of course everybody did. It kind of annoyed Agatha, but sometimes it came in handy too.

Agatha, who had just walked in the door, looked down the bar at the object of her affections, perched with one massive elbow on the bar, in serious and no doubt mystifying conversation with Stumpy Parker. There was a Donovan's in front of him with a napkin wrapped neatly around it and sticking to its wetness. She thought that this was the first tear he'd been on in quite a while and, like Patchy, tried to remember how long ago the last one had been as she moved to the juke box and picked out the country songs he liked best.

You really couldn't say that this first Saturday in June ended in a blaze of glory; it would be more accurate to say it kind of sputtered out, like an old lamp running out of lamp oil.

Desmond, being out of training, managed only 43 bottles of Donovan's Downtown Stout before retiring from the field. Bingo and Stumpy, the former on his best behavior and the latter helping out, dined on roast chicken in the dining room at the Milk House with their wives, all parties careful not to in any way derail the healing process that had set in that morning as the feed can tops clanged together.

The Brookings, charming guests at an informal and spontaneous gathering at the Woodbine Inn, had undergone a healing process of their own this day, the magic elixir being the seamless success of the wedding in the face of seemingly overwhelming odds.

Both the Reillys, at the foot of the hill, and the Brookings, well up on the shoulder of the ridge, slept the blissful sleep of the happy and exhausted, especially the menfolks, who were truly running on empty by the time their heads hit their respective pillows.

Starlight Spotsworth was released on her own recognizance pending a court appearance scheduled for Monday. She was charged with resisting arrest, assault on a police officer, assault with a deadly weapon, disturbing the peace, and inciting to riot. In the hullabaloo at the Village Green she had got to using the picket sign the way Sir Lancelot used his lance, jabbing at the enemy with the butt end. It was one of those lucky discoveries, the molecular biologist looking for the secret of life discovers a cure for dandruff sort of thing. She had dropped the sign in the melee and, scooping it up in haste, had the message end in her hands when Manfred Livingstone lurched in her direction trying to escape her coreligionists. A determined straight-away jab into the gut by Starlight and he went down like he'd been sledge hammered. Her downfall came when she used the same tactic on the next person she saw, who turned out to be an off-duty State cop named Joseph Tunkerman. Officer Tunkerman did not take kindly to the incident and pressed hard for the incarceration of Ms. Spotsworth in the lockup in White River Junction over the weekend. Starlight was delighted at the prospect, having developed plans months before for organizing an inmate hunger strike. One of her young supporters had been briefly held there after some demonstration or other and had pronounced the food "icky," although her only specific complaint was the unavailability of banana bread. The judge, noting with some suspicion Starlight's eagerness to go to the pokey, wisely turned her loose with a warning to show up promptly at Monday's hearing.

Patchy Flaxon had his best night ever behind the bar of the Milk House, pocketing $173.68 in tips at the end of the night. "Busier 'n' a one-legged man in an ass-kickin' contest," was the way he described it. The exceptionally strong Saturday night business was due to a number of factors: The full moon, both the spectacle and the historical potential of the Desmond Kiley bender, the last minute honing of darts proficiency by contenders in the up-coming tournament, and the dregs of the Brookings wedding, referring to some of those who had worked at the affair and got their beaks into the leftover booze while cleaning up.

Jake and Hernando spent the late afternoon and evening moving north along Mt. Harriet towards Woodbine. They didn't see anybody and nobody saw them. By the time darkness came they had passed above the Brookings and Hickham houses and were nearly to the outskirts of the village. Even with the full moon it was dark in the woods so they slowed and stopped in the shelter of some cedars and slept at last.

SUNDAY

B ingo was up and out and through with the morning
chores by 5:30 this bright Sunday morning, stepping
back into the kitchen just as Milly started cracking eggs on
the side of the spider. He still wasn't used to a Jakeless
barn; it was an amazement to him what a difference an
empty pen made, even when you were in a part of the barn
where you couldn't see it.

But, talking to Milly over a three-egg omelet, he had to
admit he was fresh out of ideas on how to get Jake back in
the barn for good. It seemed that no matter what they
tried, Jake managed to avoid even being seen. Matter of
fact, the only times he was seen he was breaking something, or causing fright and uncertainty to crest in somebody or other, or tearing up somebody's lawn, or something along those lines. Damn discouraging, it was, and his
friends were getting tired of the whole thing too. Of helping look for Jake, that is. They weren't at all tired of needling Bingo about the situation. But with Telford getting
hurt bad like he did, the first enthusiasm of the chase had
sure enough worn off.

"Well, you and Stumpy allus like to hunt alone anyway," Milly observed. "Might could do better just the two
of you."

Well, by golly, never thought of that.

"By jeez, mebbe you got something," Bingo exclaimed.
"Been dashing to and fro all week like that General Custer
whilst I shoulda been acting like a Indian scout."

Two minutes later he had Stumpy on the phone.

"STUMPY! MILLY SAYS WE SHOULD GO AFTER
'IM LIKE WE GO AFTER A DEER! WHADDAYA
THINK?"

He listened for a few seconds, frowning.

"WAL, KEEP THAT SQUIRT GUN HANDY 'N'
WE'LL GIT AFTER 'IM SOON'S WE GIT A LINE ON
WHERE THE HELL HE IS." He had another thought.
"BE SURE TO KEEP YER TWO-WAY ON YA, SO'S WE
CAN GIT A TRUCK IN, WE NEED IT!"

The receiver clattered back on the phone. This is more
like it. Jake weighed about seven times the weight of the
biggest deer Bingo ever shot; that 250-pound eight pointer
up in the northeast kingdom near Newport back in '78 or
'79. On top of that he's clumsy and heavy-footed compared
to a whitetail deer, and only got about one tenth the brains
and maybe one third the speed, not to mention that his
natural habitat is a barn, not the woods.

Bingo began to whistle *Brennan On The Moor* as he dug
gear out of the top of the closet in the pantry. Optimism
had returned. This's more like it, he thought, we'll git 'im
now.

Whether it was his cheerful whistle or her own pent
up resentment or something else entirely, something
pushed Milly to action right then and there. Bingo figured
afterward it must have been *Brennan On The Moor*.

Whatever prompted her, she bopped him right on top of the head with a bundle of laundry she was carrying to the cellar door to pitch down the stairs. Laundry was washed and dried on Monday, but whenever a pile accumulated in the corner of the bedroom, it would get pitched down the cellar stairs to wait for Monday.

"What the hell was that all about?" Bingo wanted to know.

"What the hell's all this 'bout you whisperin' all close to Bernadine Sisler back in the pet food aisle of the feed store?" Milly shot back.

"Who told ya' that crap?"

"Lucretia Benjamin tole me and she don't lie!" Milly was standing right there within arms length with that scrapping look on her face. "That's who!"

"Aw, that old bag couldn't ..."

"Bingo Reilly, now you listen to me! There'll be no more o' this! Ever! I ever catch you again it'll be a carvin' knife and it'll be the last time! YOU HEAR ME?"

Oh, oh. This was different than ever before.

"I hear ya, all right, what's the knife ..."

He was talking to her back as it disappeared into the kitchen. "Just think about it," she said quietly, "and believe it!"

Bingo had his mouth open to say something more when the outside door slammed. He thought about the carving knife. It made a kind of an uneasy feeling, when you added it all up. If he could just get Jake back in the barn, then maybe he could spend some time paying attention to Milly, calm her down or something. He kept thinking about that knife.

Jake slept well into daylight; weariness was setting in as he adjusted to the itinerant life of the vagabond bull. What finally woke him was the crunch, crunch of Hernando's chomping on some shrubs at the edge of a small clearing at the highest point of Mt. Harriet. The clearing, which commanded a marvelous view of the countryside to the north of the village, was actually a Woodbine Town Park and, in addition to several wooden signs admonishing against littering, boasted a trash can and three picnic tables for community dining.

When they reached the other side of the clearing they moved onto the wide path down toward the village, with Hernando leading the way.

———————

Thad and Laura slept the sleep of those for whom a long-anticipated and nerve-wracking milestone has come and gone successfully. A deep and untroubled sleep; a dreamless, healing sleep; a sleep that seemed to end almost as soon as it began.

He awoke at 8:30 as the sun, by now up over the barn roof, crept up from the floor to reach the pillow and his face. Rolling over, he slid his hand companionably beneath Laura's hip and drifted into a pleasant drowsy state between sleep and full consciousness. His touch edged Laura out of her deep slumber to near consciousness, a gathering of awareness of time and place and company. Lying there side by side, not speaking yet, they came independently to the conclusion that life was good.

A noise drifted in the window on the June breeze. Clunk, boonk, thump, thump, clang. Somebody was out in the barn seeing to the horses. Thad padded to the window to investigate, seeing Collier's Triumph parked next to the Saab.

"It's your son, God bless him, feeding the horses this morning," he said to his wife, thinking that she was still as pretty as the day they were married. Well, maybe put on a pound or two, but nearly the same. Just about then, the coffee smell from the kitchen registered on them both. They were both in the kitchen five minutes later, bath-robed and teeth freshly brushed, seeing to breakfast for the three remaining bridesmaids, helping pack their cars, giving instructions on how to get to the Interstate.

Finally the girls were off in a swirl of goodbyes and laughter and expensive perfume.

Collier was to leave tomorrow and would stay over-night at the house, now that the bridesmaids were off.

Calm had returned, and the three of them sat at the table in the kitchen.

"Thank's for taking care of the horses," said Thad.

"A pleasure," said Collier, "that I seldom experience in Chicago."

"Well, when you get the Master's you can look for a job in a country bank someplace," Laura said. "Any bank would be glad to hire you, I'm sure," she added, typical proud parent.

"Please, Mother!"

"Well they would! Smart, handsome boy like you, what company in their right mind wouldn't hire you?"

"Mother, for God's sake . . ."

"Leave the intelligent, handsome boy alone, Laura; he's easily embarrassed," interrupted Thad. "And what do the two of you know about the ancient and honored game of darts?"

They both stared at Thad blankly, unable to connect the game of darts to their lives in any way. He had their attention.

"I am to participate, perhaps later today according to Mr. Reilly, in the local equivalent of the Super Bowl, namely, the I-don't-know-how-many annual Milk House End of the Season Darts Tourney," he announced, standing at attention and saluting. "At least it appears to be the Super Bowl to a major stratum of the multi-layered community in which we have taken up residence." Dropping the pedantic tone, Thad added seriously: "I had no idea this little community was so complicated.

"For instance," he continued, "most of the people with whom we might be expected to mingle probably consider that the most important event on today's schedule is the Mixed Foursome at the Country Club, although a strong minority would no doubt favor the Polo Match in South Woodbine. But not one of these people is even aware of the Milk House Darts Tournament." He paused. "Nor was I until Friday night."

"That must have been the only thing you were aware of Friday night," Laura said dryly, causing Collier to glance apprehensively at his parents. Grown children don't do well in the presence of parental spats; they're too accustomed to dealing with their parents as a unit, playing one against the other, manipulating, that they can't relate to them as two individuals working things out.

"Well you'd certainly have been impressed with my melodic tenor and its sensitive exploration of the emotional nuances of *Lili Marlene*, if you'd been lucky enough to be present Friday evening," Thad responded. Collier moved from apprehension to bewilderment to a belated recognition that mutual mention of the notorious Friday episode amounted to putting it in its proper perspective as an incident in a 26-year marriage.

"Late-breaking news, such as the exact day, time and opponent will be coming in today, via Mr. Reilly, or perhaps I should say, good old Bingo," Thad said. "I thought of just not showing up, defaulting the match, but that wouldn't be right. So I'll go and take a public licking, I guess." They were silent over their coffee, his wife and son still trying to adjust to Thad in a saloon darts tournament.

"Good Lord, Dad, you'll probably have to drink beer along with it." Collier was aghast at this.

Thad bristled at this snobbishness. "Well now, I tasted some very respectable stout the other evening, rich and full-bodied and the color of coffee. A very good brew, and you know I might not do so bad in the tournament at that. I used to throw some pretty good darts back in Kenya; it's one of those things like riding a bicycle, you know, that you don't ever forget, so maybe I'll be a little rusty but there's no reason to assume that I can't recover the old touch." He frowned at Collier. "Maybe you ought to come along this evening. Might learn something."

"I'd like to," Collier said quickly, surprising himself and his parents. Especially Thad, who privately considered his elder child something of a stiff.

"Me too," said Laura firmly, moving Thad from surprised to astonished. "I'd love to watch you play in a tournament."

"Well I don't know about that, it's kind of, well, you know, there's some rough talk along the bar in a place like that." He was trying to picture Laura perched on a bar stool at the Milk House making small talk.

"Thaddy dear, people go there all the time to eat; the food's said to be quite good. And, you know, I'm not ex-

actly a sheltered little girl." Laura was enjoying Thad's confusion, and suddenly was actually looking forward to going.
Something that wasn't the same old thing. It might be fun.

And so it was decided. Thad Brookings would visit his
dart-throwing skills upon the Milk House crowd, complete
with a cheering section.

———

At the Woodbine Inn old P.J. Callanan hosted a
sumptuous buffet breakfast for his family: Sons, daughters,
sons in law, daughters in law, a maiden aunt or two, various nephews, grandchildren and other shirt-tail relatives.
The only non-family members were of the clergy, the Callanans' parish priest and an Auxiliary Bishop.

By special arrangement with the management, the
affair was held in a private meeting room on the "garden
level" of the Inn, a room whose many windows provided a
lovely view of the putting green and the extensive flower
garden, blooming now with the last of the tulips, which
would be dug up next week and replaced with impatiens
and other summer flowers.

The special arrangements for the affair included old
P.J.'s morning dollops of Bushmills served in coffee cups
and enough food for a troop of the guard.

Breakfast was a loud and raucous affair, Hibernian in
tenor, starting at the ungodly hour of 7 a.m.–old P.J. was
in the habit of rising early and it was, after all, his treat–
and lasting nearly two hours, after which the family group
broke apart, some packing, some touring the village, others
heading for the pool or their cars for the return home.

By nine o'clock, only P.J. and his sons, including P.J.
junior, remained in the room. John Kevin Callanan, the

oldest of the "normal" sons, notified the waiters and bus-
boys that there would be no more entry into the room until the Callanans were out of there, saw to the final replen-
ishment of coffee, and, when the kitchen door was safely
locked and the drapes closed, swept the room for listening
devices and other surveillance paraphernalia.

Then the movers and shakers of Callanan Construction Company (Quality, Reliability and Integrity Assured)
sat down to talk a little business.

On the Woodbine village green, tents were filling up
with pottery, jewelry, lacework, oil paintings, woven arti-
cles, hand-carved musical instruments, hand-made jewelry
boxes, silver candlesticks, pewter napkin rings, macramé
plant hangers, maple cutting boards, weird jellies made in
somebody's kitchen, garlic ketchup made in somebody's
garage, Vermont maple syrup, hand-made tools, hand-
whittled clothespins, wicker baskets, chainsaw sculptures,
dried wild flowers, wooden toys, strong smelling potpourri
bags, herbal teas blended in somebody's barn, color photographs of Vermont scenes, yarns hand-woven from Ver-
mont-raised sheep wool, crude sandals, shawls, commemo-
rative junk such as billed caps with insolent messages, all
manner of second-rate, hand-made irregular merchandise
that was rejected three generations ago by Vermonters who
recognized that machine-made was in nearly all cases better
designed, longer lasting, cheaper and easier to replace if
lost or damaged. The tourists ate it up.

As Craft Fairs go, this one on the Woodbine village
green this first week in June was of the fair to middling, or
slightly less than fair to middling, variety. A bit on the early

side–the heavy waves of tourists wouldn't hit Vermont until the Fourth of July weekend–it was unjuried, indicating that the organizers had less interest in the quality of goods offered than in selling booth space to benefit the St. Bartholomew Clothes Bin and Family Counseling Center, a hotbed of do-goodism and both amateur and aspiring professional "care givers" who saw their mission as ministering to the unfortunate "locals" as missionaries a century ago ministered to the "heathen Chinee."

At the east end of the village green the Woodbine delegation to the Worldwide Organization of Women had set up a food tent, hoping to knock a few dollars into the treasury as well as raising the community consciousness on a variety of issues, all duly represented on the pamphlet rack. Hot dogs, hamburgers, sodas, and a selection of home-made potato salads and macaroni salads were offered, along with coffee, sticky buns, donuts and Danish. The first shift of counter workers included Alexis Lexington, chairperson of the Woodbine Zoning Board and rising star in the legal firmament, alongside Helen Ridsome, Executive Director of the Woodbine Chamber of Commerce, a cliche-spouting ninny.

Across the street on the front lawn of the Woodbine Free Library volunteers were hard at work setting up the early summer book sale, lugging musty books up from the Library cellar, arranging them on tables marked with prices. The offerings ranged from a small and nearly bare two dollar table to seven banquet-size 25-cent tables covered with layers of tattered paperbacks. Clearly, the Library was saving the good stuff for the Autumn Color Book Sale which has become a tradition on the green in mid-October. Foliage time was when the money rolled in.

Diagonally across the village green from the Library, the long-awaited annual pet show of the Woodbine Parent-Educator Confederation was also getting underway. There had already been one dog fight, with an extraordinarily truculent miniature wire haired terrier going after an astonished St. Bernard, and two other entries had encountered an untimely end due to a leak which developed in their tank. By the time the ebb tide was noticed, the two tetra were flopping on the bottom and although emergency life-saving measures were attempted, they failed when it developed that tropical fish do not do well in ice cold Pepsi Cola. Mrs. Phillipa Genevive Huntington-Pilderson, who organized and administered the event, was trying to decide which cute little child with a cute little pet would be maneuvered into posing with her for the photographer from *The Word of Woodbine*. A three-column photo of Phillipa, looking tolerantly amused, along with a child and an unusual pet was a cinch to make the front page year after year. Nearly all the entrants had arrived, although there was still much confusion and milling about, and she had pretty much decided on the little blond-haired girl from South Brooktown with the pet crow. She mulled over different ways to get the little thing to comb her hair without being insulted at the suggestion. This was an important picture to Phillipa and she wanted everything to go just right.

Down at the Central Vermont Equestrian and Driving Association headquarters in South Woodbine, the members of the Woodbine Polo Club were assembling, seeing to their horses, checking their gear, and in general getting ready for a match set for 1 p.m. with the Podenford Polo Club from someplace in western Connecticut.

At precisely 8 a.m. Horace Bogart, the Head Golf Professional at the Woodbine Country Club, stood midst the wooden rockers on the Clubhouse verandah that overlooked the 18th green and vigorously applied himself to the bellrope of the original Paul Revere brass bell in the belfry above. The sound of golf balls ricocheting off trees, splashing into brooks and ponds, and occasionally thudding onto fairways was immediately heard about the course as the bell signaled the start of the annual Kickoff Mixed Foursome Tournament. This would have been called a shotgun start at any other golf club in America but was known as simultaneous tee off at the Woodbine Country Club, owing to significant gun control sentiment among the membership. Up until two years ago a shotgun was actually used to signal the start, but a well-planned initiative at the Club's annual meeting put a stop to that. The annual meeting, held on the third Sunday in January each year, was ordinarily a routine and sparsely attended affair. Here's the budget, wham, bang, the ayes have it, and adjourn to the bar. But that year the anti-gun members, mostly summer people, made it a point to attend, flying in from Cancun and Palm Beach and Sun City, carefully scheduling the Caribbean cruises so as not to conflict, and, after a tumultuous three-hour debate, carried the day. Both as a celebration and to heal the breach with the rest of the membership, the gun control faction themselves ponied up the money to strengthen and restore the belfry on the renovated carriage house that served as the Clubhouse. They also arranged to acquire the bell and pay for its installation.

At about the time the Paul Revere bell was doing its stuff in the Clubhouse belfry, First Constable Euclid Armstrong hollered "PLAY BALL" at Duxton Field, and the

opening game of the Woodbine Softball League was underway, with Woodbine Auto Parts taking on the Gas 'n'
Goodies Mobil Stop. Constable Armstrong was the least
favorite umpire of the players in the league, since he had a
tendency to misplace the limits of his authority, confusing
the spheres of rule-enforcement and law-enforcement. He
led the league in player ejections every year and one time
even had handcuffs on Bobby Simmons during a debate
over a called third strike.

Play was held up for a minute or two this morning in
the bottom of the first when Tranquillity Emerson led the
Walk Out For Fitness Society (WOFFS) off on their first
organized hike of the summer, right smack across Duxton
Field into the woods at the foot of Mt. Harriet. Her course
entered the outfield along the third base line, crossed into
the infield between second and third, passed just behind
the pitching mound and exited across the first base line
near home plate. There were nine WOFFS in attendance
this morning and they marched briskly along ignoring
Umpire/Constable Armstrong, who stood behind home
plate roaring "HALT!" Just before crossing the first base
line the defiant and daring little band stopped while Tranquillity delivered a consciousness-raising speech about how
Duxton Field is a public park that belongs to the people
and that means all the people not just stupid softball players and we are the people and we have every right to walk
on the people's property which is this grass that we are now
standing on. Then she took a deep breath and went on to
Part II, an analysis of the question of the right of softball
players to take up so much room all for themselves and
crowd out the public which has every right to enjoy the
Field and was never consulted as to the softball arrangement and we need more community involvement so that

our rights are not trampled by the fascists of the sports world who hate women anyway. Then they marched into the woods and onto the trail up the flank of Mt. Harriet, leaving Umpire/Constable Armstrong sputtering through his mask. None of the players or spectators made much of an objection to the intrusion; there was no tension in the game at the time, Junior Henderson from Bridgewater was mowing 'em down for the Auto Parts aggregation so no spell was broken or anything like that. Besides which, the WOFFS were what you might call militant walkers. They really worked at walking. They had their WOFFS tee-shirts on and Spandex shorts and they had three-pound dumb-bells in each hand and they swung those arms with vigor. And no dawdling along smelling the roses, either. No sir! Left, right, left, right, left, right, just like in the Marines. So the ball players and spectators just stood and watched them march through bim, bam, boom, and, what with the swishing Spandex rumps and the perfect posture, found themselves enjoying the sight. The men, that is; the women spectators were mostly frowning.

Tranquillity was anything but. Many things in American society are incorrect, in her view, and it is the duty of the responsible citizen to correct them. She took what might be called a spectrum view; so many causes, so little time. In order to effect corrections everywhere in society where they are needed, she had formed a group called the Activists Axis, which acted as a clearing-house for groups pushing for this or that change. Where Starlight Spotsworth loved life in the trenches, battling cops and howling at anyone in authority, Tranquillity enjoyed the staff work, drumming up extra pickets, keeping a list of right-thinking lawyers, publishing her monthly newsletter. No savvy agitator would plan a demonstration anywhere in the state without first checking with Tranquillity to see if there were any scheduling conflicts, line up a list of potential legal assistance, and generally sniff the wind.

Her one personal focus was the WOFFS, getting and staying fit through aggressive, authoritative walking. She had created the organization to spread the gospel of walking, and was in the process of setting up other chapters throughout the state. The WOFFS did no harm, and probably did some good; after all, it's better to be fit than not to be fit, and walking is supposed to be the best exercise of all. Their confrontations were brief, they threw no paint, formed no picket lines, broke no plate glass windows. That was the way she wanted it because her father had been very specific when she moved to Vermont: "Get arrested and the checks stop!"

Truth be known, Tranquillity didn't recognize Constable Armstrong in his umpire's mask this morning. If she had, she probably would have led her troupe the long way around, not interrupting the game. The newsletter was starting to make money, but not enough quite yet.

The Central Connecticut Antique Automobile Society was up and out early for the traditional June "early spin" around the Woodbine area, indulging themselves in great revving of antique engines and tooting of antique horns, many of the "ougha, ougha" variety. Manfred Livingstone, belly adorned with an ugly purple bruise, had nonetheless been able to make it to the cocktail party, banquet and annual meeting of the group on Saturday night and was rewarded for his heroic actions in the melee on the village green by election to the coveted post of First Driver, who gets to lead the way in all parades the group participates in for the year. He was considered to have suffered in a noble cause, defending with courage and resolution his precious

Aston Martin. Nobody mentioned that the person who laid him low was a 26-year-old woman weighing 118 pounds.

And individuals went about their business as well, puttering in cellars, scraping about in gardens, washing cars, making bread, trimming hedges, tinkering with lawnmowers, painting the kitchen, washing windows, packing the winter woolens away, fixing the roof, planting rosebushes, hosing down the lawn chairs, changing the oil, jogging, sweeping the porch, making a pile for the yard sale, sleeping in, playing tennis, thinking about the next drink, fixing leaky faucets, putting up shelves in the garage, getting the store open, heading for the supermarket, heading for the dump, taking a tennis lesson, cleaning rifles, dropping a dry fly just next to that rock 30 feet across the stream, taking piano lessons, doing all the things that free people do.

Just your ordinary, country village, dull and boring, early summer Sunday morning in June.

———

Jacob Mulligan's Meticulous Rumpus III followed his little buddy Hernando across the line into the village of Woodbine shortly before nine a.m., although neither noticed the change of venue. They were in Rutherford Hutchinson's back yard which extended across the village line and part way up the side of Mt. Harriet. A retired mail carrier and deaf as a post, Rutherford was off on his daily seven-mile constitutional or he would surely have spotted the two interlopers. Although his ears were out of business, he had eyes like a hawk, and, when not striding around town at four miles an hour, Rutherford could usually be found puttering in his backyard garden.

So Jake and Hernando just browsed their way into his yard unnoticed. There was traffic on the highway, but at village speed the noise wasn't anything remarkable. It was quiet, in fact. Bees buzzed and hummed about, and occasionally a hummingbird made a singing passage, really peaceful, you'd have to admit. Jake and Hernando relaxed and settled in to work on Rutherford's shrubs and flowering crab apple trees. Tender new growth with the tiny light green color of the first week of June beckoned. They became absorbed in their breakfast, so different from the growth on the wooded flanks of Mt. Harriet, so much more tender and juicy.

———

Melody Winchester, cook and housekeeper for the Jonathan Carruthers Rockingham household in West Woodbine about two miles out of the village, put the last of the breakfast dishes in the dishwasher and contemplated the problem of waste disposal for the ecologically self-aware. The Rockinghams, along with their friends and acquaintances, regarded the United States as a rogue criminal among the nations of the world for what they saw as its negligence in dealing with the crisis of waste disposal. With the exception of old Jonathan himself, who was a principal in a brokerage firm and saw enough of the real world to know better, the family believed that unless drastic steps were taken soon the entire nation would be covered in eight feet of fetid garbage and life as they knew it would cease.

So one of Melody's daily tasks, and one that she found most irksome, was to sort the vast quantity of garbage produced by this idle and virtually useless group of people.

There was garbage garbage, such as coffee grounds, naked T-bones, apple cores, table scraps, and the like, which would go on the compost heap down behind the equipment shed. There were newspapers. There were glossy magazines such as Time, Newsweek, Esquire, People, and the 15 to 20 other yuppie cribsheets that were delivered to the house each month. Plastic milk containers had their own bag. There were bags for brown glass, green glass, and white glass. Odd plastic and other packaging went into a separate box, folded and flattened or otherwise compacted.

Melody was the administrator of this vast system, which took up one entire bay in the four-car garage, and her bulky body the flattener. Once a week Melody's husband Alan came by with his truck and took everything to the recycling center and the dump.

The family practice was to pitch everything into one large plastic-lined garbage can in the kitchen with the words: "I'll just put this in here Melody, so as not to foul up your system." The family was very proud of their efforts on behalf of the environment and were tireless in urging their friends to adopt similar measures. Rarely did an issue of The Word of Woodbine appear without an acerb letter to the editor from one of the Rockinghams scolding the community for its wasteful ways or scornfully reporting some heinous crime that had come to their attention, a beer can along the highway, perhaps, or a plastic garbage bag set out on Monday when everybody knows that garbage is picked up on Tuesday.

This morning, with the family off at church and the golf course and the tennis courts, Melody availed herself of the opportunity to detour from the road to ecological perfection. She took the pop tart boxes and ice cream containers and soft drink cartons and assorted other such plasticized cardboard contraptions into the great living room fireplace and began burning them. Melody did this at every opportunity, aware that it would go badly for her if she were caught, since the Rockinghams were also quite passionate about not fouling the air. The one exception they allowed in their crusade for ecological purity was the fireplace fire burning comfortingly on a chilly evening. This was a pesky exception indeed, one that inspired a good deal of soul searching in the household, since it involved not only air quality but also the destruction of trees for fuel. The Rockinghams had stilled their consciences by temporarily tabling the matter of fireplace fires some years ago and there it stayed, an insoluble difficulty.

Anyway, here's a week's accumulation of food packaging burning pretty good in the fireplace and Melody popping in every now and again to add more and things are going along as usual. She tossed in several greasy pizza containers from the night before and went back into the kitchen. A couple of minutes later she heard a noise like an approaching freight train. But Melody knew that there were no railroad tracks near Woodbine. She knew she was hearing a major chimney fire and that the jig was up. She reached for the phone, called the Fire Department, then grabbed the table salt and ran in to throw it on the blaze. Too little, too late. Damn those greasy pizza boxes, she thought, God damn those greasy pizza boxes.

She stood back and wished the firemen would hurry.

Dispatcher Margaret Otis toned out the Fire Department at 9:17 a.m., energizing beepers all over town. The softball game was immediately suspended as 11 players ran for their vehicles. Hammers dropped to workshop floors, chores were abandoned, the Woodbine Volunteer Fire Department was on the way.

The golf tournament further down the road was unaffected by the emergency.

Bill Tyler was painting his front porch when the alarm went off. He hurried into the house to quickly change out of his painting clothes, stripping his painting gloves off and dropping them on the way. Moments later, in jeans and with his shirt flapping unbuttoned behind him, he galloped down his driveway, leaped into his truck, started it, and jerked it into motion.

Now there are a number of reasons folks join Volunteer Fire Departments, some of which are noble, but surely the fact that you are allowed to have your very own siren ranks high on the list.

And Bill Tyler loved his siren. It was his practice-regardless of traffic or lack of traffic or time of day–to engage it as he careened down the driveway and leave it on all the way down the road to the Fire House. It made an ear-piercing racket, irritated a few people, but was otherwise harmless.

Well, usually, but this day was different.

You see, Bill Tyler is neighbor to Rutherford Hutchinson and they don't get along so well since that misunderstanding about the property line so there's a eight-foot wooden fence between the two houses. The fence runs right along Bill Tyler's driveway, and when that siren of his kicked in Jake and Hernando were no more than eight feet away on the other side, enjoying some very tasty new growth on a flowering crab apple tree.

Well, you might as well have touched them with a damned electric wire. The two of them went into an instant sprint away from the sound, headed down the fence. They beat Bill's truck to the street end because Mrs. Tyler ran out hollering to him to pick up some hamburger rolls on the way back and that slowed him down some. Anyway, he swung out on the street, trusting the siren to clear the way for his right turn and there's this huge bull right in front of him. Bill instinctively swerved to miss the animal, it had to be instinctive because he was too surprised to do anything on purpose, but the maneuver wasn't a complete success because he glanced off a big old maple tree on the other side of the street and careened across the lawn and crashed into the Vandenbergs' front porch. Did quite a bit of damage to the porch and knocked the daylights out of Bill's truck that was his pride and joy. One good thing, it sure did shut down that siren.

The village of Woodbine isn't but four blocks north and south, two on either side of the highway, and about six blocks east and west along the highway, the square village green in the middle, and then trailing away to gas stations and such at the east end, where the Fire Station is located. So once Jake and Hernando were flushed out of Rutherford's yard toward the green they got there in fairly short order, not long after they got up to speed. And there were things to keep them up to speed, such as Mrs. Hopkins kneeling in her rose garden looked up and saw them and gave a great keening screech, and the Vandenbergs' dog, a skimpy overbred golden retriever with more courage than brains, made a big growly charge at them.

So Jake and Hernando went busting through the Vandenberg's yard, through the Hopkins' rose garden and yard and arrived at the east end of the village green at full throttle and holding. And there sat three 18-wheelers in a row, trying to get around the green and through the village, hardly moving what with one-way traffic around the green and vans parked everywhichway unloading for the crafts fair. Jake saw the wall of trucks and turned left toward the green, which was surrounded by a picturesque old iron fence. The fence had an entrance on each of the four sides, big enough to drive a riding lawn mower through. As luck would have it, the east entrance was right in front of Jake's nose and he barreled right on in. Some stories got going afterwards about how he was charging the feminine aura around the WOW hot dog stand, but that was all invention. He saw the trucks and turned and there was the entrance and he went in. Hernando was different, he went in because he was just following Jake. He was frightened by the noise and screeching and people and vehicles and buildings–the commercial buildings at the west end went three stories high–and Hernando, unaccustomed to being frightened, just wanted to stay close to Jake.

It was one of those things where everyone who wasn't there wished later that they had been. It would have been worth it just to hear the WOW ladies cursing. Cyrus Peckham, who had just dropped off the coffee urns and fired up the gas grill at the WOW food stand, said he was shocked to hear such language out of a collection of lawyers, college graduates and other upper crust ladies who were working the first shift at the stand.

"I thought for a minute I's in the beer tent up to the World's Fair in Tunbridge," he told Desmond that afternoon. "Where d'ya s'pose they learned them words?" he wondered.

"The effluvium of advocacy coagulates mannerisms and dislocates ethical particulars," Desmond explained.

The WOW ladies had set up their food tent right smack in front of the east entrance to the green, figuring they could stare down some business if people had to walk close to their table. Anybody that didn't stop and buy something to eat was obviously an enemy of womankind and worthy of being on the receiving end of some heavy duty glowering.

But their location had the unforeseen disadvantage of giving Jake no chance of avoiding it. He busted right on through it, uncooked hot dogs and hamburger patties going everywhere, tables flipping, feminists diving for safety and screaming like regular ladies, and the tent came down and pretty quick the gas grill caught it on fire.

Jake kept right on going into the maze of half-erected tents, folding tables, boxes of merchandise, display contraptions, booths and paraphernalia that covered the green. Hernando kept pace with him but off to the side, like a water skier who is way out to the side almost up even with the towboat. So he was making his own parallel swath of destruction that would be of lesser value in the later retelling of the event. If a potter saw three months work worth of earthenware destroyed by Jake, he could tell the story in terms of D-Day on Omaha Beach. But a glassblower whose three months work was destroyed by Hernando would somehow sound as if he was in the supply corps and didn't get to France until some time in the first part of 1945. Donkeys never get the credit they deserve.

Anyway there was chaos on the village green, everybody running this way and that. And the noise was terrific.

"Hadn't heard nothin' like that since them three hogs jumped offa Charley Chiverton's pickup truck during the Veterans' Day Parade in 1981," Officer Harkness declared at the annual Peace Officers Picnic and Target Shoot later that summer. People were screaming and diving under tables and hiding behind one another and running for the fence and some of them were so scared they were just frozen, doing nothing at all for themselves. There was the tinkling and shattering of broken glass and the rending of metal and the explosive fracturing of wood and plastic and fiberboard.

When Jake arrived at the Pet Show at the west end of the green you'd have thought that he'd have sensed some affinity with the creatures so proudly displayed, but if he did it wasn't apparent to any of the onlookers. He was forced to veer to his left by two major oak trees, and thus missed crashing through the cages and fishbowls and the maze of tangled leashes and tethers and very young pet owners that seemed to cover the west end of the green. This put him heading toward the fence, and when that hove onto his consciousness he simply continued his left turn until the fence no longer figured in his perception before straightening out his course and concentrating once again on speed. Jake was in a total panic. The more he ran, the more hullabaloo he encountered. This was contrary to his experience during the week, when running had always led eventually to peace and quiet. But he kept running because that had worked before and he certainly didn't have the time to stop and figure out something different right then.

Just as Jake completed his 180 degree turn, rolling his wings straight and level you might say, Engine Number Two of the Woodbine Volunteer Fire Department roared up from the east with five men aboard, heading for the Rockingham estate in West Woodbine where a chimney fire was in progress. Since the Rockinghams considered themselves God's gift, and took no pains to conceal that conviction, all five men on Engine Number Two carried negative opinions of the family and were looking forward to the opportunity of putting 500 gallons of water down their chimney.

Engine Number Two arrived at the village green at an imprudent speed, driving half on the sidewalk to get around the traffic, siren at a piercing screech and crew unaware of the complicating presence of Jake and his little buddy. The irritation level was high in the cab of Engine Number Two at the traffic.

"God damned flatlanders!"

"Might'swell be the Fourth of July!"

"Try the other side, where there ain't no big trucks!"

Martin Harris, who had won the race to the station to take the driver's seat, yanked the wheel to the left, lunged through a hole in the line of traffic and started to go around the green on the left or wrong side, against traffic. The street seemed to be fairly clear, the siren blasting, why not? He put his foot down, and Engine Number Two zoomed forward.

Near the south entrance of the green stood young Bert Grantham with the exquisite Beatrice English. Bert had some experience dealing with Jake, tutored of course by the inimitable Bingo Reilly, and knew that if you do something that involves fairly dramatic movement the bull would probably shy away. So he grabbed a big straw hat off a fleeing potter and waved it around his head like John Wayne starting a cattle drive.

Jake veered right from the threatening motion, through the south entrance onto the street right in front of Engine Number Two. Firefighter Martin Harris, the driver, was focused at the far end of the green where a traffic problem was likely to emerge and so was surprised by Jake's sudden appearance directly in front of him. That split-second lost to astonishment made it out of the question to stop in time and Martin sure didn't want to hit an 1,800 pound bull, so Engine Number Two veered shriekingly to the right, into the green's metal fence, the rending of bright red metal against old black-enameled cast iron fence sounding like fingernails on slate to the firemen, who revered their equipment with a strange combination of trust, respect, awe and admiration that amounted to true love.

Jake, unscathed, bolted across the street into the front parking lot of the Woodbine Inn, which occupied the entire south side of the green. G. Algernon Leicester, top down and white silk scarf in place, at the wheel of his 1936 Auburn 852 supercharged phaeton with right hand drive and oblivious to any untoward happenings in his vicinity due to the revving of engines about him, looked up as he backed out of his parking space to see an enormous bull bearing down on him and Mrs. Leicester, who occupied the left hand seat. It was over before he had a chance to react: Jake vaulted the low slung vehicle, hooves barely missing the Leicester domes, and continued on into the confusion of antique vehicles maneuvering to organize themselves into a nifty parade.

More rending of metal, but considerably less damage, owing to the quality of materials used in automobiles 60 or 70 years back. Still, even a minor dent is a rabbit punch to the owner of an antique car. So Jake, with Hernando at his heels, left grief and consternation behind him in the ranks of the Central Connecticut Antique Automobile Association. Once Jake had passed from the parking lot, veered slightly to the right and headed down the South Road, the members of "Double C, Triple A," as they referred to themselves, could have relaxed and assayed the damage. But they had no knowledge of the ways of animals and so remained in a state of high anxiety, believing themselves under attack and expecting Jake to make another pass any minute. Indeed, Mr. Laughten Treadley boosted his gleaming 1931 Cadillac Roadster out of the parking lot in great haste to find himself smartly tagged and spun about by Engine Number One of the Woodbine Volunteer Fire Department, Captain Raymond Turley commanding. This collision was a bit more serious, involving near total destruction from the windshield forward. Mr. Treadley was livid, not least because Engine Number One, pleading a higher purpose, raced from the scene of the accident to the Rockingham residence without even so much as slowing down or exchanging license numbers or insurance company names or anything. Spotting Engine Number Two across the street half on and half off the green, Mr. Treadley stomped over to bellow his outrage at the five men who were clambering out of the now silent machine. First Assistant Lieutenant Martin Harris was taken back by the fury of this unexpected attack from the flank, as he was already under considerable fire from the family of weavers upon whose booth, loom and entire spring production he had inadvertently guided Engine Number Two.

Under attack from both sides, Lt. Harris and his men were delighted to notice flames shooting up from the collapsed WOW tent, gratefully adopting the fire as their first priority. Ignoring Mr. Treadley and the irate covey of weavers, they grabbed fire extinguishers and began deploying firehose to deal with the conflagration at the east end of the green.

In the parking lot of the Woodbine Inn, Manfred Livingstone, acutely aware of his responsibility as First Driver to conduct a safe and ostentatious parade, gave five quick toots of the horn, led the line of antique automobiles out onto the highway and turned right, toward White River Junction. He had decided that the best thing Double C, Triple A members could do was get away from the mad scene on the green, where strange and dangerous things were happening and there was every indication that violence was imminent. He was to be sharply criticized at the July outing of CCAAA by a faction led by Laughten Treadley and G. Algernon Leicester, who felt the organization had legitimate interests in the events on the green and should have worked as a group to advance those interests with the authorities on the scene. Manfred easily won the day by pointing out that all those who had ventured to advance their interests with the authorities on the green had ended up under arrest and the CCAAA's interests had been best served by avoiding the fracas and hoping to benefit from whatever wreckage remained after things quieted down. This was a particularly telling point, since Mr. Treadley had been incarcerated for several hours that day while awaiting processing under charge of preventing a fireman from the lawful performance of his duties, simple assault, refusing to obey a police officer, obstructing traffic, resisting arrest and using loud and profane language in the presence of minors.

Mr. Treadley's hours of detention were passed in the company of seven WOW members who spent the time quoting various amendments to the U.S. Constitution, not to mention three dozen craftspeople with weird body language and strangely serene attitudes. A particularly galling subplot of his incarceration was the cavalier attitude of both the WOW members and the craftspeople to his personal property; specifically his pocket comb. A perfectly well-spoken, apparently successful, seemingly responsible WOW person had borrowed it to comb her hair. The gallant Mr. Treadley, a man of the old school, was swift to agree to the loan. "Anything to help a little lady in distress," he chirped brightly, reverting to his pre-1960s Princetonian persona.

He was discomfited to note that the comb passed from WOW to WOW without even the courtesy of asking his permission for the sub-borrowing, and was shocked to the cuffs of his $750 Brooks Brothers worsted wool charcoal gray slacks when he finally, with some diffidence, asked the original borrower if she could see to the comb's return and she instructed him to "Screw off, Gramps," in tones of flat finality. As he left the group to face the Judge, he noted that one of the craftspeople had wrapped several layers of toilet paper around his comb and was humming out atonal versions of Bob Dylan favorites. It was just a cheap drugstore pocket comb, but the unconcealed contempt for property rights chilled Mr. Treadley to his very bones.

Jake, beginning to run out of breath despite his extraordinary physical condition, eased up a bit as he left the grounds of the Woodbine Inn headed down the south road. This allowed Hernando to pull alongside and the two settled into a steady gallop, past the gaping gallery on the Inn's side verandah, past Duxton Field and the staring stragglers from the softball game, drumming their hooves on the macadam down the middle of the road towards the golf course.

When the two reached the golf course they left the road for the softer footing of Penncross grass and headed south, swerving among the trees. They were trying to get across the narrow course to the safety of Mt. Harriet's forest but they kept coming upon competitors in the mixed foursome tournament, all of whom were waving long-handled weapons in a menacing manner. Golf carts made crazy maneuvers to avoid the two galloping animals, Ms. Sissy Mellen-Pierce even driving into the brook, although there was some debate later as to whether it was the animals or the three Mimosas with which she enlivened breakfast each day that put her in the water.

Finally, more than a half mile south of where they entered the golf course, Jake and Hernando thundered over a wooden bridge, across the 12th green and into the welcome tangle of brush and woods on the steep flank of Mt. Harriet. Traces of their passage through the golf course would still be visible and subject to special ground rules when the annual Member/Guest Tournament was played six weeks later, in mid-July.

Ernestine Cartwright later reported that Bippy Walker, the golf course maintenance chief, actually broke down and sobbed when he saw the damage, especially to the 12th green. She had stopped at the office to pick up her paycheck and rode out on the golf cart with Bippy to check the damage. "Tears runnin' right down his cheeks, the little wimp," she told Stumpy later. "You'd a thought the god damned sky was fallin'."

Frank Hickham, who had been putting on the 12th green when Jake and Hernando appeared, cautiously raised his head, peering over the lip of the sandtrap into which he had flung himself at the sight of the two animals, wondering for the first time if Mrs. Hickham and the other couple in the foursome had survived. As he rose to his feet, sandy from chin to the toes of his shoes, he was chagrined to see the others standing exactly where they had been standing, and none the worse for the wear. They had waved and shouted and thrown clubs at the two animals, causing them to veer off and into the woods. Mrs. Hickham was not impressed with her husband's reaction to the unexpected danger.

"I guess we'd better make sure not to ever stand between Frank and the lifeboats," she drawled. "Might get trampled." Mr. and Mrs. Harrington Witherspoon said nothing. They just stood expressionless, watching Frank brush sand from his brightly colored clothes.

Jake and Hernando were naturally preoccupied with their own reactions of terror during their intimate brush with the Woodbine community. It never occurred to either of them that they had sown terror of their own during their abbreviated tour of the village.

Well, at least it was terror at the time of the destruction. But before Jake and Hernando had cleared the golf course, the mood was changing to outrage and, as the litigious possibilities began to dawn on people, a toting up of damages both economic and emotional. "There ought to be a law!" folks declared. "Somebody should pay!" others agreed. "Who's responsible for all this?" they asked. "My back hurts!" the more foresighted of them cried.

Stumpy realized that Jake had surfaced in the village before Bingo did, because as First Assistant Chief of the South Woodbine Fire Department he always carried his two-way radio on his belt. So he heard the call go out to the Woodbine Fire Department for a chimney fire in West Woodbine and thought little of it. Fairly routine event. No need to stop what he was doing, which was moving Sophie's tomato plants from the kitchen to the garden.

Well it's just a natural thing that if your radio is saying something, you listen. So while he got the stakes ready and made sure there was plenty of baling twine to tie the plants, he heard Engine Number 2 leave the station with five men, followed shortly by Engine Number 1 with six men aboard. He heard Fire Chief Quenton Musgrave inform the dispatcher that he was proceeding directly to the scene of the fire. Nothing out of the ordinary in all that, except that a fair man had to say that it was sort of a peculiar time for a chimney fire, a beautiful warm Sunday morning in early June.

Then the transmissions turned testy, about the clogged traffic situation at the village green, then turned to a tone you might call "evasively excited and upset," as the various forces in play around the green engaged one another. For example Martin Harris, driving Engine Number 2, reported his crash into the cast iron village green fence with the message: "Ummm, Woodbine Dispatch this is Engine Number 2 and, ah, we've, ah, run into, ummmm, a little complication here."

Well, it wasn't long before even Dispatcher Margaret Otis, sitting in her windowless office back at the Fire Station, knew they'd run into more than a little complication because she could hear the weavers screaming and carrying on in the background, along with the bellowing of Mr. Laughton Treadley of the Double C, Triple A.

By this time Stumpy was standing motionless in the garden, listening hard trying to make sense of the chatter on the radio. Both engines were yakking away, cutting one another out, hollering into the mikes, agitated and excited, and Margaret Otis yelling for information on "what the hell's going on up there to the green."

There seemed to be an accident, or maybe two accidents, and there apparently was some kind of fire at the green, not the one they'd been called out for, and the background noise was terrific, horns blowing and shouting, and Margaret yelling for Officer Harkness to get to the green right away and find out what's going on.

Stumpy wasn't alone in trying to dope out the situation. All the other members of the South Woodbine Fire Department–standing in barns, sitting at kitchen tables, lying under vehicles, standing in the back of the church–were all trying to decipher the chaotic and mysterious messages. Not to mention the other groups that monitored the Dispatch channel. Nearly 20 members of the Ambulance Service listened with furrowed brows. Every employee of the Woodbine Town Highway Department was trying to puzzle it out. First Constable Armstrong had flung off his umpire's mask and hustled to the green planning to help with traffic control. Although he was on the scene, his bellowing radio transmissions were no help in understanding what was going on. The Second Constable was in the dark like everybody else, although he was in his pickup and headed for the green because it was obvious that something big was going on. Throw in a couple of hundred scanners in kitchens around Woodbine and it was easy to see that CNN couldn't have spread the news as fast as it spread this Sunday morning.

The first mention of Jake was almost offhand.

"Traffic's a god damned mess 'n' we took the south side 'n' we tryta miss the sonuvabitchuvabull and touched the god damned fence," gave the first indication that Woodbine's most famous farm animal was at the scene.

It was enough to send Stumpy running for the telephone.

"Big ruckus up to Woodbine Green and Jake's got sumpin' to do with it," he said when Bingo answered. "Be right up," he added.

On his way up the South Road to the Reilly house, Stumpy stopped briefly at the South Woodbine Fire Station to pick up the spare two-way radio for Milly. That way he and Bingo could communicate with her from deep in the woods if they needed any help or equipment.

And by the time he rolled into Bingo's driveway he had gleaned some additional information from the radio chatter, such as that there was apparently a second animal and maybe even a third. "Jake's got himself some recruits," he told Bingo.

About the time Stumpy arrived the phone started ringing off the hook. Bingo picked up the first call, said hello, listened for awhile, then yelled "GO PISS UP A ROPE!" and slammed the receiver down. After that Milly took over answering the phone.

Between phone reports and the chattering on the Dispatch Channel, a picture began to emerge. Jake had definitely passed through the green. And the parking lot of the Woodbine Inn, headed south toward home. And, if Milly correctly interpreted the anguished, outraged, sobpunctuated vehemence of the Country Club Manager, through the golf course as well.

The boys waited around just long enough to get confirmation that Jake had exited the golf course to the east, across the brook and onto Mt. Harriet. That settled, they mounted Stumpy's truck, which had the better tires, and

drove up the hill past the Chester place where the Brookings lived, moving on up the hill past the Hickhams'
charming post and beam beauty, following the road until it
petered out up near the ridge. Stumpy turned the truck
around so it was headed toward home.

Leaving the vehicle they carried quite a load. A pound
or two of grain. A ten-foot length of strong chain. Two dart
guns, loaded and ready. Two pair of binoculars. Couple of
sandwiches Milly had made. The two-way radio, turned
way down so they could just barely hear it. Slickers for laying on the damp ground without catching pneumonia,
hunting knives, an extra wool shirt, and other little odds
and ends that probably wouldn't be needed but only a
damn fool would step into the woods without. No need for
a map, though. Bingo and Stumpy had been tromping this
ridge for over 50 years, with their fathers, by themselves,
and with their own kids–Stumpy's 28-year-old daughter,
now a school teacher up north, got her first deer almost
exactly where the Hickhams had built their house.

The two men entered the damp freshness of the
woods, going easy because there was really no reason to
hurry, the still incomplete leafing of the trees giving an
open feeling that would be gone in two weeks time. They
moved along near the top of the ridge, stopping now and
again to listen for sounds of movement, guessing that Jake
would come south away from the village once he cleared
the golf course. Their plan was to head for the ledges that
scarred the west flank of Mt. Harriet and whose steep and
rocky terrain would force Jake to either stay low along the
brook or work high up on the ridge. They figured he
wouldn't even slow down until he was well up on the ridge
and planned to intercept him above the ledges. Despite
everything, Bingo was surprised to realize that he was en-

joying himself, relishing the feel of the forest floor under his boots, welcoming the smell and feel of June.

Out at the Rockingham estate Fire Chief Quenton Musgrave found himself the only firefighter on hand and he was trying to find out why. "Where's the apparatus?" he kept hollering. "Damnit, where's the apparatus?"

But the radio traffic quickly became less colorful and more cryptic as the full dimensions of the debacle emerged. Fact was, the Fire Department wasn't all that proud to be jabbering on the public airways about two expensive pieces of equipment getting banged up on one fire call. All those folks out in scannerland were quick to jeer at the slightest foul-up and, truth to tell, this foul-up wasn't all that slight. In fact, all three fire engines responded and only two ever reached the scene and only one got there unscathed. That was Engine Number 3, which circled north on back streets and gravel town roads to avoid the village green.

So the Fire Department chatter died off, leaving just the reports coming in from the two Constables and Officer Harkness and a State Policeman named Coleman Henderson who picked up the ruckus on his radio and was on his way from White River Junction to take a peek.

As near as Bingo and Stumpy could make out, moving along the ridge of Mt. Harriet listening to the talk, some folks in the area of the village green were really enraged. Had every right to be, most of them, but as First Constable Armstrong explained later, "There's just so much crap I'm gonna take from these artsy-craftsies."

Justified or not, the vociferous plaints of the smocked and sandaled crowd led to unpleasantness in all directions. The crew of Engine Number 2 made the WOW food tent fire out to be more than it really was, which enabled them to ignore everyone, refusing even to acknowledge friendly hellos, since fire, one of mankind's great fears, was obviously of a higher priority than some busted pots. When the fire was snuffed out all too easily, they declared a gas grill emergency, calling for the Constables to clear the area, yelling authoritatively at everyone and roping off that end of the green. The WOW contingent, resenting the preemptory tone of the proceedings and protesting that decisions were being made without their input, caught the mingled scents of fascism and male chauvinism on the morning breeze and went into immediate and automatic opposition to any instruction at all from any source whatsoever. The Fire Department/WOW hassle quickly became loud enough that Constable Armstrong left off threatening the mass arrest of 47 craftspeople and their dependents to take a hand. Soon he and Alexis Lexington, Esq. were snoot to snoot quoting various Vermont statutes at one another at the top of their lungs.

They heard him before they saw him, since Jake wasn't exactly the most graceful animal in the kingdom. He was quite a ways off when they picked up the first snapping of twigs and scuffing of leaves. After a quick conference they split up and climbed trees, Stumpy over the ridge to the east and Bingo near the crest, both handy to deer trails that provided the easiest going and so would be Jake's most probable routes.

Bingo's first glimpse of his prize bull in nearly a week was sobering. He looked some gaunt, and the ugly deep scrape on his brisket along with the dried blood down his leg and side contributed to the air of alert and suspicious wildness that had overtaken Jake during the week. Might not be so easy to handle at that, Bingo thought.

Meandering along behind Jake was a scruffy, dirty gray burro, looking like he could use a coffee can of grain and a good rubdown with a handful of hay.

"Where'd that damn thing come from," Bingo muttered to himself. He resented useless animals and often declared that he wouldn't provide a roof for a critter that didn't pay its way. "What the hell's the use of a damn BOO-row?" had been his reaction when news reached the Milk House of Mrs. Billington's burro adoption. "All ya' git to do with 'em is feed 'em!" It was a subject that touched a nerve with him, sorta set him off. "Can't ride 'em, they won't haul nothin,' can't eat the meat, don't lay no eggs, can't shear no wool off 'em, hide ain't worth nothin'." He would have gone on and on like that, but Stumpy recognized the problem and changed the subject.

But on this bright and sunny 11 a.m. on the first Sunday in June in the year of our Lord nineteen hundred and ninety three, Bingo didn't waste time stewing about the burro. He concentrated on Jake, not looking directly at him–that might somehow alert him–but keeping him in sight, willing him to get close enough for a shot in the hip from the dart gun.

The two animals were in no hurry. The panic of their horrifying voyage through the heart of Woodbine had subsided, although they were still a bit edgy, stopping to listen now and then, heads cocked and still. But hunger was returning, the powerful urge to continue the breakfast that had begun on the flank of Mt. Harriet and continued into Rutherford Hutchinson's back yard before the siren put an end to it.

They wandered this way and they wandered that way and pretty soon Bingo had a terrific ache in his tractor leg from staying so still for such a long time. Finally, sick of waiting, Stumpy tried a long shot from his tree and the dart smacked perfectly into that broad hip.

Jake exploded into forward motion, banging into a tree and gouging the soft ground with his hooves. He burst along the ridge, fortunately headed south toward home, and disappeared into the brush with Hernando-panicked because his big buddy was panicked-right behind.

Bingo and Stumpy descended from their perches, thankful to be moving, and cautiously followed the animals.

The trick now was not to spook Jake any more than necessary, so that his excitement didn't hinder the effect of the tranquilizer. Left alone, he would slow and stop and get dopey and maybe even lie down and sleep. At some point in the process it should be possible to snap a chain on his nose ring and anchor him to a tree. Then when he woke up he would get a nice dollop of grain and be hand fed a little hay and it then should be possible to walk him along the ridge to the truck.

And that is exactly what happened. When Jake began to come out of his daze an hour later he seemed to be almost relieved to lose his freedom. Being led around had its advantages, not being faced with decisions being the principal advantage. The boys didn't even feel the need to call on the crooning of Hyacinth Spencer to get him to the truck. They didn't pay any attention to the burro lurking back in the trees.

"Let 'im go ta' hell!" said Bingo Reilly.

Jake was back in his pen at two p.m., exactly six days, 13 hours and 16 minutes after leaving it.

———————

The first darts in the 1993 Spring Finale Tournament were scheduled to fly at four p.m. sharp, and business at the Milk House started to pick up in early-afternoon, boosted as well by the morning's astounding events on the Woodbine village green.

Thad, Laura and young Collier pulled into the Milk House parking lot shortly after three p.m., followed by Bingo's old pickup truck. Early enough to get seats at the bar, where the action was near and present.

All three boards were in use, last minute practice and warm up throws thunking smartly into the bristle, as anticipation of the coming matches mingled with an uncertainty over the scene at the green this morning.

When extraordinary events occur there is an automatic reaction which folks can be fairly certain will be shared by their neighbors. Fire is bad, for example, and a car accident is a shame, and a healthy new baby is wonderful, and nobody to argue otherwise.

But the debacle on the green had too many elements. It was a cross-cultural nightmare and you couldn't quite predict where any particular person might stand on any part of it. Would they say it served the damned artsy-craftsies right? Or would they think the Fire Department reckless? Would they focus on the plight of the WOW ladies, who were nearly run over by an 1,800-pound bull? Or would they expend their supply of sympathy on Bill Tyler for the extensive damage to his beloved pickup truck?

So much had transpired in so short a time that the community didn't yet have it in focus, had reached no common conclusions, drawn no lessons from events. It would be a few days before all the testimony was distilled into a coherent version of what had occurred. That final version would be fairly close to the truth and in the short run would be accepted with minor reservations. In the longer term it would first be altered slightly here and there just to make a better story. Then, over the next couple of years, it would be completely revised into a modern myth, with heroes and villains and just desserts and poetic justice and perhaps a touch of tragedy here and there. By the time a few years had gone by the story would be totally misshapen and there would be people claiming to be eye witnesses who hadn't even been in the State of Vermont that day.

But this Sunday afternoon folks were still sorting things out.

"By God that lawyer lady sure enough went ass over teakettle . . ."

"She'll probley sue everybody from the Governor on down . . ."

"Wouldn'ya think the damn firemen'd git through the village without hittin' somethin' . . ."

"Wouldn'ya think they'd keep them hippies from blockin' the damn streets . . ."

"Them flatlanders got a little closer to nature'n they figgered . . ."

"Johnny Watkins'll be tough today . . . just put three darts in the triple 18 . . ."

"Heard Bingo finally caught 'im. That right?"

"Bet he's glad to git back in the barn at that."

As he stepped into the room Bingo launched a program of spin control.

"GOT 'IM BACK, BY GOD, FAIRLY SOUND AND SCARED SHITLESS BY ALL THEM FLATLANDERS," he roared, kicking off his campaign to take the onus off Jake. "IF IT WA'NT FER ALL THE GOD DAMNED GOLFIES AND HIPPIES WE'DA HAD 'IM 'FORE NOW," he added. That statement didn't really hang together too well with the facts, but in molding public opinion you sometimes have to be flexible as to what actually happened and what didn't. Interpretation is needed so people understand what's important and what isn't.

"Interdisciplinary confrontations ventilate transcultural similarities while pulmonary transactions reverberate," Desmond declared as he placed bottles of Donovan's Downtown Stout in front of Bingo and Thad. Looking at Laura, he raised his black bushy eyebrows high, furrowing his forehead clear to the hairline in patient anticipation of her order. She and Collier both opted for Donovan's, surprising Thad, who hadn't seen her drink a beer in 20 years. Milly ordered a Black Russian, causing Bingo to look carefully at her. The last time she got into the Black Russians was several years ago when he took her to the Cedar Grove Saloon over Rutland way, for an evening of dining, country music and dancing. They were celebrating their anniversary.

Stumpy and Sophie had been late, having blown a tire on Route 4 and no air in the damned spare, so the Reillys repaired to the bar to wait. Time went along, then came another round, a little dancing, two or three games of pool with another couple sitting there, and Bingo starts being charming to the woman. Pretty soon Milly's steaming pretty good and working on her fourth Black Russian, and she "accidentally" rammed her pool cue into that other woman's kidney region, giving it a little twist to boot, wishing it was a big old butcher knife or something.

Well it turned out the other woman was none other than Mary Beatrice Shanahan, a well-conditioned middle-weight who was unbeaten in the saloons of Caledonia County, not to mention three or four towns across the river in New Hampshire. Mary Beatrice was between husbands at the time, and auditioning a potential candidate in the Rutland area. A woman of action, she retaliated smartly with her own pool cue.

Bingo moved quickly to break it up, but the dumb bunny with Mary Beatrice-never did get his name-misinterpreted everything and joined Mary Beatrice in the fray. It only took one good shot in the snoot to convert Bingo from conciliatory peacemaker to hell on wheels with a split lip. The place was fairly crowded but the fight didn't become general because all four principals were strangers, unknown to the regulars.

"I ain't got a dog in that fight," one of them declared, and that's how they all felt. Besides which, they all knew the bartender.

His name was Herbert Smith and he looked about like you'd expect a Herbert Smith to look; on the scrawny side, with big eyes like an owl, hair combed right straight back from his forehead, and big ears sticking out to the sides like Prince Charles. But the eyes were cold.

The fight quickly reached the point where it had the attention of everybody in the bar, which was fairly crowded, and right about then Herbert Smith reached down between the sink and the beer cooler for the shotgun-double barreled and trimmed a bit for easier maneuvering in cramped quarters-and let a round off into the ceiling.

The fight stopped right then, everybody frozen, and quiet as all hell.

"Pay your bills and git out!" Herbert Smith's quiet voice was like a knife on a whetstone. Bingo and Milly and Mary Beatrice and her latest candidate paid and left, none of them saying a word. Nobody felt like resuming hostilities in the parking lot. The sound of a shotgun in a closed room can even overcome four Black Russians.

So this afternoon Bingo looked carefully at Milly when she ordered a Black Russian. She looked normal; not overjoyed about anything but not as grumpy as the last few days either. Could be a good sign after all.

Desmond put the drinks on the bar, then took the envelope marked "Bingo friend" out of the register and put it in front of Thad. "Aggressive husbandry obviates a multiplicity of onerous reformations and perspicacity intimidates the resultant repercussions," he intoned at Thad's bewildered look. Looking into the envelope, Thad put two and two together and kept his trap shut.

The hubbub increased as the crowd grew. Soon there were regulars and occasionals and hardly evers three deep behind the bar stools occupied by the early arrivals. Patchy Flaxon went behind the stick to help Desmond, taking over the half of the long bar furthest from the darts room.

Little by little, the shattered mosaic of Jake's passage through the village of Woodbine that morning was reassembled. Each bit of testimony was evaluated as to the reliability of its source, how many layers distant from an actual eye witness it was, and how it fit in with the bare outlines of the incident upon which all were agreed.

The tale of the stalking and taking of Jake on Mt. Harriet served as a sidebar to the main narrative of the awakening, reawakening was more like it, of Woodbine-a village grown comfortable with its boutiques and pricey restaurants and art galleries-to the reality of life on the farm.

As the role of the Tyler siren in the initial acceleration of Jake towards the green became clear, the consensus opinion of Jake began to improve for two reasons. First, this crowd was mostly men of the country, with few illusions about animals. No one present believed that animals could hold grudges, dislike this or that person's looks, act out of vindictiveness, do anything at all with humanesque motivation. Well, maybe one or two extraordinary animals out of their own pasts, but not as a general rule. An occasional individual seems almost human, but when it's all boiled down, dumb animals are dumb animals. Let off a piercing siren six feet from a bull's ear and all bets are off; he's going to get to highway speed in a hurry and run over whatever is in front of him.

The second reason was that the Tyler siren had annoyed more than just Jake. When a fire call came, Bill roared out of his garage with the siren on and he left it on all the way to the station. Four o'clock in the morning? Siren on full blast! Middle of mud season, not a tourist within 50 miles, no cars on the road? Siren on full blast! Church service in progress, final exams, funerals, rain or shine, didn't matter, that siren halted conversation, started headaches, raised blood pressure, created indignation and discontent whenever the Woodbine Volunteer Fire Department was called to action.

Letters to the editor in *The Word of Woodbine* had fulminated against that siren. Its volume and intensity had been discussed at Town Meeting. Complaints had been forwarded to the Chief. All to no avail, because Bill Tyler pointed out that it was in the first place legal and in the second place he was insuring his own safety while hurrying to the assistance of the community in his capacity as firefighter as well as warning pedestrians and other motorists that an emergency condition existed before which they must give way for the general good. His colleagues on the Department stood with him to defend the use of sirens–they all had them–although privately nearly all of them agreed that Bill overdid it.

Although Woodbine had changed over the past 30 years, it hadn't changed that much. Simply telling Bill Tyler to "knock it off, or else" was more than any elected official could be expected to do. As in any small community, the Woodbine Volunteer Fire Department was a powerful political force.

Bingo Reilly had never been a member of the Department, although he had been asked to join in his younger days. At the time he didn't fancy going in as a private, so to speak, and getting told what to do by somebody else. To Bingo, being an adult was not having to do what somebody tells you to do.

So there they were at the bar, Milly and Laura on bar stools, Bingo, Stumpy, Thad, and Collier standing behind them, Bingo jawing away at everybody passing by, getting and giving the latest versions of the morning's events, amending casualty lists, adding a pro-Jake spin to the tale wherever possible, needling and being needled.

"How much it cost ya' ta' put Jake in that pet show up to the Green this mornin'?"

"We got robbed," was Bingo's answer, "and I'm gittin' one of them lady lawyers to sue fer Jake."

"I heard Jake run second to a goldfish, that right?"

"Wal, gotta admit, it was one helluva goldfish."

Thad listened with admiration as Bingo skewed the telling and retelling ever so slightly so as to bring Jake's concerns parallel with those of the Volunteer Fire Department. By the time he got through buying drinks for people, and thanking people for all their help, calling in little favors, and exploiting minor intra-departmental personality conflicts, and cajoling, and blaming, and calling up the specter of outsiders telling folks what to do, and talking farming talk, and telling the ladies how nice they looked (carefully though, with Milly sitting right there over her Black Russian), he was well on the way to rehabilitating Jake's position in the community.

The excitement over the goings-on at the green was such that the Darts Tournament got underway almost as an afterthought. Folks hardly paid attention. Which took the pressure off Thad, especially in the first match. Throwing darts in competition before a crowd of mostly strangers would be enough to make a body a little whippy, but with hardly anybody paying attention he breezed to a win, helped by the fact that his opponent was Basil Mallary, who couldn't throw darts sober, much less the way he was this afternoon.

As he ambled back to the bar after his win, Thad for the first time thought seriously about the Darts Tournament. "By George, that wasn't half bad," he mused. "Might even get in the money sort of thing," he ventured to himself.

"Bit of all right, those darts of yours," he informed Bingo as he went back to work on his Donovan's. "Fly true as a bloomin' Irish girl." The victory, in combination with the Donovan's Downtown Stout, had somehow activated his English gland or gene or whatever it was.

The hands of the old schoolroom clock high on the wall behind the bar moved inexorably on their slow rounds, the afternoon faded into late day, the noise level in the Milk House slowly rising as the crowd grew and its thirst was slaked.

"Well as I live and breathe here comes old Plutarch," said Bingo, who had been watching and hoping for just such an arrival. "GIVE MY OLD FRIEND PLUTARCH OGLESBY HERE A HEALING SHOT OF LOUD MOUTH WITH A LITTLE OF THAT TONIC WATER THROWED OVER IT," he yelled to Patchy, making room in their little group for the newcomer. "Meetcher new neighbors, Pluto," he went on, "who's bought the old Chester place and made a fine lookin' place of it at that, doin' some work that needed doin'."

"Howdy," said Plutarch, taking off his hat and nodding. Laura looked to him like a pretty fine city lady for sure. "Pleezed ta meetcha," he said.

"Well, Mr. Oglesby, we've heard a great deal about you," said Laura, "it's a pleasure to finally meet you in person. I hope you don't mind our trespassing on your land from time to time on our rides and our walks."

"Go right to it, you wanna," said Pluto waving his arm like a traffic cop. "Help yourself!" he added grandly.

"Mr. Oglesby, I was over there last week on an early morning walk and I do believe I saw a row of asparagus poking up. You shouldn't let it go to waste."

The Reillys both looked quickly at Plutarch, wondering what he would say to that. Here was a man who hadn't hardly been back to that cursed piece of land since the day he knocked on the Reilly door back in 1934.

"Ain't seen the place in some little time, maam, but as I recall Mother was a great one to have a garden, 'n' she'd of sure enough had asparagus in it." Plutarch looked off, through the wall and away from the noisy saloon. "Mother surely loved vegetables."

Bingo and Milly were astonished at this exchange. Everybody always shied away from talking about Pluto's family, and his mother, and the fire, and the land, and every other thing about his terrible heritage. Time was, you could get yourself in a hell of a fist fight just by bringing those subjects up with Pluto. Now here he was going on nice as pie with Laura Brookings about all that stuff.

Little by little, the Reillys joined in the conversation, which both of them considered a delicate subject, a tinder-box, although Laura and Pluto were jabbering on about all these things everybody had considered taboo for the last 50 years. The flowers, and the patch of lilies near the cellar-hole, and the view from what must have been the barn, and the meadow among the first to melt down to grass in early spring because of its south-facing tilt. Collier, mean-while, was dividing his time between inspecting the Milk House clientele for attractive females and watching his father win his first dart encounter, and paying no attention to the conversation.

"Flatlander livin' up there wants to buy the land," Pluto said abruptly.

"I hadn't heard it was for sale," Laura said, surprised.

"It ain't been," Pluto replied, "but alla' sudden every-body wants it." He looked at Bingo. "'Cludin' Bingo here."

"Wal, I been workin' up a proposition, Pluto," Bingo began, "and it's based on the knowledge that you and I both know, that money ain't nothin' but paper with num-bers written down on it and the god damned bankers'll git it away from yu' ever' time." Pluto had been approached occasionally over the years by folks interested in the land but he had always turned them away. Except when he knew they were bankers; then he not only turned them down, he was likely to take a swing at them.

Bingo paused, cleared his throat, and wished that Laura wasn't sitting there so interested. He would rather not have presented his proposition at the bar in the Milk House, either, but it was so noisy and crowded it almost amounted to privacy.

"Now I got a use fer that land," he said, adding seriously, "Father always said to never buy a piece of land less you got a use fer it figgered out. Wal, I got a use fer it figgered out, and I believe I can figure out how to git onto that land 'thout too much trouble and expense.

"I was thinkin' along the lines of some kinda swap, with a piece of my property along the brook, and I build ya' a little cabin, I was thinkin' it could set on that little knob just south of the road down there, couple acres, plenty room enough fer a garden, nice spot, summer or winter . . ." Bingo's voice trailed off, wondering if a garden appealed to Pluto at his age, not doing too good here presenting the deal.

"We swap and I own it, I still got taxes to pay," Pluto pointed out.

"That's part of owning land, god dammit, is payin' taxes."

"I die, I'll swap it back to ya," said Pluto seriously.

"In that case you might consider paying the taxes yourself, Mr. Reilly," Laura chipped in.

"If it were me, I might even consider providing a lifetime supply of firewood," added Thad, who had rejoined the group.

"Gittin' some long in the tooth," Pluto declared. "Don't know how many years I got left."

"Wal, the Oglesbys allus was long livers," Bingo put in. He didn't like the idea of this negotiation taking place in front of the Brookings but he couldn't think what to do about it because apparently it didn't bother Pluto one bit. "So they say," he added, belatedly realizing the only

Oglesby he had ever laid eyes on was the one right in front of him now. But he had heard the talk; they all lived to be 90 or 100.

"You ain't got no serious miseries yet, though, have ya?" Bingo hadn't thought of that.

"Nope. But the time'll come, the time'll come."

"Wal, I might throw in five thousand dollars, so's you could have something going with the bankers, too," Bingo said.

"Make it ten thousand," said Plutarch, who knew his man.

"Seven thousand and not a penny more."

"Nine thousand and I won't go down another cent."

Laura thought both of them were getting their backs up a bit, caught up in the competitive heat of negotiations. "Split the difference. Make it eight thousand," she said firmly.

The two men looked sourly at one another for a moment, then nodded.

"Eight thousand it is, but I ain't decided yet on the whole deal," Pluto declared.

"NOW WHAT THE HELL YA WANT?" Hope had soared for one brief moment, now replaced by disappointment equally vivid.

"I can see that we have two top notch negotiators here," Laura said to Thad, speaking across the two men. "They're both doing quite well."

Bingo and Pluto looked at her and then went back at it.

"What's this cabin like?"

"It ain't like nothing yet, it ain't even there."

"You gonna put electric in it?"

"Wal, I ain't thought about it, but I spose so."

"Good water piped into the house?"

"I spose so."

"Flush toilet?"

"Jeez, Pluto, what the hell ya want?"

"Flush toilet, fer sure!"

"All right, but that's it!"

"How many rooms?"

"I dunno. . . two maybe . . . maybe three . . . what d'ya need a lotta rooms fer?"

"Spose I git sick?"

Bingo was taken by surprise at the shift from the cabin to Pluto's health. "What if ya git sick? Whatta ya spect me to do?" He looked at Laura, wondering if she had any more bright ideas.

"Mr. Oglesby is worried what will happen to him when he gets old," Laura put in gently, "just as we all worry about the same thing." She looked from one to the other. "Surely something can be worked out."

"I think I should get two hunnert dollars a month on top of all the rest," said Pluto.

"TWO HUNNERT MY ASS," said Bingo Reilly.

"Watch yer mouth," said Milly.

"Tally-ho, old chaps, time for another round of the Donovan," said his lordship, moving quickly to salvage the negotiation. "And whatever you're having my good fellow," noticing that Pluto was not drinking beer.

"Predomination buckles the pluck of evenly-matched adversaries, exsanguinating possibilities of accomplishment and serenity," Desmond intoned with a significant look on his face as he provided refreshment.

There was a tension-filled silence while they all tried to figure out what that meant and how they individually figured into it. Nobody got anywhere with it, but the moment of dangerous conflict had passed, Desmond's weirdness once more proving a positive influence on the lives of his constituency.

The whole thing went on for quite a while, into the dining room where the six of them had a nice chicken dinner on the Brookings, and back again to the bar where the second round of eliminations were underway. And it wound up this way: Bingo to get the Oglesby land. Plutarch to get $8,000, plus two to three acres along the brook (the boundaries were established precisely in their minds but they would need a survey to determine the size of the piece), a three-room log cabin to be built for him by Bingo on a knoll just up off the brook. Bingo would pay the property taxes. The cabin would include electricity and running water, including a flush toilet. Kitchen appliances, guaranteed working but not guaranteed new, would be supplied as would a good wood stove and sufficient firewood for the winter. The cabin would be ready for occupancy by the beginning of deer season in early November. Land, cabin, and all appurtenances would revert to Bingo Reilly if and when Pluto should croak. With a straight face, Pluto insisted on the "if and when" language since it left open the possibility that he might never do so, a comforting notion. Pluto lost his bid for a monthly stipend but he gained a certain grandfather status, perhaps great uncle status would be more like it. When he got his miseries, it was agreed, he would be maintained in the log cabin as long as possible. The head of the Woodbine Visiting Nurses, Milly Reilly, and the Brookings would be the judges of when it was no longer feasible for him to stay in the cabin, the majority to rule, at which time he would go to a nursing home or whatever dismal fate awaited.

Bingo thought it was a pretty good deal, wouldn't draw down his cash too much although he would lose some productive time building the cabin and probably wouldn't be able to push ahead with his access plan for the Oglesby property until next year. The main drawback was he didn't look forward, as he commented to Milly just before they went to bed that night, to being "a goddam housemother" for Plutarch.

"Don't be so snippy 'bout motherhood," Milly snapped, "if it wa'nt fer Mother Brookings tonight you wouldn't of gotcher precious land."

Bingo sputtered a little bit about that, but he knew it was true.

For his part, Pluto figured he "skuned Bingo Reilly good," as he confided to Patchy Flaxon a week later. He had secured a permanent home of his own, established a nest egg of cash just in case, and provided as best he could for care in his declining years. It would never occur to him to ask for a better break than that.

The deal was done on a handshake, although the men asked Laura to "git it all written up just right so it's legal." This she promised to do. Bingo would pay for the survey and the costs of the deed work.

By the time his second match arrived, Thad was filled with chicken and Donovan's, and feeling comfortable on the hockey, toe planted exactly against the line, wrist and arm flicking the darts in a swift flat trajectory to thunk into the bristle. Relaxed, nothing to lose, not expected to go far in the tournament, he zapped two darts into the triple 18 and the third in the double 18 to open the match. His opponent, a finish carpenter named Marsden Ellinger, never recovered and Thad joined the other five survivors of Division III.

On the ride home in the Saab, Thad congratulated the driver on her deft handling of the delicate negotiation. "You certainly brokered the swap deal from beginning to end, my dear. The U.N. should ship you off to the Balkans."

"It's just a matter of figuring out what each party really wants, which is to say what each party will settle for, and then working it around until both sides get the important things that they really want," Laura replied as she swung the car onto the Oglesby Farm Road. "That's what makes a good deal: when both sides are happy." She muttered something under her breath when the car hit a pothole. "Really, Thaddy, the Town should do something about this road."

"They will, dear, when they get to it; they can't do all the roads at once, you know," he sighed. A few ruts in the road constitute a federal case, while negotiating a unique land transaction was just something that happened that day. Thad shook his head in wonder, and went back to musing on the land deal.

"It still seems to me that Bingo got an awful good deal," he declared as they pulled into their driveway. "Our friend Hickham would cough up a lot of cash for that property, I bet."

"Thaddy, you're impossible! If I should die, be sure to get a good accountant."

Collier chimed in. "Well, I thought he got it pretty cheap too, Mother."

In the house, Thad opened a Donovan's to split with Collier and the three of them sat down at the kitchen table.

"Neither of you were listening the whole time," Laura noted, "since Collier couldn't keep his eyes off the waitress and you were excelling at the dartboard, so I'll explain the whole thing.

"I know for a fact that the property is appraised by the Town for tax purposes at $1,100 per acre." She paused, looking at Thad intently. "That's low for this section of town and the excuse is probably the difficult access and the lack of improvements, and maybe the fact that a lot of it's steep and there's a lot of ledge. But $1,100 is still low for that piece of land so the chances are the listers are giving Mr. Oglesby a break, and why shouldn't they?

"If you approached Hickham, his first offer would be around $500 per acre, because he's the kind who isn't happy with a purchase unless he practically steals it. And he'd cry about the gully and this and that, and maybe he'd go up a little, but not much.

"Now in my opinion, $1,800 an acre is a fair price for that piece, because of the bridge that has to be built to get to it, the state gets involved in that and you have to build to their specifications. Plus you need to drill a well and put in a road, and on top of that a septic system could get very expensive if the land doesn't perk properly.

"So $1,800 is fair, and I suspect we could maneuver Hickham up to $2,000, maybe a little more. It'd be a hassle, but you could do it. First you'd list it with the most highfalutin' real estate office in town, an exclusive listing but not an exclusive right to sell, and you'd put a big price on it, $3,000 an acre, maybe more.

"Then you'd put signs all along the road, drive him crazy ever time he drives up the hill. Then you'd make a big thing about showing it to someone, maybe your brother Jimmy, and ask him to come in the Jaguar.

"That should be enough to get Hickham out and about, looking for Mr. Oglesby. And he'd be real sly, talking confidentially out of the corner of his mouth, 'I'm gonna save you some money' claiming that because his first interest in the land came before it was listed, Plutarch has no obligation to pay a broker a commission, which may be legally true but isn't necessarily an ethically attractive position.

"Meanwhile you keep showing it. Every broker in town has a list of serious prospects looking for either estate-type properties or big pieces of land with dramatic views—just like the views from Mr. Oglesby's land—so they can build a showplace and become gentlemen horse farmers. Just like you and me Thaddy, when you think about it.

"Now Hickham's got to be getting nervous. Maybe you let it be known that we, as Plutarch's representatives, are considering an offer and trying to decide if we should recommend that he accept it.

"Now he's not only nervous about who might turn out to be his neighbor, he's thinking maybe he should have some more land to insure his privacy. Of course he lived 25 years on Long Island in a house about 40 feet from the one next door, but times have changed. And, although it's by now clear to him that he can't steal the land, his eyes have been opened to a potential profit greater than he thought.

"Now things are getting serious for him. He finally has to either make an offer or be left in the dust. And he's dealing with me, us, which is different than condescending to Plutarch. so it can't be some preposterous figure; it has to be within a legitimate range or we'll just scoff at it and walk away. He strikes me as a man who has spent his whole life trying not to be scoffed at.

"Let's say we dicker with him and finally settle on $2,000 per acre, which amounts to $124,000. A lot of

money for old Plutarch? Well, not as much as you might
think. Take out ten percent for the real estate commission
and two percent for the lawyer and you're down to, let's
see, about $109,000. Hickham will want it surveyed and
that cost is usually split, so Plutarch is down another fif-
teen hundred."

Laura was figuring on the back of a shopping list,
frowning and biting her lip.

"Next in line is the tax man. Tax men, I should say.
The Feds want . . . let's see, Plutarch's income is social
security and that's it, so he'll have over $105,000 in capital
gains because when he inherited it back in the 1930s it was
worth about $2,000. So he'll owe maybe twenty five per-
cent. That's over $25,000 to the Feds. Now here comes the
State of Vermont with its hand out looking for twenty five
percent of the Federal tax, which is over $6,000. So . . . the
net to Plutarch is something under $70,000."

Laura stopped and looked across the table at Thad
and Collier.

"Now," she said sharply, "there he sits on the sidewalk
with a check for $70,000, perhaps a bit less, and all his
belongings piled around him in three feed sacks." Another
pause to let that sink in. "How would you boys manage
that seventy grand for him? How could you take that
money and do as well for him as he did in the swap with
Mr. Reilly? Don't forget he ended up with $8,000 in the
bank, a life estate on a nice piece of property complete
with a house and flush toilet, no tax burden, no heating
cost, and he finally acquired a family of sorts when the
Reillys and us agreed to monitor his capacity to live alone.
If you read the real estate ads in the paper you know that
in this up-scale Vermont area a beat-up old mobile home
perched on a cinder block foundation in the flood plain

253

somewhere is going to cost $50,000 to buy and $650 a month to rent. And the cheapest hamburger in town costs $8.95.

"How does his deal with Mr. Reilly differ from that assisted living development that Hickham is always trying to peddle? Plutarch's situation is actually better. It cost less to start with and will cost little to maintain. He should be able to get along fine on social security, since his housing costs are taken care of once and for all."

Thad and Collier stared at her, thinking about it.

Collier wasn't convinced. "Seventy grand is a lot of money, Mother, and over time he'd be much better off with it soundly invested," he said.

"He's in his 70s Collier, so all his investments are short term, which means either they carry a low return or are extremely risky. And he doesn't need to build capital, he needs to see to the next few years. The deal he made accomplishes that."

Thad thought of something. "What about major medical expenses? Who'll pay?"

"He can meet reasonable costs himself, with the help of Medicare. He's mentally together and physically in pretty good shape. He doesn't want to linger on in a hospital bed anyway. If some hospital decides to ignore his living will by hooking him up to a bunch of machines to keep him technically alive, they'll be doing it on their own account, because he doesn't have anything for them to sue for."

"What about the land and house; they certainly have value."

"Don't forget the life estate," she cautioned. "In effect, the land and the new house have already been sold to Mr.

Reilly, it's just that the sale doesn't take effect until Plutarch dies."

"When and if," said Thad, conceding the debate. "And it's past my bedtime," he added as he finished his stout and rose from the table.

AFTERMATH

K nowing that news of the land transfer from Plutarch
Oglesby to Bingo Reilly would spread like fox
mange, Bingo moved quickly the following Monday to
obscure the facts, acting for no better reason than that they
were "nobody's damned business." By one p.m. he had
stopped at the Mobil station for coffee, picked up an un-
needed bag of grain at the feed store, chatted up a number
of people in the Woodbine Post Office, and popped into
the Milk House for a noontime Donovan's. At each stop
he revealed the transfer of land, offered misleading descrip-
tions of the negotiations, hinted at this or that figure, nodded sagely in reply to leading questions, and managed to
launch four different versions of the price and terms of the
affair.

As the word spread, real estate agents all over Woodbine held their heads in their hands, no matter which er-
roneous version they happened to hear. The Woodbine
legal community did the same. All were mourning the fees
and commissions that would not now be deftly extracted at
the closing ceremony; the solemn meeting of bankers and
real estate people and lawyers and buyers and sellers at
which papers are passed with a reverence proportional to

the money involved. It was a damned shame, a dangerous and foolhardy move, very nearly a criminal act to accomplish such a transaction without the expert guidance of dedicated professionals in the field.

Frank Hickham heard about it in the Pro Shop at the Woodbine Country Club, some five minutes before his tee time. His first drive broke a window in Johnny Polk's house clear on the other side of South Street. The mulligan nearly beaned Mrs. Archibald Thrush-Macklington, the bubble gum heiress, who was standing on the eighth green waiting for her husband to complete his elaborate pre-putt ritual of wiggle-wagging his backside. All in all, Hick had a bad day, losing forty simoleans to a pair of dubbers he could usually count on for lunch money.

The first property damage suit resulting from Jake's reconnoiter of the village green was filed by Alexis Lexington first thing Monday morning on behalf of the Woodbine Chapter of the World Organization of Women. It was followed in the next few days by many more such claims, owing to the efficiency with which Tranquillity Emerson's Activist Axis connected crafts people with legal counsel. There was plenty of the latter available, since the real estate market had been depressed for over a year, resulting in a dearth of the Vermont lawyer's bread and butter: title searches performed by their secretaries.

Widespread hopes for juridical enrichment were dashed quickly, however, when Judge Praxiteles Bismarck Smith cited an 1899 case concerning crops damaged by a pair of escaped hogs. The case had been dismissed when the judge ruled that, in order to dignify the claim, the plaintiff's field had to be protected from the occasional escaped animal by a fence that was "hog tight and bull strong." The Woodbine legal fraternity retreated, grumbling, but not too loudly. Some even went so far as to point out that Judge Smith himself raised purebred Angus cattle on his farm in Randolph.

The legal attacks were a surprise to Bingo. He had assumed that everyone would be happy that Jake was back in the fold, none the worse for his experience, and that would be that, since Jake wasn't the first bull to ever get out of his pen. Instead it seemed as if everybody was just jumping all over him until, taking Stumpy's advice, he drove the old truck up to Bethel to contract the services of Phidias Metternich Smith, Esquire, a world-class conniver hiding behind a genial country facade and the judge's brother to boot. Fiddy, as he was known, achieved the rout of the plaintiffs with three phone calls, counting the one that was a wrong number. In fact he spent more time drawing up his bill, which when completed ran three and one half pages, than he had in fighting the case. When Bingo coughed up the dough a few weeks later, Fiddy commiserated with him at the seemingly unnecessary expense and the two had a long conversation on the terrible changes being brought down upon honest Vermonters by the flatlanders moving in.

The Word of Woodbine published a day early the week after Jake toured the village green, and the editorial page was practically frothing at the mouth. The paper, established in 1915, had been sold three years before to a couple from Massachusetts named Tiffany and Seth Botz, in their 30s and yearning to leave their Boston apartment for the true and wholesome life of the country. The children would be brought up with a respect, nay, a veritable reverence, for nature and its wonders.

The special edition wasted no respect or reverence on Jake, however, since the Botz family had been represented at the pet show by Tiffany and the girls, seven-year-old Allison and nine-year-old Kaitlin, not to mention the family Guinea Pigs, Bert and Ernie.

Seth, who was listed in four different places in the paper as Editor in Chief, was turned away from the Reilly barn when he arrived bright and early Monday morning with a photographer. "There was no mistaking Mr. Reilly's ill will," he confided to Tiffany later that day, which was an understatement.

Seth and the photographer proceeded to the Hopkins Farm, which was really a fake farm for tourists to visit, to inspect and photograph a bull, any bull. It was Seth's first close-up exposure to farm animals and an eye-opener. Before they were done they had also photographed a pair of oxen that towered over them, and a sow the size of a sports car.

The Word of Woodbine's expanded editorial page proposed an elaborate plan to protect tourists, business owners, and ordinary citizens from such barnyard behemoths. The plan involved establishing a special subcommittee of the Zoning Committee to propose bull-free areas, boar-free areas, and a registration system of such animals showing their location in the town and other particulars, such as weight, height, a recent photograph, and a short assessment of the creature's disposition. It called for a preliminary proposal to be amended and enlightened at a series of public hearings, all duly warned in advance, with a final proposal to be approved by the voters at Town Meeting. The plan was well-received at the Chamber of Commerce and the Activist Axis, a strange and unusual alliance, but the Town's elected officials were lukewarm at best and nothing came of it.

Late Monday afternoon, on Jake's first full day back in the barn, Hernando showed up in the Reilly yard bawling and bellyaching. Jake, hearing him outside, set up a bellering of his own and Bingo finally put the little donkey in the barn just to get some peace and quiet. Hernando's soothing effect on Jake was apparent and when Bingo notified Mrs. Magda Billington Smithers of her donkey's whereabouts he mentioned in an offhand way that the little critter seemed to get along well with his roving bull.

"Well, perhaps I might consider selling him to you," Mrs. Billington said cautiously.

"Thought mebbe you'd consider givin' 'im to me," Bingo replied, "seein's how he bit ya in the ass and all." Then remembering his manners, "Less ol' Stanford Lamphere made that part up."

The negotiations were over quickly. Mrs. Billington simply held no cards in her hand. So Hernando became a fixture in the Reilly barn. Bingo rationalized buying feed for a useless animal by considering the donkey as nothing more than an increased appetite on the part of Jake. In his mind he didn't feed the damn thing; he just fed Jake a little more. Hernando, unaware of this mental self-delusion, settled easily into his new home and, through some instinctive caution, was careful never to bite Bingo Reilly.

The Darts Tournament was an artistic success for the dart-throwing community as well as an economic boost for Desmond Kiley. Bingo was eliminated early by Geraldine Larkpester, who had been practicing for months in her kitchen. Distracted by the lawsuits and the unexpected resentment of many segments of the community, he had figured Geraldine for a pushover and went into the match overconfident. She beat him decisively, against a deafening background of derision coming from the bar. Thad won his division, beating Wendell Coates in a close and exciting match, but was ousted from the finals without ceremony. Still he was amazed to end up with a hundred dollar bill for winning the division.

Stumpy played for the Championship against a young student from the Law School up in South Royalton and lost, although it was close. But he was the biggest winner among the Milk House regulars, making $100 for winning his division and the $400 runner-up prize. "Not bad for losin,'" he grinned.

The Word of Woodbine reported the results of the Kickoff Mixed Foursome Tournament, all the way down to tenth place, spelling the names correctly. A brief item noted that the local polo team had also won its match in South Woodbine. Scores of the softball league games were displayed in bold type under a standing headline and a chart showing the team standings. The darts tournament didn't make the paper, although Millicent Buchanan had planned to provide opening day coverage. But the Sunday morning carnage on the village green had so taxed the paper's staff that the darts tourney was out of the question.

Millicent did attend two of the later sessions of the darts tournament, however, including the final night. The first trip led to an insightful essay on sports as a violence-deflecting outlet in the life of the average working man. Her second trip to the Milk House, the one when Hank Swenston pinched her bottom, gave rise to a 1,400 word meditation on the decline of civility in everyday life, attributing the alleged decline to a rising tide of insolence and savagery stirred up by talk radio and the desperate mood of a public overwhelmed by rising medical bills. Both essays went into the Editor's waste basket, the first because it was trendy claptrap and the second because it libeled 16 local citizens who were cited by name, not to mention three doctors at the Woodbine Health Center and the entire faculty of the Dartmouth Medical School over in Hanover.

Frank Hickham was enraged at Bingo's snatching the Oglesby land away. The more he thought about it the more it made him mad and the bigger the price he decided he would have paid for it if he had had a chance to put in a bid. He conveniently forgot that he had refrained from mentioning a figure when he first talked to old Plutarch, thinking he could maybe get it for practically nothing. Also forgotten was the fact that he had no use for the land. The whole affair bothered him so much he broke down and spoke to Bingo about it, stopping him on the street in front of the Post Office and hinting that he might be willing to pay pretty good money for it. Bingo, merciless in victory, not only refused to entertain the notion of selling but also let it be known that he was considering putting a pig shed on the property and going into the hog business. "Good money in hogs, by God," he told his neighbor. "Might even set up a slaughterin' operation," he added. Hickham, shocked speechless and face the color of putty, threw an arm around a parking meter for support and watched Bingo walk jauntily away down the street.

"Asseverations evanesce when porcine vernaculars collide with posturing patriciate contumelies," Desmond commented when he heard about the encounter.

At just about the time the darts tournament was over, folks got busy. May had been a perfect month, chilly and rainy. The old saying was: "Cold, wet May, barn full of hay." Serious haying started during the third week in June, although some fields wouldn't be cut until after the Fourth of July. But haying is an important thing to a farmer, and a gambling thing too, taking a chance it won't rain for three or four days in a row. Once you get going you don't stop for several days, and though it's true you don't get going until 10 a.m. or so, the chances are you'll still be throwing bails up on the truck at dusk.

So summer came along, starting with the haying, people's lives scuffing ahead through time, moving on, and Jake's run receded into memory.

THURSDAY, JULY 22, 1993

T he couple who stepped into the dimness of the Milk
House this boiling summer afternoon were tourist-
dressed and camera-laden, probably staying at the Woodbine Inn and out for a walk around town that had worked
up a thirst.

"Kitchen's closed!" Patchy Flaxon was in command
this afternoon, alone in the place and a man who liked to
get things clear at the outset.

"We're just looking for something cool to drink," the
man said pleasantly.

"We can sure enough fix ya up with that," the little
man replied, wiping the bar in front of them with a clean
rag as if it needed it, which it didn't.

"What have you got for beer?" The *succès d'estime*
achieved by the "Gambrinian umber" in recent years had
changed that potable from a symbol of scorned middle
America to a subject on which it was permissible, even
necessary, to speak knowledgeably. Indeed, being a wine
snob was getting to be old hat; beer snobbery was not only
the latest thing, it also established you as a regular guy with
lines of communication out to the common man.

"Donovan's Downtown Stout or Tinker Mountain Pale Ale is what most of 'em drinks around here," Patchy said. "Stout's the same color as coffee and gotta strong taste," he added.

The man ordered one of each and Patchy put the Donovan's in front of him, the ale in front of the lady. "Want glasses?" When they nodded, he added, "A lot of 'em don't."

After the first long swallow and the relieved sigh that followed it, they looked around the place, eyes now accustomed to the dimness, seeing it for the first time. The framed maps, some old and others recent, along with the low beamed ceiling and the dart room made for a pubby feeling, a sense of being in a definite neighborhood.

"So what's new around the village of Woodbine?" the man asked, looking for conversation.

Patchy scratched his head, not bothering to remove his Caterpillar cap. "Wal, ya'know they caught the damn bull." It was half way between a statement and a question.

"What bull?"

Oh oh. These folks must be from another planet.

So Patchy launched into the story of Jake's hegira through the sensibility of Woodbine, embellishing here, smoothing things out a little there, stressing the extent of his own consultation with Bingo Reilly throughout the crisis.

"I told old Bingo ta hunt 'im like a deer, stalk 'im, and him and Stumpy finally did, but that bull sure raised hell in Woodbine before they caught 'im, 'n' everybody's suing fer damages and old Bingo's takin' it hard, seemed like he was down, ya know, wan't saying much to nobody, he'd just set there with his Donovan's lookin' glum, couldn't nobody cheer 'im up, we was all gettin' worried, ya'know, mebbe he's sick or sumpin.' Lotta things come down on 'im to once, like the vet bills, cause the bull was all slashed up on the brisket, and the goddam lawyers, beggin' yer pardon Maam, and the newspaper blamin' 'im fer everything, and a girl beat 'im in the darts tournament right in front of everybody, and he hadda lay out a lotta cash fer the land he bought from Plutarch. He felt like his own town had turned on 'im, ya know? Tough as he is–and he's sure enough tough–it got 'im down and we's all of us worried 'bout 'im." He paused, looking off. "Wal, right up ta last Sattidy we's worried about 'im. Then the fever broke, ya might say.

"Bingo's here at the Milk House, see, settin' apart and lookin' glum like he has lately, with a couple of pops under his belt already, when old Morgan Perlick from up to Bethel come in to wet his whistle. Old Morgan ain't called "old" 'cause he's old, but on account of he acts old. He's always whining about this and that and complaining, and he has the knack of being able to see the bad side of even the best things that happened to 'im. He's known as a pretty good man with mules; growed up with 'em, dealt with 'em all his life, got so's he acts like 'em sometimes. Well he's always got a couple of teams of mules in different stages of training and he swaps 'em around, and trades, and generally does pretty good at the World's Fair in Tunbridge, so he's got a good name in mules. But with all his bellyachin' and groanin' and moanin' about everything you wouldn't think he'd ever owned a decent mule. And he's also got a reputation as being tighter'n Dick's hatband. Well that afternoon he gits his beak dipped into a Tinker Mountain Pale Ale and he starts complaining about this team of mules he's got, how they's hard to handle and don't earn they keep and ornery as hell and so on.

"Pretty soon Bingo pipes up.

"'Morgan,' he sez 'you talkin' 'bout that team of red mules I seen last month over there to the Hopkins Farm?'

"'Yup.' Morgan was kinda surprised, ya know, cause Bingo usual didn't pay him no attention, or anyway damn little.

"'Wal by God,' Bingo sez, real strong, 'I'll give ya eighteen hunnert dollars fer them mules. Best goddamn pair of mules I ever see.'

"'You wouldn't!' sez Morgan. 'They ain't worth that.' You could tell he was real surprised, 'cause if he'd thought about it he wouldn't a said that last.

"'The hell I wouldn't,' sez Bingo. And he reaches in his pocket and takes out his wallet and he distangles 18 big, green hunnert dollar bills from it and he lays 'em right there on the bar. By God that got everybody's attention right away, I'll tell ya. Then he grabs a napkin off the bar and he starts writin' out a bill of sale on it. 'Sign this and take the money,' he sez, 'or goddamn it shut up!'

"Come to find out later that Bingo'd just got paid by some Connecticut flatlander for working on a old barn at his country place down in Reading way last fall and Bingo'd had a helluva time gittin' the check out of 'im so he went right to the bank and changed the check for cash money. So that's why he's carryin' all that money, which made sense, but at the time it just about knocked everybody on their backsides that was there.

"Morgan pounced on that money like a fox on a field mouse, cause he knew them mules wasn't worth that much. He signed the napkin and stuck that money into his jeans real careful, so it wouldn't anyway fall out, and he started lookin' some smug. 'Helluva deal,' he's thinkin' to himself.

"Bingo starts in crowin' like a banty rooster. 'By God,' he's sayin' to Desmond Kiley, that's the boss ya know, owns this place, 'By God, I just stole the best damn pair of mules in Windsor County.'

"Then he turns back to Morgan. 'Now Morgan,' he sez, 'I'll be over ta pick 'em up first thing tomorrow morning and don't you be gittin' any ideas 'bout backin' out of this deal cause you signed the paper and everybody seen ya do it.'

"Morgan's got his mouth open to repeat that them mules ain't worth even one thousand dollars when here comes Stumpy through the door into the Milk House.

"'By God Stumpy, I just pulled off the deal of the century,' Bingo hollers. 'Jest bought the best pair of mules in Vermont off of poor Morgan here, fer a lousy eighteen hunnert smackers, 'n' once I git through winnin' all the prize money this summer and fall at the Fairs by God I'll sell 'em fer three times that.'

"Now Stumpy's pretty quick between the ears and he fell right in with the game, cause he knew the last thing Bingo Reilly wanted was a pair of mules. 'Sorry to hear you're so short ya hadda sell them wonderful mules,' he sez ta Morgan, acting kind of sorrowful ya know. Then he turns to Bingo and starts giving 'im congratulations and ain't you lucky and how come you get all the breaks and like that.

"'BUY THE HOUSE A DRINK, BY GOD,' Bingo's bellerin,' 'WE'RE CELEBRATIN' THIS ONE.' He's whoopin' and hootin.' 'BUY THE PICTURES ON THE WALL A DRINK, LONG'S YER AT IT,' he hollers. And he goes on laughing like he'd really put one over on old Morgan and joking and talking about being the King of the Fair Circuit this year and how he'd had his eye on these mules ever since Morgan first got 'em and so on like that. Everybody comes in he buys 'em a drink and tells 'em all about it real excited and all the time he's kind of ignoring Morgan, paying no attention to 'im atall. By the time 30 minutes was gone by them mules had growed to being the best mules in all New England.

"Pretty soon the expression on Morgan's puss goes a little sour. 'Them are good mules, sure enough,' he sez. 'Could be prizewinners,' he sez. 'Mebbe,' he sez.

"All this time Bingo's fussin' and crowin' and carryin' on about this wonderful pair of mules. Along about the fourth time through the story of them wonderful mules and what a great buy they was, Morgan starts lookin' a little sick around the edges.

"Pretty soon he's movin' over to where Bingo was, tryin' ta get a word in. 'Thought you's takin' them Belgians of yours to the Fairs this summer,' he piped up, 'how ya gonna do both?'

"'I'll figure somethin' out Morgan, don't you worry,' Bingo sez.

"'Be a shame ta slight one or t'other,' Morgan sez, sounding wistful like.

"'Wal I ain't slightin' them mules, not with all the money I'll be makin' with 'em.'

"'Now they AIN'T that good a pair Bingo!' Morgan's talkin' like he really believed it, sounded solid, them words. But ya' could feel the doubt creepin' in around 'em. He's startin' finally 'membering some good points 'bout them mules. All of the sudden he had an idea. 'Ya' got a place to keep 'em mules?' he asked. 'Them's used to a big double-size box stall, ya know.'

"'Plenty o' room in my barn,' Bingo sez, 'Plenty o' room.'

"'Well I ain't sure,' Morgan sez, 'might get kickin' and jumpin' around there and hurt one another.' He put on a concerned look about all the danger. 'Tell ya' what,' he sez, 'I'll come look at yer barn,' he sez, 'and I'll see if ya' got a good enough place fer 'em,' he sez. 'Meanwhile,' he sez, 'you'd best hang onto the eighteen hunnert dollars,' he sez, 'till we're SURE ya got a place for 'em,' he sez.

"Well right away Bingo starts makin' a big stink about that idea. 'Not a chance,' he sez, 'because,' he sez, 'everybody in the whole place seen ya' sign the paper AND,' he sez, 'ya' can't weasel out of it,' he sez."

Patchy was getting into the story pretty good, windmilling his arms around and yelling and imitating voices, first Bingo, then old Morgan. When he accidentally rapped his knuckles on the back bar it brought him back to earth.

"How's that stout? Need 'nother one?" When the man nodded, Patchy removed the empty, fished a new one from the cooler, opened it, and slid it across the bar the way he had seen Desmond do it so many times. Pretty soon, by God, people will be saying that Patchy Flaxon really knows his way around a back bar, he thought.

Then he picked up the story again, not wanting to overdo the dramatic pause.

"But by now Morgan has decided he's made a mistake and he wants them mules back and he's latched onto the idea of not doin' anything that ain't in the mules' best interests. Mules like that, worth a lot of money, thousands of dollars, ya' can't just stick 'em in any old barn and throw 'em some hay. Ya' gotta take care of 'em and it takes an experienced mule man to do it right.

"Now Bingo's still protestin' but he's comin' off of it just a little bit, know what I mean? Stumpy picked up on it right away and he chimed in with the voice of reason and good sense.

"'Now hang on here jest a minute Bingo,' he sez, 'Morgan's brought up a interestin' point here,' he sez, 'and you don't want to be too hasty,' he sez, 'in puttin' the kibosh on it,' he sez.

"Now Stumpy and Bingo get discussing the situation and arguing and back and forth and by this time old Morgan's got the hunnert dollar bills back on the bar all neat and pressed out flat, the pile scuffed just a little to one side so's ya could see there was really all of 'em there.

"So the argument went back and forth for twenty or thirty minutes, or at least it was supposed to be a argument but Morgan was the only one really thought it was one, and they wouldn't even let him have a say, but Stumpy gradually seems to be winnin' and finally it comes down to Bingo arguing with Stumpy over the bar bill, which by now has a number on it so big Bingo claimed when he glanced at the tab he mistook it for his Social Security card.

"Stumpy was still the voice of moderation, ya might say, an island of good sense in a situation that was gettin' more and more het up. 'Tell ya what,' he sez, 'how about if Morgan here,' he sez, 'returns the money in full,' he sez, 'AND,' he sez, 'pays for the bar bill too,' he sez. 'How about that?'

"'THEM MULES IS WORTH MORE'N JEST A LITTLE DAMN BAR BILL,' Bingo hollers. 'THEM'S PRIZEWINNERS, FOR SURE,' he sez.

"But Morgan seen the light at the end of the tunnel in Stumpy's plan and jumped at it. 'Fine idea,' he sez, 'a fine idea indeed.'

"Well the hollerin' and yellin' and argyin' dragged on for most of the rest of the afternoon, with the eighteen hunnert dollars laying there on the bar and all the while the bar bill growin' like Jack's beanstalk, as Stumpy said later, what with Bingo still celebrating by buying everybody drinks, but finally Morgan had his mules back that had never budged from their stall up in Bethel the whole day, and Bingo had his eighteen hunnert dollars back, the bill of sale all tore up and burned in an ashtray, and half of Woodbine drove home singing, most of 'em takin' back roads and shortcuts so's to avoid having to drive past Officer Harkness, settin' on the village green bored to tears in the police cruiser lookin' for somebody to arrest to liven up the afternoon.

"And Bingo! Well Bingo and cupla others, Stumpy was one of 'em, was tighter than a little red musket and Desmond hadda call Artie Strong to come with his van, he's got a seven-seater, and haul em off to home. They was all singin' and yellin' and the next day they said when they went by Officer Harkness one of the younger fellas wanted to moon him but he didn't think of it till the last minute and couldn't git his britches off in time. Don't know how true that is, but that's what they said.

"Morgan was relieved and pleased at getting his mules back. The bar bill didn't amount to but $261.90 and, he's braggin' a couple days later in the feed store up to Royalton, that's a helluva price for a pair of mules as valuable as these ones. 'Cheap at twice the price,' he claimed. 'WutImean Bingo Reilly himself, who knows his critters, Bingo Reilly himself said they's worth a small fortune.' Morgan's decided he made himself one helluva shrewd deal.

"But Desmond and me and prit'near everbody else was happy, well, relieved was more like it, that Bingo Reilly was back to his ownself again."

Patchy paused again, looking at his audience. "That old Bingo Reilly sure is somethin,'" he declared. "He sure is somethin'!"

The End

Printed in the United States
59218LVS00002B/370-471